JUST O

"I do not thi[...] murmured.

"Why not?" Remo asked, looking down at her perfect body.

"Because you cannot."

"Wrong," said Remo. Lifting his right hand, he made the stiffening fingers into a spear point. "It's my job."

The seductress spread her legs apart, and her scent filled Remo's head. She lay open to him like a burst plum.

"Kill me, then—if you can," she said. "Or else mount me. Take me."

Remo felt his killing hand freezing. He felt another part stiffening. It was against all his training, but his mind kept flashing back to their succulent lovemaking the night before.

It was like they said in the ads. You couldn't stop with just one. . . .

FEEDING FRENZY

The Destroyer

#94

FEEDING FRENZY

Created by
WARREN MURPHY & RICHARD SAPIR

A SIGNET BOOK

SIGNET
Published by the Penguin Group
Penguin Books USA Inc., 375 Hudson Street,
New York, New York 10014, U.S.A.
Penguin Books Ltd, 27 Wrights Lane,
London W8 5TZ, England
Penguin Books Australia Ltd, Ringwood,
Victoria, Australia
Penguin Books Canada Ltd, 10 Alcorn Avenue,
Toronto, Ontario, Canada M4V 3B2
Penguin Books (N.Z.) Ltd, 182–190 Wairau Road,
Auckland 10, New Zealand

Penguin Books Ltd, Registered Offices:
Harmondsworth, Middlesex, England

First published by Signet, an imprint of Dutton Signet,
a division of Penguin Books USA Inc.

First Printing, October, 1993
10 9 8 7 6 5 4 3 2 1

 REGISTERED TRADEMARK—MARCA REGISTRADA

Printed in the United States of America

For David and Lee Burton, for baking tasty peach pies and stuffing mighty Teddy Bears, without confusing the two. (Knock on wood!)

And for the Glorious House of Sinanju, P.O. Box 2505, Quincy, MA 02269

1

Later on, no one would remember who was actually the first one to eat the bug, but a lot of them tried to take credit for it.

Brother Karl Sagacious said that he remembered it clearly. He had been hiking around the hills north of San Francisco while on sabbatical from his professor's job at UCLA where he taught a history course titled "Egyptians, Phoenicians, Romans, Greeks, and other Black Folk," and as he was pitching his tent one night to sleep, a brilliant light appeared in the sky.

And then a thin voice came and it said, "All your science is false. But I will show you the true way."

It was a woman's voice, Brother Karl Sagacious later recalled.

He remembered he had been blinded by the light, but impelled by some force he could not understand, he staggered sightlessly from his tent and pushed his way through the forest, until the voice commanded him:

"Kneel and eat. This is your truth."

Still unseeing, he obeyed. His hands found tiny nuggets of food which he popped into his mouth. They were delicious. They tasted like miniature lobster tails. He could not stop eating and when he did, he finally fell asleep where he knelt.

He woke with the morning sun and found himself in the middle of a field of weeds. The weeds were covered with brown, soft-shelled bugs. Was that what he had eaten?

He looked closely. The bugs were not moving. They were asleep. Or dead. His stomach rumbled at the thought that he might have chosen to eat dead insects for supper.

But then he remembered the voice.

"This is your truth," She had said.

Slowly, with trembling fingers, he reached out and plucked one of the bugs from the weed. He examined it carefully. It even looked benign. It had a round head, but no pincers, and its legs were but little hair-like stubble on the side of its inch-long body. And it *was* dead.

He gulped once, swallowed, and then popped the bug into his mouth and bit into it.

It tasted exactly like lobster tail. It was wonderful. Nirvana.

He stayed in that spot for breakfast, and then when he was full, he returned to civilization to spread the word.

At least that was how he remembered it.

Brother Theodore Soars-With-Eagles remembered it quite a different way.

No modern man, he insisted, had been the one to discover the bug. It had been part of the collected wisdom of the Native Americans who had ruled these lands before the white man came to despoil it with his cities and schools and churches and toilets and homes.

And he, Brother Theodore Soars-With-Eagles—as the spiritual and physical heir to those noble Red Men—had known since childhood of the magical properties of the thunderbug, so named because they invariably lifted their tiny heads quizzically whenever it thundered—and had been eating nothing but them since he was little more than a papoose on the Chinchilla Indian reservation in Sedona, Arizona.

Some reporters found out later that Brother Theodore Soars-With-Eagles had never so much as seen an Indian reservation in Arizona. Instead, he had been raised in Pittsburgh, Pennsylvania, as Theodore Magarac, the son of an immigrant Latvian steelworker. He had spent fifteen of his forty years in jail for petty theft.

His last known scam had been perpetrated in the wake of the U.S. Postal Service's pick-an-Elvis-any-Elvis campaign. Theodore thought that if they're going to put a junkie on a stamp, they ought to put a fag on too, so he started a 900 number to lure people into paying for the privilege of voting on whether Liberace or Rock Hudson should have his gummy backside licked by the Postal Service's patrons.

The scam collapsed when the Postmaster General called the number, got an answering machine and no callback, and subsequently discovered a $49.99 tele-marketing charge on his office phone bill. He got steamed and sicced the Inspector General and the FCC onto Theodore. Magarac did a year in Folsom.

However, the reporters decided that running a story on Theodore Magarac's pedigree would add nothing to the public's necessary store of knowledge on the subject. And since the new bug was obviously going to be such a boon to mankind, it would not do to confuse the discussion with a lot of extraneous non-issues, and so the story was never published.

They were saving it for when the story peaked.

But while the history of the bug's discovery might have been in doubt, what was certain was that somehow Brother Theodore Soars-With-Eagles and Brother Karl Sagacious had come together and created an organization called PAPA—People Against Protein Assassins—and it was their stated goal to make the bug the new staple of the world's diet.

"The world no longer needs chicken farms or cattle ranches or hogs raised for meat. With the discovery of the Miracle Food, we have ended forever the specter of hunger and starvation on our planet," read one of their press releases.

Even in California, where people will sign up to do almost anything, it was a tough sell convincing people to eat bugs. But as time went on, more and more came aboard.

Soon PAPA was taking over the entire membership of the state's hundreds of New Age groups. Crystal-strokers, cosmos-guiders, rain-foresters, Harmonic Convergers, Pyramidologists—all decided that the Miracle Food was the way of the future. They joined by the hundreds and the movement slowly crossed the Rockies and came into America's heartland.

It could no longer be ignored.

The Miracle Food was tested and examined in scores of laboratories, and the preliminary reports were almost as glowing as Brothers Karl and Theodore made them out to be.

The bug was a little-known insect named *Ingraticus Avalonicus*. It was able to live in all climes but in the past had been slow to reproduce and therefore had not ever been previously found in large numbers.

The entire body of the insect was edible, high in protein, carbohydrates, and essential amino acids, but without fat and with the added property of apparently lowering the blood cholesterol of someone who ate it. People could eat them like popcorn and actually lose weight.

The bug's habits were also peculiar. It did not sting and there were no known allergies exacerbated by it. It did not eat valuable crops. Instead, the lowly and insignificant *Ingraticus* fed only on common weeds that grew everywhere, and it would simply light on a weed and eat until it died.

A panel from *Consumers News* magazine made a test of the Miracle Food, both raw and cooked, and reported that the thunderbug tasted better than pizza.

In every state in the union, PAPA groups sprang up. The United Nations called for action. Official

Washington decided the lowly thunderbug was now worth its consideration and it ordered redone, at a hundred times the original cost, all the tests that had been done privately. But first a new laboratory had to be built at a cost of six hundred million dollars in the Arkansas district of the Speaker of the House. With cost overruns, the lab ultimately cost four billion dollars, but eventually it got around to studying the thunderbug.

"Is the Millennium Here?" the *New York Times* wondered in a front-page editorial. "Has mankind really found the answer to worldwide starvation?"

Back in California, in the wooded clearing where the original one hundred members of the very first PAPA group still lived, there were rumblings of internal problems.

Brother Theodore was unhappy because Brother Karl Sagacious had been on television too much of late, depriving him of equal-opportunity face time.

And Brother Karl had been heard to complain that he thought Brother Theodore was raising too much money for "research" that never seemed to get done.

It got so bad that the two stopped talking to each other.

And then came the Great Schism.

One day, Brother Karl came out into the clearing to address the faithful.

"You will remember that I was the first to eat the Miracle Food. And I ate it raw. And now, it seems that many of you are under the misapprehension that the sacred bug must be cooked first. This is heresy. From this moment on, the dietary rules are set by me. And not anyone else."

Brother Theodore entered the clearing an hour later to address the same faithful.

"My people," he said, meaning his imaginary Chinchilla forebears and not the Latvian steelworkers, "have been eating the thunderbug for centuries. It must be cooked. We let it die on the vine and then cook it. It is the only correct way."

Brother Karl was back a few minutes later. "The Miracle Food is better eaten fresh. Cooked dead food is no better than beef stew."

In the morning, the hundred earliest disciples had split into two camps.

Brother Theodore called his people The Harvesters. They waited until the insects had died on the weed of overeating and they cooked them in a clear broth like chick-peas.

Brother Karl said that hereafter there would be only one approved way to eat *Ingraticus Avalonicus*. "Pick up the bug, snap off its head, and pop it into your mouth. Fresh and good. The way She wants it."

Brother Theodore dismissed Sagacious's followers as heretics, calling them "Snappers."

Sagacious gleefully picked up on the name. He had T-shirts made for his Snappers, in six designer colors and silkscreened with a legend rendered in what he claimed was genuine Phoenician calligraphy:

SNAP OFF THEY HEADS

AND EAT THEY RAW

He proclaimed Brother Theodore and his Harvesters to be hopelessly New World and therefore counter-progressive.

Theodore told his followers that the Snappers were practicing the kind of cruelty to living things that all thinking people must protest. He had his own T-shirts made up for the Harvesters. They read:

ALL IN GOD'S GOOD TIME

The calligraphy, he claimed, was fourteenth-century Mohican. They sold like hotcakes at $29.99.

The next day, Brother Karl's followers moved out of the communal clearing into the next clearing. Both groups continued to share the slit trench latrine, and one evening Brother Karl and Brother Theodore met there, quite by accident, when both came to squat.

"Karl, you're screwing things up," Brother Theodore said.

"I am following the way that She set out for me."

"Forget her," Theodore snapped, "whoever the hell she is. We've got a good thing going here and if we start fighting about it, we won't have anything left."

"I'm not interested in 'a good thing,'" Karl said. "I am interested in truth."

"All right, all right. You want truth. Try this: How is it that somehow it's wrong to kill a freaking chicken, but you can snap the heads off the thunderbug and swallow it down warm?"

"Because that is what She told me to do."

"That's your answer? She told you to do it? What kind of an answer is that?"

"A truthful answer," replied Brother Karl Sagacious.

"You know what's wrong with you?" Theodore snapped. "You're a nut. You never should have left the campus. They like nuts at UCLA. That's why it's called macadamia."

"The word is academia," said Karl, "and yours are the remarks of a desperate man."

"Look. Can't we get together on this and stop bickering? Let everybody eat the way they want. No skin off anybody's ass."

"You're a charlatan, Theodore."

Brother Theodore Soars-With-Eagles growled, pulled up his pants, and left, wondering what he was going to do about Brother Karl Sagacious.

He did not intend to let this one get away from him. He had been on the wire all his life, scratching to make a wrinkled dollar. Con games had put him in jail. Anointing himself as a Chinchilla Indian had gotten him room and board and a little good press for a few years, until his thick black hair began thinning and falling out. Male pattern baldness, a specialist had told him.

"Well, fix it," he had insisted. "I can't be no freak-

ing Chinchilla Indian without hair. You ever see a
bald spot on a Mohawk? Or a Dakota Sioux with a
receding hairline? Everybody knows the noble Red
Man had the follicles of a grizzly bear. That's why my
Chinchilla ancestors were so heavy into scalping. Hair
was their totem. They ate hair, thus insuring abundant
buffalo and no unsightly dandruff on their noble Chinchilla shoulders."

"Sorry, friend. *Your* hair's going."

Shortly after that, the Indian movement went up in
smoke signals when most of its members went to jail
for murder, and Brother Theodore drifted West where
he lived on the fringes of assorted loony movements
until one night, in a restaurant booth, he heard another man—who turned out to be Karl Sagacious—
talking about the wonderful bug food he had
discovered.

"Tastes just like lobster," the man kept repeating.

Theodore decided that there might be some way to
turn a buck from it, and after the people had left, he
went into the north California hills the man had been
speaking of and, trying hard not to vomit, ate a couple
of dozen bugs until he found one that tasted like
lobster.

He went immediately to the press, concocting his
story about the ancient Chinchilla thunderbug-eating
tradition as he talked, and created PAPA right on the
spot. A few weeks later, Sagacious—who never quite
understood that the discovery had been stolen from
him—showed up, and the two men agreed on a part-
nership to lead the new organization, People Against
Protein Assassins.

And it had worked well enough until now . . . until
this damn stubborn display by Sagacious.

Something was going to have to be done about him,
Brother Theodore thought as he was falling asleep
that night.

By morning, something *had* been done.

"Wake up, wake up, Brother Theodore," a young woman called, rushing into his tepee.

"What's the matter? What is it?"

"He's dead."

"Who's dead?"

"Brother Karl is dead."

"Oh, no. How sad. Oh, what a loss is ours," Theodore moaned and turned and buried his face in his pillow so the woman could not see him smile.

"And that's not all."

"What's not all?"

"Others are dying too," she said. "They're dropping like flies."

"Oh, what a pity," Brother Theodore said. And this time he meant it.

2

His name was Remo and his favorite movie was still *Gunga Din*.

He thought about it as he was sitting in the Harvard University auditorium, waiting for the start of the film tribute to Hardy Bricker, Hollywood's newest wonderchild.

He had liked Sam Jaffe in *Gunga Din*. But Cary Grant and Douglas Fairbanks and Victor McLaglen were good too. What other movies did he like?

He saw *Fantasia* once and really liked the dancing hippopotamuses. And *Casablanca* was okay except he never liked that fat guy who was in it. But *Citizen Kane* was about a sled, for crying out loud, and he had seen three minutes of *Batman* once, but the picture was so dark it looked like it had been filmed in a cave. He hadn't seen much else, not even in the various apartments he had lived in all his life, because while he had a VCR, it was always being used by Chiun, his trainer, to watch old soap operas.

It wasn't as if he hated movies. He didn't hate them. He didn't care enough about them to hate them. He just didn't think about them at all.

But he was willing to make an exception for Hardy Bricker.

Hardy Bricker had made five films and was now being called the hottest director in Hollywood history. "The thinking man's director," some critic said on television and Remo thought that might be true if the thinking man involved never thought about anything but bullshit.

Bricker's first film had been called *Frag*. It showed how American soldiers committed atrocities in Vietnam, pushed to perform them by an evil military-industrial complex intent upon enslaving the world. Remo had been in Vietnam for a while and he knew that the soldiers there were no better or no worse than any America had sent anywhere else. They just wanted to stay alive.

To call them criminals was in itself criminal. But it had rung just the right note for Hollywood. That city, run by people so dumb that they thought conspiracies explained everything, had found in Hardy Bricker an eloquent new spokesman. They bombarded him with picture offers. He took only the ones that paid him the most money.

Frag was followed by *Dependent Day*, showing how America was an evil racist country that turned its back on the noble soldiers who had fought in Vietnam— the same noble soldiers who were murderers in *Frag*.

And then he did a movie called *Horn*, about some jazz musician who killed himself with a drug overdose brought on by his worrying about America turning into an evil racist country.

Then his movie *Jocko* told the story of a rising young politician who was killed by an evil racist secret power structure of the United States, in a conspiracy involving 22,167 people. It won Bricker his third Academy Award.

And tonight was to be the preview of Bricker's latest epic: *Crap*, which proved that all organized religion in the United States was the tool of an evil racist secret power structure trying to promote fascism in America. To be followed by remarks from Hardy Bricker himself, for those who needed even pictures explained to them.

Does anybody believe this bullshit? Remo wondcred, then looked around at the bearded, hairy Harvard underclassmen who had packed the auditorium, and he nodded sadly to himself. *These zanies would swallow anything*.

Remo could tell that it was eight o'clock, and right on time the house lights dimmed and the elegant title *Crap* appeared on the screen, the individual letters apparently made by arranging dog turds on a white background.

Then the camera pulled away and the white background turned out to be a priest's cassock. The priest had it pulled up around his waist. He was sexually molesting a preteen girl. In the first five minutes of the film, the same priest sexually assaulted three more children. Then he shaved, put on expensive aftershave lotion, and went to lunch with an evangelist at an expensive New York City restaurant, where they talked about following the secret orders of their military-industrial masters. Before lunch was finished, both clergymen had ducked into the hatcheck room to ravage two waitresses.

When they finished and came out of the hatcheck room, they sprinkled Holy Water on the restaurant and blessed it as a Place for God's Work. Then they argued with management about the luncheon bill, refused to pay it, and went outside to their waiting block-long limousines, in each of which three street hookers had been gathered up to make sure the ride back to their churches wasn't too boring.

Remo rubbed his eyes in stupefaction at what he was seeing. The sound was scratchy. The film looked to be out of focus. The dialogue, what little there was beyond sexual grunting, seemed to have been written by an imbecilic fourth-grader.

And all around him, students were cheering, laughing, and applauding.

"Tell them, Hardy. You tell them, man," a black man next to Remo stood up to shout. He punched a clenched fist into the air.

"Sit down and shut up," Remo said.

"I . . . beg . . . your . . . fucking . . . pardon," the man said coldly. He was older than most of the others in the auditorium, so his dumbness couldn't be written off as the ignorance of youth. He wore a goatee, tortoise-shell glasses that might have been swiped from Hedda Hopper's cold corpse, and a black baseball cap with the Roman numeral ten on it.

Remo recognized the man then. He was a famous film director who after running ten million dollars over budget trying to film the life of a burglar-turned-pimp-turned-martyred-civil-rights-leader, cried racism after the film company refused to kick through the shortfall. When other black film personalities ponied up, he publicly demanded that black people all over the country skip work and school and breakfast to see his movie about black responsibility, or risk being branded as Uncle Toms themselves.

Harvard University immediately hired him to teach a humanities course called "Black Values."

Remo reached out and touched the back of the man's left knee. The leg collapsed and the man slumped back into his seat.

"Hey—!" he started.

"One more word out of you," Remo warned, "and I'll do the same thing to your head that I did to your leg. Shut up."

The man did. He whipped off his cap and started chewing on the bill.

Remo could put in only five more minutes of watching *Crap* before he stood and slipped quietly out of the row and walked around to the back of the theater. Although it was dark, he was able to adjust his eyes so that he saw as clearly as if it were high noon. There was a flight of steps at the side of the small stage and a door behind them.

Remo walked down quietly and let himself backstage through the door.

There were a half-dozen students running around,

apparently busying themselves with errands of some sort, but Remo saw no sign of Hardy Bricker.

He walked down a long hall. While he made no effort to eavesdrop, any sound from inside the rooms would register on his sensitive ears. He stopped outside the last door. Inside he could hear sighing and heavy breathing.

The two guards could hear the breathing too. They were Harvard University campus police and they were paid not to remember things they heard or saw, and, occasionally, smelled.

"Hey, get away from that door!" the first guard shouted. "You know who's in there?"

"Another Bolshevik," Remo said.

"Hardy Bricker, that's who," the second guard said.

"Well, la-di-da," said Remo.

They were a Mutt and Jeff pair, one tall and reedy as a flagpole with the blue flag twisted around it, and the other short and squat like a squash ball stuffed into a shapeless blue sack.

They had been standing in their dark blue uniforms at the far end of the corridor, before the fire door and under the darkened EXIT sign, their hands clasped behind them, at parade rest.

Except now their hands were swinging at their sides and they were moving in on Remo with all the purpose of high school corridor monitors and, to Remo Williams, the first white Master of Sinanju, about the same threat level. Which was to say, none.

Remo lifted his hands to show that he had no weapon and wasn't a threat. He didn't look like a threat. He didn't look like much of anything—merely a man of slightly more than average height, very average weight, wearing a white T-shirt and tan chinos that fit tightly enough to suggest he carried no weapons, concealed or otherwise.

While the police were sizing him up with their eyes, satisfying themselves that this lean-bodied intruder was unarmed, Remo reached out with the deadliest weapons on his person—if not the universe—and got his fingers around the police throats. The thin-necked one was easy. The thick-necked one needed an extra two seconds of squeezing before his nervous system shorted too.

Still holding them by their necks, Remo carried the pair over to the fire door and dropped them there. Then he reached up to wave one hand over the EXIT sign. It winked on.

"Take a penny, give a penny," Remo told himself.

The sounds were still coming from behind the closed door. He took the knob, twisted it with deceptive slowness, and slipped in.

Hardy Bricker was standing in front of a mirror, making faces at himself. He had a puffy, spoiled face, the face of somebody with too much money and a private school background. So the way he snarled and frowned at the mirror was funny. It was as if he were trying to put on his tough face for the speech he was scheduled to give to the Harvard undergrads.

Remo stepped into the light so the mirror caught his reflection.

Hardy Bricker caught the reflection too. His face froze with his upper lip curled à la Elvis Presley and his lower lip pushed out in a hemorrhoidal pout.

He pulled both lips into line and turned.

He began, "Who—?"

"—Me," Remo shot back.

"Leave!" said Hardy Bricker, testing his tough voice.

"No," said Remo.

"Don't make me call the guards."

"Don't think you have the lungs to wake them," Remo said casually.

"They dead?"

"Asleep, and so will you be if you don't listen to me."

"Listen to what?"

"I've got this idea for a movie," Remo said.

Bricker groaned. "Everybody's got an idea for a movie," he moaned. "What's yours? Little green men in a spaceship who captured you one night in Iowa? Or a tender love story about a sixteen-year-old and an eighty-year-old checkout clerk at the local Acme? Or maybe a ghost story about a guy who comes back to save his sweetheart's life from killers? I've heard them all. What's yours?"

"Naaaah, nothing like that. I've got this story about a big government conspiracy. To wipe out whole races of people. To promote fascism. Racism. The whole military-industrial conspiracy—stuff like that."

Hardy Bricker's soft features quirked into attentiveness. "Conspiracy?"

"A conspiracy with fifteen thousand people in on the secret," Remo said.

The tension went out of Hardy Bricker's overfed body. "That sounds like something more up my alley," he said, sitting down suddenly. He waved Remo to a chair.

"Alley's the right word," Remo mumbled, adding in an audible voice, "I thought you might like it." He took the other chair. Remo leaned over and whispered conspiratorially, "You know how your movies are always about government conspiracies?"

Hardy Bricker learned forward too. He looked Remo in the eye. "Yeah?" he said, his tone equally conspiratorial.

"Well, I've got the biggest one." Remo pretended to look to see that the door was closed and then that there were no strange faces or shotgun microphones at the only window. "There's a secret government agency, see, and it hires contract killers and they go around knocking off everybody who pisses them off."

"Sounds about right. Who are the killers?"

"Well, one of them is this misunderstood American guy. He grew up in an orphanage in Newark and used to be a cop until they conned him into working for the Feds."

"And he's a racist, right?"

"No, no," Remo said. "He loves everybody. He's really kind of sweet. Thoughtful. Gentle, even."

"Screw all that sweet and gentle. I want some racists. That's what I make movies about. Racist evil Americans. Who's the other guy?"

"You'd like him. He is a racist. He hates everybody."

"Good. Now we're getting somewhere," Bricker said, his puffy face relaxing like a sponge absorbing water.

"Okay," said Remo. "He's about a hundred years old, see? Although he'll only own up to eighty. And he's from this small village and his family have been supporting the village by being professional assassins for a couple of thousand years. See, he gets into it because this secret agency hired him to train the young American and make him into a great assassin too."

"Right. Got it. Where's the village? Upstate New York?"

"No, actually it's called Sinanju. That's in North Korea."

Hardy Bricker's interested expression soured. "You mean this eighty-year-old great assassin is some dinky North Korean?"

"Right," said Remo.

"That's ridiculous! I don't want a Korean racist. I want an American racist. Somebody put you up to this, didn't they? One of the major studios, right? They're trying to con me with this cock-and-bull story about two secret assassins. All right fella, tell me. Who are you?"

"I came on my own," Remo said truthfully.

"Good. Then leave on your own. Interview ended. Good-bye."

Hardy Bricker started to rise, but a hand he couldn't see coming pushed him back down into his chair. The hand stayed there. It was firm. It wasn't clutching or pinching or squeezing, but a numbness filled Hardy Bricker's soft shoulder like Novocaine invading a healthy tooth.

Hardy Bricker noticed then that the hand was attached to its forearm by a very thick wrist. He looked at the man's face again, as if seeing it for the first time. It was a strong face, dominated by deep-set dark brown eyes and very pronounced cheekbones. The man's hair was as dark as his eyes and his mouth was a thin twist that suggested cruelty.

"Not until I finish pitching my story," the thick-wristed man said casually. "So these two work for this secret government agency called CURE, and their job is to kill America's enemies."

"And they get away with it?"

"Of course," the man said, as if it was no big deal.

"Well, that's the part I like. But as for the rest of it, sorry, pal, it just won't fly."

The man said, "I haven't told you the best part."

"What's that?"

"You know how you always say that there's a secret government that really runs America and goes around killing people?"

"Yes."

"You were right."

"I knew that."

"No, you were really right. In fact, it's bigger than you dreamed." The thick-wristed man made his voice conspiratorial again. "The President is in on it."

"Which President? Give me names."

"All of them."

"Since when?"

"Since CURE started. Back in the 1960's."

"You don't look old enough to go back that far."

"Macrosymbiotic diet," said the other. "Keeps me young. Besides, I didn't come in until later."

Hardy Bricker was trying to process the information coming into his barely wrinkled brain. Every President since the sixties. Mostly they were Republicans. Hardy was pretty sure about this, because in his forty-odd years of life only twice had he ever voted for a winner.

"Your story has a tinge of truth to it," he allowed.

"I thought you'd think so."

"But tell me this—if every President for the last four decades has known, how come none of them have talked—or shut you down?"

"They haven't talked because they can't."

"You kill them? Is that it?"

The thick-wristed man looked insulted. "No, no. We just erase their memories after they leave office, so that they think they remember everything about their term in office, but they don't."

"That must be an incredible machine that does it," Hardy Bricker said.

The guy blew on his wriggling fingers and said, "It is."

Hardy Bricker started to scoff but then remembered how numb his shoulder had gotten after the skinny guy had touched it.

"That part doesn't sound so plausible," he said.

"Sure it is. All over the human body are nerve centers. Sensitive nerve centers. It's just a matter of putting negative pressure on those nerve centers while reminding the subject of what he shouldn't remember."

"Reminding him of what he shouldn't remember? That sounds awfully Zen."

"The Zen guys overheard something they shouldn't have and that's how they got where they are today— which is to say playing with themselves."

"You're losing me."

"It's like this. I just the other day had a nice chat with the last President."

"Oh, him."

"Yeah, that one. I reminded him that he was supposed to forget all about us when he left office, and he let me pressure the nerve that sort of blocks the bad thoughts."

"This nerve—is it in the shoulder?"

"On some people."

"What kind?"

"Ones without a working brain." Hardy Bricker blinked his watery eyes rapidly, and Remo could tell by his expression that last part hadn't quite sunk in.

"If this is true, why are you telling me?" Bricker wanted to know.

"Because I got to thinking if we make every President we work for forget that there is a secret government agency that really runs America, even though we know they'll keep their mouths shut, we really shouldn't leave a blabbermouth like you out."

"Out of what?" said Hardy Bricker as the hand he couldn't see move came back to his shoulder and squeezed so hard he thought he heard his rotator cup pop.

The pop seemed to pop his eardrums too. And out went his brain.

Hardy Bricker lost consciousness so he didn't feel himself being thrown over a lean shoulder that was as hard as petrified bone or feel the coolness of the evening as he was carried out into Harvard Yard and across Massachusetts Avenue to a park where he was set down with his back to a bus port.

Remo scrounged up a discarded paper coffee cup, splashed out the last congealing brown liquid, and placed it in Hardy Bricker's limp fist. Digging some loose change out of his pocket, he shook it in his palm until a thick subway token showed its brassy face. He picked it out along with a shiny quarter and poured the rest into the flimsy cup.

Then he touched the exact center of the man's forehead, right where the caste mark would be if Hardy Bricker were a Hindu untouchable and not an American unmentionable.

Hardy Bricker's eyes flew upon. He looked around. He did not see Remo, because Remo had slipped behind him and was doubling around so that he could casually pass Hardy Bricker.

Hardy Bricker was still seated on the sidewalk when Remo pretended to come up to him. Remo stopped, dug into his pocket for his last quarter and dropped it into the paper cup, where it rattled the rest of Remo's change.

It rattled Hardy Bricker too. He peered into the cup, and then looked up at Remo's face with big uncomprehending eyes.

"I—I don't understand. . . ."

"Understand what?"

Bricker looked around. He seemed in a daze. "Understand anything. What am I doing here?"

"Well, that depends on who you are."

"Who I am?"

"Yeah, who you are. You know, what your name is, where you live, where you work."

"I—I don't think I know."

"I guess that makes you one of the growing legion of homeless, jobless, penniless unfortunates who fill our streets, public parks, and subways, the cruel victims of a heartless military-industrial conspiracy," Remo said. "Any of it coming back now?"

"Yes, I think I've heard those words before."

"Well, there you go," said Remo happily.

Hardy Bricker looked behind him. There was a park, sure enough. "I don't see any others like me."

"Then you're in luck. First one in has squatter's rights."

Hardy Bricker looked down. He was squatting, sure enough. It was beginning to make sense to his dull, foggy brain.

"What do I do?" he asked, watching the cars and buses zip by.

"You could say thank you."

"For what?"

"For the quarter I dropped into your cup. It was my last quarter too."

"Oh. Thank you." Confusion crept back into his face. "What do I do now?"

"It helps if you shake the cup every little while," Remo suggested.

Hardy Bricker gave it a shot. The cup shook, the change jingled and instantly a woman stepped up and dropped a Susan B. Anthony dollar into the cup. She walked on.

Hardy Bricker looked up. A slow smile crept over his puffy features.

"Thank you," he told Remo gratefully.

"Glad to help the dispossessed of the earth."

And Remo walked off, whistling. He did not walk far—only to the closest subway stop, where he took the Red Line through Boston to the city of Quincy, where he now lived.

He wasn't a big fan of the subway. But he had driven in Boston traffic enough by now to understand he had a better chance of survival if he went over Niagara Falls in a Dixie cup.

3

From the North Quincy stop, it was a short walk to the place Remo Williams called home.

The sight of it made Remo long for the days when he lived out of a suitcase. Remo had always envisioned that one day he would live in a nice house with a white picket fence—not in a baroque monstrosity of sandstone and cement.

It had once been a church. It still looked like a church. Or more like a church than anything else. Depending on which compass direction you were approaching it from, it resembled, variously, a Swiss chalet, a Tudor castle, or the condominium from hell.

Right now, it looked like a Gothic warehouse because of all the delivery trucks parked around it. There was a UPS truck, a Federal Express van, another from Purolator Courier, and numerous other package delivery service vehicles.

"What's Chiun up to now?" Remo muttered, quickening his pace.

He caught up with the UPS driver as he was dropping off a plain cardboard box.

"This for a Chiun?"

The man looked at his clip. "The invoice says M.O.S. Chiun."

"I'll take it."

"If you sign for it, it's yours. My responsibility stops at the front steps."

Remo signed "Remo Freud" and took the box. He had to put it down in order to climb the steps. The steps were piled with boxes of all types. He was clearing a path as the other drivers came out of their trucks, their arms laden with boxes of all shapes.

"What is all this stuff?" Remo demanded after he had finished signing for six more packages.

No one knew. Or cared. So Remo reluctantly accepted the boxes and added them to the pile.

He carried what he could inside and set them down at the mailbox buzzers. In the days when Remo was a Newark cop and he had to get into an apartment building, he had used a little trick. Press all the buzzers at once. Usually, somebody would ring him in.

In this case, there were only two inhabitants distributed among the sixteen units that made up the church-turned-condo—himself and Chiun, Reigning Master of Sinanju, the ancient house of assassins which had operated at the edges of history for thousands of years, and to which Remo now belonged.

A squeaky voice called down from above, "Remo, is that you?"

"No," Remo called up, "it's me and the entire Sears gift department."

"My packages have come?"

"They're piled to the freaking ceiling."

The Master of Sinanju floated down the steps. He was a frail wisp of a little Korean with a face that was like a wrinkled-up papyrus mask. The top of his head shone under the lights, bald but for the patches over his ears, where cloudy white tufts of hair clung stubbornly. He wore a chrysanthemum pink kimono bordered in white silk that made him look like a thousand-year-old Easter egg.

His wizened face puckered up in pleasure, bringing a twinkle to his clear hazel eyes.

He fell upon the box with long fingernails that were like X-acto knives. They sliced plastic packing tape cleanly and flaps popped upward like ugly cardboard-colored flowers.

"Where did you get this stuff?" Remo asked, curious.

"From the television."

"Say again."

"It is a new custom. One watches television and one merely calls certain individuals and reads to them certain useless pieces of information and in return they send interesting presents."

"What useless pieces of information?"

"Oh, mere numbers."

"Charge card numbers!"

Chiun made a small mouth. "Possibly."

"Little Father," Remo said patiently, "you know Smith's been on our case about spending. The new President's been after Smith to cut his budget and help reduce the deficit and—" Remo stopped. The Master of Sinanju was holding up a silver utensil like a spatula.

"What's that?" Remo demanded.

"It is a cheese fletcher."

"Cheese! We don't eat cheese. We *can't* eat cheese."

"We might one day have company who does and they will be insulted if we do not fletch their cheese properly."

Chiun continued picking over his booty. One box he regarded disdainfully and passed to Remo saying, "This is for you."

"It is?" said Remo, his face momentarily softening. "You bought me a present?"

"No. It is from Smith."

"Why would Smith send me a present?"

Chiun shrugged. "He said something about it the other day. I believe it is a pox."

Remo's face went blank. "Pox? Isn't that a disease?"

"I do not know, for I do not get diseases."

Remo knelt down and ripped open the box. Inside a roll of bubblewrap was the largest, ugliest telephone Remo had ever seen.

"This is a fax machine!" Remo blurted. "Why would Smith send us a fax machine?"

"Possibly because he could not obtain a proper pox."

Remo carried the fax upstairs to the main room of the building, a huge four-windowed crenellated turret that corresponded to the steeple of the former house of worship. It was crammed to the high rafters with all manner of knickknacks and electronic equipment, ranging from microwave ovens to blenders.

In one corner was a stack of televisions. All were turned to the Home Shopping Network. The sound was off.

"When did you get started on this kick?" Remo asked when Chiun came in, bearing boxes balanced in both uplifted hands and atop his shiny amber skull. The combined weight should have slammed him to the pine floor, but Chiun bore them as if the boxes were filled with daydreams.

"I must have some solace in my bitterness and deprivation," Chiun said. "Now that all the light has departed my life and it is barren of love and hope."

"Oh," said Remo. And suddenly he remembered. For years, the Master of Sinanju had been infatuated with Cheeta Ching, the Korean network anchorwoman who had just had a baby. She was no longer on the air. Normally, that would have been enough to plunge Chiun into a killing rage, dismembering network presidents until the flat face of Cheeta Ching was restored to the TV screen.

But after nearly a decade of distant infatuation, the Master of Sinanju had finally gotten to meet the object of his affection, had in fact rescued her from kidnappers, with the end result that he had been horrified by the real Cheeta Ching, an ambitious unfeminine harridan with eyes only for Remo. Chiun's crush had been crushed.

It had been a relief to Remo, who had suffered through Chiun's earlier infatuation with Barbra Streisand. He had been wondering who was next. And now this. Maybe, he thought, looking around at the piles of unboxed electronic equipment and appliances, this was preferable to Chiun falling in love with Dame Edna Everage.

Remo decided not to press his luck. He hoped the subject of Cheeta Ching was closed forever.

"Need any help with that stuff?" Remo asked.

"I am the Master of Sinanju, sun source of the martial arts."

"That's what it says on your credit card—M.O.S. Chiun—but maybe I can take a few of those for you."

Chiun abruptly dipped and stepped back. The three vertical stacks of boxes, like silverware on a tablecloth that had been whisked away by a parlor magician, suddenly stood on the floor, perfectly balanced. It had seemed like magic. It was not. It was Sinanju—the complete control of mind and body and physical surroundings that had inspired the original karate fighters, Ninja warriors, and Zen masters to their achievements—impressive only to those who had never experienced the real thing.

Remo set the fax machine on a taboret and dug out the instruction book.

Chiun was slicing open boxes. "You have not told me how your meeting with the famous Bardy Hicker went," he said.

"It's Hardy Bricker—or at least it was."

Chiun looked up from examining a juice machine. "He refused your entreaties to make a film of my glorious life?"

"Chiun, I told you when I went out the door that making a movie of your life was the furthest thing from Hardy Bricker's agenda," Remo said wearily.

"And so you dispatched him for his gross insensitivity. Good."

"No, I did not dispatch him. I got him a new career."

"He no longer makes movies?"

"You got it."

"Then who will commit my glorious tale to the silvery screen?"

"Nobody," said Remo. "It's not filmable."

"If they waste millions of dollars telling about some scarlet woman in the south whose plantation burns down and other unimportant matters," Chiun retorted bitterly, "why will they not make a film about the most kind, gentle, and gracious assassin who ever lived?"

Remo shrugged. " 'Bricker Balks at Boffo Biopic Bucks.' "

Chiun narrowed his hazel eyes. "What language is this you speak?"

"*Variety* talk."

"You are just jealous. You do not wish me to become famous."

"You got that right."

"You admit it?"

"Look, we're supposed to be a secret operation. If the whole story's playing in every movie house from here to Guam, everyone will know."

"Everyone now knows who murdered your most famous politician, thanks to Bardy Hicker," Chiun retorted.

"Bricker was full of manure. He wasted one hundred-eighty minutes of perfectly good film accomplishing what most people do every day sitting on the john in twenty."

Chiun sighed. "It is probably just as well."

"Good. I'm glad you agree."

"They probably would not have cast me in the role," Chiun said resignedly.

"Count on that."

"Or gotten Robin Williams to play me," Chiun added.

Remo raised an eyebrow.

"They probably would have gotten someone terrible," Chiun added.

Remo blinked. "Who did you have in mind to play me?"

The Master of Sinanju shrugged unconcernedly. "I do not concern myself with the casting of bit parts."

"Come on, you obviously had this all figured out."

"Perhaps Andy Devine."

"Andy Devine!"

"Or possibly Sydney Greenstreet."

"Sydney—!"

"All those fat white people look alike anyway," Chiun said dismissively. And Remo thought he detected a rare twinkle in the Master of Sinanju's eyes.

Frowning, Remo turned his attention back to the instruction manual. It was eighty pages long and divided into chapters. He read along, one hand resting on the wall, and after twenty minutes the only thing he understood was the part that said, "When the phone rings, lift the handset to answer call."

Remo threw away the book, saying, "What the hell. It's a telephone. How hard can it be to install?"

He pulled out the modular plug of his old phone.

"So far, so good," he said happily, inserting the modular plug of the new phone. There was another plug, like that on the TV. This, he reasoned, obviously went into a wall outlet.

He plugged this in. Nothing happened.

Then he discovered that there was an On switch. He turned the fax phone on and a green power light went on. Unfortunately, so did a red paper light. He wondered what that meant.

He started to hunt up the instruction book, then realized it would probably be easier to ask Harold Smith, who after all had sent the thing to him in the first place.

He picked up the handset and prepared to dial. Instead, he got a loud conversation.

"What is this—a party line fax?"

He listened a moment and on came, of all things, a commercial.

"I think this overfed phone is picking up the TV signal," Remo muttered.

"What good is picking up a TV voice when there is no picture?" Chiun wondered. "You must have gotten a defective pox."

Receiver in hand, Remo grabbed the remote and ran up and down the channels of the nearest TV. None of the voices matched.

"Maybe it's a radio station," he muttered. "You by chance order a radio?"

Chiun was slicing open another box and excavating a Veg-O-Matic. "Yes," he said absently, "I ordered one of everything."

"It looks it."

"I deserve it."

"Tell it to Smith," said Remo.

"You are just jealous because all you have is a pox," said Chiun. "A defective pox at that."

Remo hung up and went looking for a radio. Fortunately most of the boxes were marked. He carried the box, still sealed, back upstairs because he knew that Chiun would insist on opening it himself.

The Master of Sinanju accomplished this with a swift slicing motion of one elongated fingernail.

Remo went to plug in the radio, but all the outlets were full.

"You order an extension cord?" he asked Chiun.

"I do not know what an extension cord is," Chiun replied.

"If I find one, can I use it?"

"What makes you think I ordered one?"

Remo looked around and made a wry mouth. "Mathematical odds are heavily in my favor."

"You may do what you wish," said Chiun, removing from a box a complete set of Ginzu knives.

Remo found, not an extension cord, but a surge protector. It looked like it would do the job, and it did. Remo turned on the radio and roved the dial.

The station was a religious talk station. The broadcast signal was coming through the telephone with greater clarity than the radio.

"You got a cheap radio," Remo grunted.

"It was free."

"Tell that to the American taxpayer," Remo retorted.

Just then the fax phone rang.

"That must be Smitty calling to check the fax," said Remo, picking up the receiver. It beeped in his ear, then tweedled loudly.

"Hello? Hello?" he said.

"Incoming fax," a voice said. Remo didn't recognize the voice, but it was hard to hear over the radio voices assaulting his ear.

"The paper light is on," Remo said.

"Well, put in the paper and I'll call right back."

Remo hung up and searched out a roll of paper. It was surprisingly simple to insert. He felt proud of himself when he got it in place. The phone rang again and the beeping and tweedling started anew.

The paper began spitting out. And spitting out. It was a long continuous sheet and Remo realized it was going to make a mess if he didn't get hold of it.

He picked up the loose end and started reading.

"This looks like the financial report of some big company," he muttered.

He read some more.

"This is the financial report of International Data Corporation," Remo said in a puzzled voice. "Why would Smith send this to us?"

"No doubt Emperor Smith has his reasons," said the Master of Sinanju, whose Sinanju ancestors had worked for the great emperors of history and assumed that Harold Smith, whose title was director, must be some modern word for emperor.

"I guess so," said Remo. He kept rolling up the greasy fax paper as fast as it was spit out. The paper exhausted itself before the report ended. When it was over, the paper light came back on, along with one saying "Error."

"Error? I didn't do anything wrong."

"You do nothing right," said Chiun thinly.

He grabbed up the receiver and hit the 1 button— the simplified code that enabled him to dial directly his superior without having to remember complicated codes like ten-digit telephone numbers.

"Smitty?" said Remo. "What's with this fax?"

Through the background voices, the lemon-bitter voice of Harold W. Smith was saying, "Fax? I did not send you a fax."

"Well, I just got a fax as long as Roseanne's enemies list."

"You must have gotten a wrong fax."

"You can get those?"

"Remo, I can barely hear you. Who is that speaking in the background?"

"I think it's the Jehovah's Witnesses."

"What?"

"It's a long story. Why did you send me a fax?"

"I just told you I did not," Smith said testily.

"I mean a fax machine, not a fax fax."

"Oh, yes." Smith cleared his voice. "Security reasons. It is best if we communicate by fax from now on. This way I can transmit data with greater efficiency."

"If this is efficient," Remo said sourly, "I say we tie a string to two tin soup cans and try that."

Smith's tone sharpened. "Remo, you are breaking up."

"No," said Remo. "I am hanging up." And he did. Remo dug up the endless fax and located a phone number at the top of the roll. He called it, got a switchboard girl, and said, "I just got your fax."

"Whom shall I inform?"

"The idiot who dialed my number by accident and used up all my freaking paper," Remo told her.

"Sir, the International Data Corporation does not misdial. All our phone calls are made via computer and verified by the central processor."

"Well, your central processor just stroked out. What I want to know is who is going to reimburse me for a new roll of fax paper?"

The switchboard girl's voice became chilly. "Sir, I assure you if you received an IDC fax, it was intended for you."

"Like hell it was."

The switchboard girl's voice cooled dramatically. "Then I must conclude that you are not authorized to use the fax you are using."

"I'm calling from my own freaking castle!" Remo shouted.

"Here, here," said Chiun, opening a plastic egg and sniffing at its inexplicably flesh-colored contents.

"Now you are becoming abusive and I am allowed to hang up without prejudice," the girl retorted.

"Listen, kid," Remo said quickly. "I just read this thing through. It's a financial report. According to this, your bottom line is a circle."

"Circle?"

"Yeah. Circle. Zero. Goose egg. You know what that means?"

The girl's voice trembled. "Bankruptcy?"

" 'Fraid so."

"Um—how bad is it?"

"I'd update your resume before the rush starts," Remo said in his best sincere voice.

"Is it okay if I tell some of the others?"

"Fine with me," Remo said cheerfully. "Good luck job hunting." And Remo hung up. "She fell for it. I'll bet IDC stock drops five points before that little rumor is squelched."

"I see you are enjoying your pox," commented

Chiun, donning a pair of headphones that made him look like a superannuated test pilot.

"I am *not* enjoying my fax. I want to break it into a million pieces."

Chiun's eyebrows quirked upward. "Would it not be better to unplug it?"

Remo did. He plugged his old phone back in and stabbed the 1 button. He got Harold W. Smith again. This time without the Greek Chorus of Jehovah's Witnesses.

"Smitty?"

"Remo, are you ready to receive?" Smith asked.

"Not since my first Communion."

"I beg your pardon?"

"Forget it. And forget the dippy fax. It's in a million pieces."

"But I was about to fax you your next assignment."

"What's wrong with what we're doing now?" Remo wanted to know. "Just talking?"

"There have been some recent technological break-throughs in telephone eavesdropping," Smith said in a suddenly soft voice, "specifically by the National Security Agency. They now have the capability to overhear anything we say."

"Smitty, there are probably fifty million telephones in this country and if the National Security Agency has even fifty clerks whose only job it is to listen in to private telephone conversations, I'll eat any fax you care to send me. If you can get it through."

Smith cleared his throat. In the twenty-odd years Remo had worked for him, Smith never managed a decent comeback.

"Listen carefully, Remo," said Harold Smith. "You are familiar with HELP?"

"Sure. It's been at the top of the news every night for the last month. You'd think the bubonic plague was back the way the media is trying to stampede people."

"The death toll has just reached thirteen people," said Smith, ignoring Remo's outburst.

"What's the big deal? If environmentalist dips are getting sick from eating bugs, then all they gotta do is stop eating the stupid bugs, and presto! No more problem. What's the big deal?"

"The big deal," said Harold W. Smith, "is that the members of People Against Protein Assassins, as they call themselves, are now claiming that according to every test known to man, the thunderbugs simply cannot be transmitting the HELP virus."

"Thunderbug?"

"It's the Indian name. I believe it is Pawnee."

"It's pap. The whole thing is pap. Pap and crap."

"The PAPA leader, Theodore Soars-With-Eagles, is claiming that the HELP virus is not a virus at all, but a result of the depletion of the ozone layer."

Chiun's voice lifted. "There is no ozone hole. The illustrious Thrush Limburger has told America this."

"What did he say?" asked Smith.

"Chiun's latest kick—or it was before he discovered the Home Shopping Network."

"He what?"

"Look, let's stay on the subject. You can have your heart attack when the charge card bills come in."

Smith sighed, sounding like a leaky steam valve. "Theodore Soars-With-Eagles has called upon the federal government to help head off the coming HELP epidemic."

"Why doesn't that surprise me?"

"The new Vice President has heard his appeals and made a plea to the new President. He has asked us to look into it."

"Isn't this kinda flaky? Don't we have better things to do like—and here is major hint number 334—taking care of the quack who likes to help sick old ladies commit suicide?"

"The Dr. Mordaunt Gregorian matter is still under review."

"Call him Dr. Doom like everybody else. And I want a crack at him."

"Later."

"Don't we have the right to refuse dippy missions from the President?"

"We do," admitted Smith. "But the President has had a good look at our operating budget, and he is eyeing us for cutbacks."

"Wait'll he finds out Chiun just doubled the budget in one shopping day," Remo said.

Smith groaned. Then he said, "I have decided it would be politic to look into this."

"Chiun isn't going to like this," Remo warned.

Chiun, in the middle of unpacking a juice machine, straightened to demand, "What am I not going to like?"

Remo grinned and saw his chance. "Smitty wants us to look into the bug-eaters who are dying out in California," he said and waited for the wail of outraged complaint.

Instead, the Master of Sinanju said amiably, "Inform Emperor Smith that we will be happy to meet with the unfortunates who are reduced to eating bugs."

"We will?"

Chiun nodded. "Happily."

Remo glowered and said into the phone, "Just tell me what I absolutely have to know, Smitty."

"Their headquarters is called Nirvana West, which is a commune of sorts near the town of Ukiah, north of San Francisco. It was jointly founded by Brother Karl Sagacious and Theodore Soars-With-Eagles."

"Soars-With-Eagles?"

"He claims to be a Chinchilla Indian."

"Chinchilla?"

"According to the newspapers, that is his tribe's name. Although I must admit, his features do not appear very Indian."

"Wait a minute. Are we talking American Indian or East Indian?"

"American."

"I played cowboys and Indians all over Newark as a kid, Smitty, and I never heard of any Chinchilla tribe. And whoever heard of an Indian brave named Theodore?"

"It's possible Theodore Soars-With-Eagles is a white man with some Chinchilla blood in him," said Smith.

"It's possible he's full of wampum too."

"There has been bad blood between the Sagacious faction and the Eagles faction of PAPA," Smith went on. "Eagles has ample motivation to have done away with Sagacious. Look into that angle, Remo. It may all be a tawdry power struggle in a fringe group. You will go in as investigators from the Food and Drug Administration, and mingle with the federal scientists who are already on site."

"Anything else?"

"Yes. Keep your expenditures to a minimum." And Harold Smith hung up.

Remo hung up too and turned in time to see the Master of Sinanju running a blob of Silly Putty through his juice machine.

"Since when are you all hot to watch a bunch of lunatics in their natural element?" he asked Chiun.

"Since I have gotten tired of watching the old lunatics," replied the Master of Sinanju, lifting the lid and looking in to see the interesting concoction he had just created.

4

It had all started on the opening day of school.

Five-year-old Kevin O'Rourke had been looking forward to school for a long time—almost three weeks, since his mother had first sat him down to explain kindergarten to him.

Kevin O'Rourke was an exceptional child. All mothers think their offspring are exceptional. Mrs. Bernadette O'Rourke was no different. She thought young Kevin quite a lad. And he was the spitting image of his dear father, like herself a native-born Irishman, but who fought for his adopted country, the U.S.A., in the Gulf War and died in a Scud missile attack, God rest his soul.

Young Kevin looked exactly like Patrick—the young Patrick whom Bernadette could still conjure up in her mind's eye whenever she thought back to the tiny Irish village of Dingle where they had grown up together. Kevin had the same open face; what one day would be the same fierce Catholic faith, the same stubbornness, but also the same willingness to trust others.

He made her feel proud even through her sharp loss.

And so on the day she drove him to the Walter F. Mondale Grammar School in Minneapolis, Minnesota, Mrs. Bernadette O'Rourke rode on a cushion of air. Oh, she was not without motherly pangs. For one thing, there had been no one with whom to talk over her decision to send Kevin to a public school instead of Catholic school. It had been an economic decision, really. The truth was she was already working two jobs and didn't have even the modest tuition the parochial schools charged. There were scholarships, certainly. Unfortunately, they didn't have any for Americans like Kevin O'Rourke. He was the wrong color for scholarships.

But this was Minneapolis, after all, where the public schools were supposed to be very good. Not like New York, where they had to have metal detectors in the school doorways to weed out the hooligans with their guns and their knives.

Mrs. Bernadette O'Rourke shivered at the very thought. Even in the north of Ireland—she was from the south—they didn't have it so terrible.

There was a crowd in front of the school when she pulled up.

"Who are all those people, Mommy?" asked Kevin with those innocent blue eyes.

"Other mommies bringing their wee children," said Mrs. O'Rourke, but when she got Kevin out of the car she noticed an unusual number of very old ladies present. They were well past childbearing age. They looked too old to be teachers, to be sure. Perhaps they were grandmothers, she thought. The Lord alone knew how many mothers had to work these days.

Mrs. O'Rourke took little Kevin by his moist hand and led him up the walk to the school door entrance where the old ladies seemed to be concentrated. They carried old cigar boxes hung with what looked like colored balloons without air in them.

Little Kevin thought so too.

"Bawoons," he cried, pointing.

An old woman in a purple hat stepped up and smiled with teeth yellowed from too much tea and not enough brushing and asked, "Would you like one, sonny?"

"Yes!"

And the woman handed little Kevin O'Rourke a blue foil packet that said "genuine latex" on it.

Only then did Mrs. O'Rourke recognize the limp multicolored things hanging off the old lady's cigar box for what they were.

"Good God, madam! Are ye daft? Do ye not realize what it is ye be handing out to the boy?"

"It's for his own good," replied the woman in a snippy voice. "Here, peewee, let me help you with that," she told the boy.

And before Mrs. O'Rourke's horrified eyes, the old woman dug apart the foil packet and unrolled a lubricated latex condom that was a watermelon red.

"Madam!" Mrs. O'Rourke said huffily, snatching the thing before Kevin could touch it. "What is the matter with ye now?"

"I want my bawoon," said little Kevin, the tears already starting in his young eyes.

"It's not a balloon," his mother and the old woman said in the same breath. Only Mrs. O'Rourke's tone was angry. The old woman's was exasperated.

The old woman fingered one of the garish things as if it were rosary beads. "It's a condom, young man. Can you say con-dom?"

"Madam!"

"It's not to play with," the old woman went on primly. "It's for little boys to know about so when they become naughty men they don't cause diseases in nice young ladies."

"I won't be naughty," Kevin promised. "Can I have my bawoon now?"

"Madam, will you stop?" said Mrs. O'Rourke, clapping her hands over Kevin's ears. "The boy is too young to be knowin' of such things. Let him be, would you please?"

The old woman practically spat her vehemence into Mrs. O'Rourke's reddening face. "He is *not* too young! If we get them before they know anything, when they grow up they'll only know what we want them to know."

"What nonsense are ye talking now?" Mrs. O'Rourke's Irish temper was rising now.

"It is education. The board of education approved it four to three, and the three slackers were later reprimanded by the superintendent."

"Come on, Kevin," said Mrs. O'Rourke, not believing her ears. She pulled the boy along, trying to stifle her anger.

But another old woman blocked the door and said, "He doesn't have his little rubber safety cap. The young boys are not allowed in until they learn how to unroll their little caps and put them on."

"Put them on what?" Kevin asked, not understanding.

At that point the first old woman bustled up, and before Mrs. O'Rourke could block her son's innocent ears with her strong, protective hands, the old woman told little Kevin O'Rourke exactly where he should put his watermelon red condom.

Mrs. O'Rourke decked her with a roundhouse right that started at her right hip and didn't stop until the old woman was an awkward pile of bones on the school walk, her uppers and lowers bouncing in the grass.

The police were called. Mrs. O'Rourke tried to explain how the old women had provoked her with their foul terrible language—and in front of a mere boy at that—and the next thing she knew they were binding her trembling-with-rage hands behind her back with flexicuffs and she was in the back of what used to be called a paddy wagon in the days the Irish were treated like common dirt in the streets of America, and a matron was explaining to her that her little Kevin, the only good and fine thing that had come out of her brief marriage to darlin' Patrick, would be going to a foster home and the chances of getting him back were not very good at all.

*　　*　　*

Up until that day, Race Branchwood was just another unhappy three-hundred-thirty-pound disk jockey playing middle of the road music and reading the news—ninety uninterrupted seconds of news as the station's promos boasted—every half hour.

It was no glamour job. Oh, some thought differently. But not Race Branchwood. He had gotten his communications degree from Emerson College and thought he was destined for greater heights than playing mush for mushheads.

As it would turn out, Race Branchwood was absolutely right.

But on this early September day in the year 1991, Race Branchwood was Thrush Limburger, a name which he hated but which was a condition of employment at Radio Station WAKO in the Twin Cities, when he chanted into the microphone for the one-thousand-five-hundred-and-seventy-seventh time, "And now, ten uninterrupted minutes of seventies music, count them, ten, nine, eight, seven, six, five, four, three, two, one uninterrupted minutes from the station that still plays with your bippy. This is Thrush Limburger, and I'll be right back."

He switched off the mike and left the sound booth, muttering under his breath as he hurried to the hall coffee machine.

"Thrush Limburger, my left testicle."

"What was that, Branchwood?" came the surly voice of the station manager.

"I said I got heartburn in my left ventricle."

"Burp. And while you're at it, try to lose a few hundred pounds. The next Arbitron book is only two months away and we're trying to project a lean-and-mean image. How can you show your face at public appearances looking like the the the Pillsbury Doughboy?"

"What do you think people expect from a guy named Limburger?" Race Branchwood snapped back.

"The Limburger was to cover our bets. I want you looking like a Thrush, not just sounding like one."

"I could do better work under my own name. Race."

"Everybody knows that Race is short for Horace. You look like a Horace too."

"I *am* a Horace, you dink. It's my name, for crying out loud."

"We've had this idiot conversation before. I'm going to be next door having my hair done."

"Must be louse season again," muttered Race Branchwood, continuing on to the coffee machine, walking on tippy toes like so many three-hundred-pounders do. He coaxed the machine to fill the cup all the way this time just by punching the C in Coffee and added two sugars—real and not that pink stuff he hated—and a dollop of real cream and was back in time to pick off the latest news script that the WAKO news writer had laid beside his mike.

Race Branchwood took a quick sip of the coffee before picking up the script and switched on his mike.

He didn't know it, but the switching on of the microphone marked the end of his disk jockey career. It was also the end of Race Branchwood. He would never be Race Branchwood again. That was the only downside, the only regret he was to feel for the rest of his natural life.

"And now," he said in a booming baritone that was redolent of the cream in his coffee, "here is the WAKO Ninety-Second News."

Race Branchwood cast his professional eye over the first item and did something he had never done in his radio career. He froze at the mike. But only for six seconds. He took a second hit of the coffee he was destined never to finish.

Clearing his throat, he tried again. "A Mrs. Bernadette O'Rourke was arrested today for—" Race stopped. "This is unbelievable," he said in a stunned whisper. "I mean, ladies and gentlemen, this is an unreal item I have just been handed. Let me—give me a moment here, please."

He tried again. "A Mrs. Bernadette O'Rourke was arrested today for assault and battery of a seventy-eight-year-old woman named Agnes Frug—that's F-R-U-G, like the dance. Now the reason Mrs. O'Rourke was compelled to coldcock the other woman is very simple. It seems that Ms. Frug—the script says Ms. attempted to force Mrs. O'Rourke's five-year-old son Kevin to put on a condom before he could enter the Walter F. Mondale Grammar School. It was Kevin's first day of school. He never got in the door. As a matter of fact, he's now in a foster home. Mrs. O'Rourke is in the county lockup. No, I am *not* making this up. This is an actual news item and it took place in our fair city."

Race Branchwood took a deep breath. He looked at the wall clock and saw that he was already sixty seconds into the Ninety-Second News spot and he had only read the first squib.

Then he said, "Ah, the hell with it." And with that he became Thrush Limburger forevermore.

"You know what really gets under my skin, ladies and gentlemen? It's the whackjobs. The whackjobs who think five-year-olds have to be indoctrinated in the scare of the month. And the feminasties who put them up to it. And the old toot grannies who get their jollies playing with condoms in public. My friends, if you were to take those old toot grannies and turn their biological clocks back fifty years to when they were twenty, and hand *them* a rubber, they would have A) slapped you right in the face and B) whistled up the cops. And you, my friend, would be doing hard time on a morals charge.

"So how is it fifty years later those same old ladies are spending their waking hours packaging prophylactics and passing them out to kids too young to even begin to understand what the hell these things are. I'll tell you why. Because before menopause hit them like a ton of bricks and took away the last shred of common sense they may or may not have had, they were terrified at the very thought of a condom. Now they can't get enough of them. And why not? They're out of the game. They can't play anymore. And these dried-up old biddies can't wait to throw these things around like bingo chips."

In the control room, the program director was turning purple. Thrush Limburger—he was Thrush Limburger now even if he didn't know it—never particularly liked the program director, so he ploughed on, hoping to get the man's face to match the particular shade of lavender Thrush happened to be wearing around his own neck that day.

The program director pointed at his watch, at the wall clock, and then at his forehead and pretended to pull the trigger of an imaginary gun, until he realized there was no stopping Thrush Limburger. He buried his head in his arms and Thrush continued on, an unstoppable juggernaut of opinion given voice.

"When are you people going to wake up out there? How many Bernadette O'Rourkes have to be hauled off and strip-searched? And how many Kevin O'Rourkes have to end up wherever some bureaucrat with the child protective services division happens to drop him before people take a stand against these idiots who think they know what's better for our kids than we do? Is everybody asleep, or am I the only one with a functioning brain? Does anyone share my moral outrage at this lunacy?"

"If this goes on, they'll be having these poor little kids simulating safe sex with one another just to satisfy these nutso do-gooders."

The WAKO station manager thought he heard the booming voice of his most problematic DJ coming through the chrome hairdrier capping his head and snapped his fingers. The hairdresser turned and looked blank.

"Is that Thrush?" he asked.

"Yeah, and he's sure telling it like it is."

"What?" The station manager flung up the hair-drier. He always got his hair done at the ladies salon because they knew how to treat the subtle wave in his hair. He also had a crush on a manicurist named Bruce. He listened with growing horror.

"What gets me, my friends, is that our taxes go to keeping these rainbow-chasers in gear. You know, those so-called free condoms aren't free. Uh-uh. You paid for them. And if you keep turning the other cheek, next year they'll have you paying for people's sex change operations, and then when they find out they're still not happy, you'll be paying for them to change back. And after that, you'll be paying again when they sue the state or the city government for malpractice and loss of quality of life because after they get their dicks sewn back on, they still won't function properly."

"Oh, my God. The sponsors will kill us," moaned the WAKO station manager, rushing from the salon in curlers.

Thrush Limburger was deep into his second quarter hour of commentary when the plug was pulled on him. The ON AIR sign went out and although he was dimly aware of it, Thrush didn't care. He kept going, a human icebreaker of public opinion.

In the control booth, the station manager and the program director were going nuts. Thrush had locked himself in the sound booth, so they could go as nuts as they cared to. He was going to speak his piece. If they wanted WAKO to be heard, they'd have to put him back on the air. After that, they could fire him all they wanted. Just so long as Thrush Limburger had an opportunity to sit on that idiot station manager during the firing.

Thrush Limburger was off the air all of seven minutes. The switchboard lit up like a Christmas tree. Thrush could tell because they were answering the incoming calls frantically. After three minutes of that, the station manager began pulling out his hair, steel curlers and all.

With a resigned gesture, he flipped the ON AIR switch.

And Thrush Limburger was back on the airwaves.

"For those of you just tuning in," he said without skipping a beat, "we're talking about Mrs. Bernadette O'Rourke, who is now languishing in jail because she thought her five-year-old son deserved to be shielded from some of life's more adult topics. Those of you who want to hear the Cowsills or Abba, or any of that tripe, we don't want you. Go find a station that does."

A groan came through the supposedly soundproof glass.

When he came off his shift, the station manager said, "Limburger, your fat ass is fired!"

"It's Branchwood, you pillow-biter."

As it turned out, they were both wrong.

Thrush Limburger became the hottest on-air radio personality in the Twin Cities. WAKO went all-talk with the next Arbitron book. And the station manager ultimately got a job next door in the hair salon, where his heart lay, anyway.

No one ever heard the name Race Branchwood again. Not even Thrush Limburger, who knew a good thing when he saw it and had his name legally changed to Thrush Limburger.

Within a year, he was all over Minnesota. From there, he self syndicated *The Thrush Limburger Show,* over his own network, the TTT Network. It stood for Tell the Truth. And he did. About everything.

 By the time he had landed on TV, he was a genuine phenomenon, with a best-selling book, *The Way the World Is,* to his credit and rumors of a bright future in national politics swirling about his close-cropped head.

On the second anniversary of the day he had irrevo-

cably become Thrush Limburger, the former Horace
Branchwood was doing a restrospective.

"On the phone with me now is a very special person," he was telling his nationwide audience.
"Now a lot of you may not know the name Bernadette
O'Rourke, but she is a very special lady. It was her
story, ladies and gentlemen, that got me started on
my meteoric rise to—shall we say—greatness? How
are you, Mrs. O'Rourke?"

"Just grand, Thrush."

"And little Kevin. How old is he now?"

"Seven. And he's now in the second grade in St.
Mary's Catholic School, thanks to you."

"Ahem. For those who don't know, it was yours
truly who brought the sad plight of Mrs. O'Rourke to
national attention, resulting in the dropping of all
charges and incidentally through the kindness and generosity of my original listening audience, the tuition
that enabled Kevin to be enrolled in St. Mary's to
begin with. Now you didn't call just to traipse down
memory lane with me, Mrs. O'Rourke. Pray tell,
what's on your mind?"

"It's this HELP nonsense, Thrush. It's starting to
sound like that AIDS hysteria all over again. And
over what? Eating bugs? Who would want to do that,
for God's sake?"

"Exactly right. Exactly right. And I've been meaning to address this matter myself. Now for those who
don't read your newspapers—and even for those who
do—HELP is another one of those viral plagues we
hear so much about. You can't get it from breathing
other people's air, touching their skin, and being bitten by a wild animal. In fact, if you want to get HELP,
you have to do all the biting. Even then you probably
won't get it. My friends, the only—and I mean only—
way you can contract this dreaded fatal, incurable
scourge is to consume in great quantities—eating just
one won't do it—a lowly bug. *Ingraticus Avalonicus* is
its scientific name. There are those who claim the In-

dians called it the thunderbug. It's a tiny thing like a dull brown ladybug and about as appetizing. Certain whackjob environmentalists are proclaiming it to be the solution to famine worldwide. All we gotta do is eat this little critter every day and figure out a way not to die."

"It's madness, Thrush," Mrs. O'Rourke said. "Sheer madness."

"And now they're claiming that the bug doesn't cause HELP. It's the thinning ozone layer. Well, if it's the thinning ozone layer, why is it only bug-eaters are coming down with Human Environmental Liability Paradox? That, my friends, is the true paradox. But it's simple. Just bear with me because here at the Triple-T Network, we always . . . tell the truth."

The retrospective show soon became the HELP show. Everyone called in. Microbiologists. Immunologists. Meteorologists. Epidemiologists. Entomologists. Everybody had a windy answer, but no one agreed with anyone else's answer.

At the end of it, Thrush Limburger had had enough.

"I have just now decided after listening to all sides of this growing noncontroversy, that only my on-site presence can possibly dispel the ridiculous myths that surround HELP, the greatest noncrisis since Swine Flu.

"Tomorrow—and you're hearing it here first—I am going to the Nirvana West headquarters of PAPA, where I will broadcast this show live and reveal . . . the startling truth about HELP."

And in a darkened office not far from the White House, a telephone rang. The handset lifted with a click. And a thin voice said, "Harpoon that whale."

The in-flight movie was *Dances With Wolves,* possibly the only thing that could make a Boston to San Francisco airline flight even more interminable than it was necessary to be.

Remo told the stewardess clutching the plastic earphones, "Thanks, but these clouds look real interesting."

The stewardess leaned closer, showed perfect capped teeth, and asked Remo if he'd like a headset anyway because the airplane had a wide range of piped-in radio programs.

"Sure, why not?" said Remo.

"And you, sir," she asked Chiun, leaning over so Remo could fully inhale her perfume. Remo held his breath. Perfumes, even the subtle ones, tended to enter his sensitive nostrils like a fragrant Roto-Rooter reamer.

The Master of Sinanju said, "If you are going to expose your udders, madam, expose them to one who is not repelled by their grossness."

The stewardess straightened like a bent bamboo pole springing back.

"I beg your pardon," she said in a chilly tone.

Remo said, "Don't mind him. He gets crochety on long flights." But he was relieved when the stewardess went off in search of another aisle to fumigate. She had been nice to look at, but stewardesses, more so than other women, seemed to respond to Remo's Sin-anju-enhanced pheromones. Usually they tried to sit in his lap. Often, they lost it completely and were reduced to tears by the simple and predictable event of Remo getting off at his assigned destination.

Remo plugged the stethoscopelike plastic plug of his earphone set into the seat jack and inserted the earpieces into his ears. He hit the On switch and began moving the numbered dial back and forth.

He got rap, rock, opera, bluegrass, country, heavy metal, acid rock, and gardening hints. The last chan-nel bellowed out in the unctious but exuberant voice of Thrush Limburger.

"My friends," he was saying, "you are being yanked!"

Remo unplugged both ends of the earphones and handed them to the Master of Sinanju, saying, "It's for you."

Chiun's wizened features grew curious, and while he was putting the earpieces in, Remo plugged in the other end.

Surprise, joy, and interest overspread his features and the Master of Sinanju settled down to listen. From time to time, he cackled with undisguised pleasure.

Remo could live with the cackling. It beat Chiun carping about the fragile state of the aircraft wing, which he invariably pronounced at the point of falling off whenever they flew.

At San Francisco International Airport, Remo rented a car and they drove north on Highway 101 past parched orchards and vineyards and into a hilly area dominated by evergreens and towering redwood trees.

"Thrush Limburger have anything good to say?" asked Remo, who really didn't care, but thought Chiun deserved a little conversation after a relatively peaceful flight.

"You are being yanked," said Chiun, who wore a simple but garish vermilion kimono.

"I think I caught that much. About what?"

"About everything. Especially, you are being yanked about this HELP."

"There, I agree with the guy."

"Thrush the Vocal is a brilliant man."

"Says who?"

"No less an authority than Thrush Limburger himself."

"Because . . . ," Remo prompted.

"Because he says so in a loud voice and accepts telephone calls from common Americans who do nothing but agree with him. They arc apparently a new emerging sect, called Rogers."

"Rogers?"

"When the great-voiced one pronounces a thing to be true, immediately, Americans in vast numbers call in and say 'Roger, Thrush.' It is apparently a secret code they have so that they recognize one another even over the telephone," Chiun added.

Remo rolled his dark eyes. "Yeah, it's pretty secret all right. Only you, me, and thirty million other radio listeners are in on it."

"He is also coming to this place."

"Oh, great," groaned Remo.

They had left the city behind and the landscape had turned piney and cool. Remo followed the signs to the town of Ukiah, where Nirvana West was located.

"This place is supposed to be only one step above a commune, so we may have a problem finding it," Remo said.

"Just listen for the whacking," said Chiun unconcernedly.

"Whacking?"

"It is their job, according to Thrush. Whacking. They are whackjobs."

"Little Father, a whackjob is a—"

Chiun's hazel eyes, younger by decades than the

surrounding face, looked to Remo curiously. He stroked a tendril of beard that clung to his tiny chin.

Traffic started to get heavy.

"Never mind," said Remo. "You keep your ears peeled and I'll keep my eyes on the road."

"No whacking will escape my notice," Chiun promised.

Further along, the traffic thickened and slowed. Before they had traveled another mile, they were bumper-to-bumper with a line of cars wending their way through the parched hills.

"Damn," Remo said.

"Let us walk," said Chiun.

"Do you have any idea how far it is to Nirvana West?" said Remo.

"No," replied the Master of Sinanju, stepping from the car. "And neither do you. So we will walk because we cannot sit here and inhale the stink of others' vehicles until our lungs and brains die."

Remo pulled over, got out, and followed. He saw that the traffic jam of vehicles was far worse than he thought. He stopped and knocked on a car window. It rolled down. A woman with thin blond hair and translucent teeth poked her head out.

"Any idea how far Nirvana West is from here?" Remo asked.

"At the end of this jam," said the woman.

"What is this?"

"This is the media traffic jam."

"It's not moving. Is there another way to get there?"

"You could hook around to the other side. But I hear the federal jam is even worse."

"Damn."

"Or you can sit on my lap and play coochie-coo," the blonde added.

"Thanks, but no thanks," said Remo, going to catch up with the Master of Sinanju.

"If we follow this to the end we'll get there," he said.

"Of course," said Chiun, who walked with his hands serenely tucked into the wide joined sleeves of his kimono.

They walked until they had rounded a piney hill and the line of cars—they saw TV microwave vans idling in the line like dejected war elephants—turned off the highway, and onto a wooded path.

They cut through the woods and started up the hill. Halfway up, they had a good view.

There were three lines of cars, all converging on a woodsy vale that might have been any patch of Northern California land except for the tents that dotted the place. Most were tents. A few were tepees. Big army tents were being pitched at one end. At the other, there were the pup tents and tepees.

The pup tent and tepee end were obviously the PAPA camp.

Most of the PAPA adherents, however, were climbing a brushy hillock in a double line. They bore three shrouded figures in stately procession. At the head of the line was a man in buckskin whose trailing war bonnet even at this distance didn't quite conceal his bald spot from Remo's sharp eyes.

As Remo and Chiun watched, the procession came to a shallow ditch at the hillock's rounded top. They lined it and without preamble, the shrouds were unceremoniously unrolled like flags, and three slightly stiff corpses tumbled out to land in the ditch with a thump.

"We commend our brethren to the earth, where they will abide in ecological harmony, nourishing the roots of the weeds that feed the thunderbugs that feed us now and by the millennium will feed the whole world," chanted the man in the war bonnet.

"Savages," said Chiun. "These people are savages."

"Because they don't bother with caskets?" asked Remo.

"No," said the Master of Sinanju. "Because they are morons. I do not care if they bury their dead in expensive shoe boxes or not. But there," he said, pointing to the hole the mourners were filling by the simple action of kicking clods of dirt in with their sandals and moccasins, "is where the dead are buried."

The Master of Sinanju pointed to a ring of stones at the foot of the hillock. A rusting bucket sat beside it.

"And over there," he added, "is their well. They are burying their dead uphill of their drinking water. In two months, it is going to taste like rancid duck. Have they no brains?"

"If they had," Remo said, "they wouldn't be eating bugs."

The ceremony, such as it was, was hastily concluded.

Someone could be heard asking, "Shouldn't we have waited for the media to set up their cameras?"

The man in the warbonnet—who Remo took to be Theodore Soars-With-Eagles—replied, "No. It will be better that they record my predictions for the endangered American people than the sight of our dead brethren. For if the federal government does not act soon, the dead will be beyond counting."

"What if they don't act?"

"They will act because the destruction of the ozone layer that is causing this will force them to act."

"They didn't act for acid rain."

"Or global warming."

"Or AIDS," someone else said.

"They will act here because it is not innocent trees, or deer, or persons who practice simple alternate lifestyles who are threatened, but the very ones who hold power in our corrupt society. For all know that the depletion of the ozone layer lets down carcinogenic ultraviolet rays, killing those who are cursed by being born light of skin. This is the first Caucasian-specific disaster in human history. The white man cannot wish this away."

Chiun frowned. "I do not understand a single word that man has said, Remo."

"Basically, he's doing a Chicken Little."

Chiun looked blank.

"He's claiming that the sky is falling," Remo explained.

"Is this true, Remo?" Chiun asked. "Will only whites succumb to this threat?"

"Only if they eat bugs. Come on, let's start looking around."

They started down from the hillside just as the first wave of press began setting up their cameras in front of a wooden dais evidently set up for Theodore Soars-With-Eagles's press conference.

"Let's try to avoid these guys," Remo whispered.

"How? There are so many."

"Let's at least try," said Remo. "Remember our last assignment, where we were up to our hip pockets in television anchormen? Smith is still trying to explain the network casualties to the President."

"It was not our fault so many died."

"Maybe not, but half these guys have your description memorized."

They worked their way around and came upon a malodorous slit trench filled almost to overflowing with yellowish offal.

Chiun peered inward. His nose wrinkled up.

"How can they live in such filth? They do not even bury the waste of their miserable bodies."

"Since they eat only bugs, I'm surprised there *is* any waste. Boy, does it smell bad in there."

"What can one expect of dead bugs that have passed through the bodies of idiots?"

They leapt over the trench and continued on to a bivouac area where preparations for a full-scale press conference were under way.

A food-service truck was in operation, manned by two men in cook's whites.

"Come get your lobster salad sandwiches here," one cried. "We have lobster salad sandwiches and lobster salad bowls. Tastes just like thunderbug. All the taste and no risk to your health."

The food-service truck was immediately surrounded. Money changed hands and sandwiches were grabbed by eager hands.

Some members of the press, already unable to get close to the truck, held up remotes here and there.

"You know, it's strange knowing we won't run into Cheeta Ching or a Don Cooder out here," Remo remarked.

Chiun sniffed and said nothing. Cheeta Ching remained a sore subject with him. Don Cooder was one of the network anchor casualties and a thorn in their side for years, until they had pulverized him.

A reporter they recognized as *Nightmirror* correspondent Ned Doppler was speaking into a hand mike and was staring into a minicam.

"Here in the rugged wilderness of Mendocino County, California, a new breed of American environmentalists are taking a stand against the despoiling of nature. PAPA. People Against Protein Assassins. They don't eat meat or dairy products. Only pure, natural food enters their systems. Only the purest water, only foods harvested in their natural habitat. Here, in one of the richest breeding grounds of the thunderbug, a valiant band, ignoring the naysayers, are deep in an experiment more monumental than the much-maligned Biosphere 2 experiment. They are the vanguard, eating a natural insect, becoming human insectivores in their quest for purity and oneness with nature."

"Stay low, Little Father," warned Remo. "This guy knows you on sight."

Ned Doppler, his wealth of hair squatting on his head like some steroid-intoxicated fur, seemed oblivious to everything but his lines, which he was reading off cue cards.

"Crap," said Remo. They moved on.

Another live remote was in progress not much further along. Remo recognized the boyish-looking newsman as Tim Macaw, who anchored the MBC evening news.

"The Thunderbug. Miracle Food or Menace? Who is to know? Who can know? The debate is already raging here in this mountain fastness between the legions of PAPA and the hordes unleashed by the Food and Drug Administration. Will right triumph? Will good be rewarded? Will the PAPA continue to nourish their bodies with *Ingraticus Avalonicus*—or . . . or will we ever know? Can we ever know? Can we ever really, really, really, ever know anything?"

"Not if we listen to dickheads like you," Remo yelled in a loud voice.

A producer called, "Cut!"

Macaw looked around angrily. "What jerk ruined my standup?"

But Remo and Chiun were no longer in sight. They had drifted on.

It was like that for the next five hundred yards. Reporters talking into microphones, giving opinions without foundation, speculating without sources, and clawing for a piney background that would make it seem as if they and only they had the exclusive story.

It was impossible to get close to the podium where Theodore Soars-With-Eagles and his adherents were about to appear, unless Remo and Chiun wanted to insinuate themselves into a growing circle of media that resembled a fast-forming mold ring, which they could, and risk having their faces televised nationally, which they preferred to avoid.

"Those big tents over to the south must be the Feds," Remo whispered. "Let's try them."

"I do not see the bugs everyone speaks of," said

Chiun, examining the bottom of one sandal. "What do they look like?"

"Search me. All I know is that they're pretty small."

Chiun stooped, brushing the dried-out grass with his long fingernails. "I see many bugs. Which are which?"

"All bugs look alike to me. Just don't eat any, okay?"

Chiun straightened. "Remo! I would no sooner eat a bug than I would go naked in public."

"Do me a favor. Don't do either."

On the other side of a stand of ponderosa pine that seemed to form a natural barrier, they found the big army-style tents.

"Damn!" said Remo. "The media's all over this place too."

"Why do you not beat them, as did the adherents of the last President?" wondered Chiun. "He would simply revile them before large crowds, and his followers would descend on the Philistines with hard sticks."

"Pass," said Remo. He was looking around, thinking that this assignment, already a pain, was fast becoming a logistical nightmare. He was about to suggest they withdraw to the nearest hotel and wait for the feeding frenzy to subside when someone with a mircrophone suddenly shouted, "Hey! Isn't that Twin Peaks?"

"You mean Capital Hills."

Remo saw what the two meant an instant later. And it wasn't landscape.

She came without a mike or sound man or minicam. She didn't need them to break a path. Her chest looked big enough to knock down an advancing skirmish line. It bounced.

Remo had seen a lot of bouncing breasts in his time. Usually they bounced in tandem. These did not. One went up as the other was going down. Sometimes they collided in passing and caromed off one another.

It was clear the woman was not wearing a bra. She

wasn't big on shaving her legs either. She wore khaki
shorts that left her legs bare. Or as bare as the legs
of a tarantula could be. They were that hairy.

And Remo had a deep suspicion that she dispensed
with underarm deodorant too. The cool California air
was becoming acrid.

The woman carried a stubby pencil and a frayed
spiral notepad, so Remo took her to be a print
reporter.

"Is anyone here not with the feds?" she bellowed.

The electronic press lifted their hands. Their eyes
stayed on her chest.

"Not you idiots!" she snapped. "I know who you
are. I'm looking for someone from PAPA."

The hands went down.

"Anyone here from PAPA?" she repeated.

Suddenly her eyes lighted on Remo and Chiun.

"Uh-oh," said Remo.

"Remo," Chiun said worriedly. "It is coming this
way."

"I know it."

The woman bounced up, seemingly oblivious to the
uppercuts her mammaries were trying to give her
pointed chin. "You! Are you the People Against Protein Assassins?"

"No," said Remo. "Go away."

"You can't tell me to go away. I'm from the Boston
Blade."

Remo groaned. It was worse than he thought. The
Boston *Blade* was notorious for the political correctness of its reporters. Although they had another
phrase for it: moral rectitude.

The woman marched up to Remo and came to a
dead stop. Her breasts continued forward, stressing
the thin fabric of her peasant blouse beyond reason.
Through the gauzy stuff, her nipples showed as big as
cow teats mounted on lopsided aureoles.

Remo and Chiun took a unified step backward.

"I'm Jane Goodwoman," the woman announced

when her chest stopped rebounding. "And when I write things in my column, great Americans from Senator Ned Clancy to the Reverend Juniper Jackman pay attention. Sixteen column inches of my copy in tomorrow's *Blade* will have America's best and brightest politicians swarming all over this place."

Remo turned to Chiun and said, "Maybe we should just get rid of her now."

"You can't get rid of the press," Jane Goodwoman snapped, "and you know it. We're eternal, the permafrost of American society."

"That explains the cultural Ice Age," said Remo.

Jane Goodwoman narrowed her thin eyes. "So who are you two?"

Sighing, Remo dug out an ID card and lifted it to her face.

"Remo Cougar Mellencamp," he said in a bored voice. "With the Food and Drug Association."

"You mean 'Administration.' "

Remo pulled the card back real fast, palming it so it couldn't be read. "No, I mean Association."

"I understand it's Administration."

Remo decided to bluff his way through this bullshit conversation. "The new Administration changed the name. Claimed people got it confused with the executive branch. Guess they were right."

Jane Goodwoman's face lost its tension. "Oh, if the Administration says it's all right, then it's all right, right?"

"Right," said Remo. "Now we have work to do."

"Well, I'm here to help," said Jane Goodwoman, who was looking at Remo's pants zipper.

"By hauling every congressman and senator from the fifty states into this?"

"How else are we going to solve America's problems?"

"It is not a problem, according to Thrush Limburger," squeaked Chiun.

Jane Goodwoman blanched. She swayed. For a mo-

ment, she looked like she was about to faint or throw
up, or possibly do both.

Remo's instinct was to reach out to prevent her
from falling on her face. The thought of touching her
repelled him. Then she leaned forward and her breasts
popped out of her blouse and he realized her face was
in no danger at all.

She hit the dirt with a mushy splat. Her pointed
nose bent to the left, but only because it struck a
stone.

Remo called over to a crew of workmen pitching
tents.

"Hey, we could use some help over here."

Their eyes went wide and their faces paled. "Did
you say HELP?" one croaked.

"Not that kind of help," said Remo. "We need a
tent pitched right here."

They came bearing rolled canvas, pegs, and tent
poles and nervous twitches.

"Put it over her so she doesn't draw flies," Remo
suggested.

The workmen noticed Jane Goodwoman's pallor.
"Is—is she contagious?" one asked shakily.

"Only if you read her column with your brain
turned off," said Remo. "Come on, Little Father."

They started making the rounds of tents. Signs were
hung on all of them. Remo saw that the Department
of the Interior, the National Institutes of Health, the
National Institute of Allergy and Infectious Diseases,
and the Federal Emergency Management Administration were on the job, among others.

"Is anybody in charge here?" Remo called into
open tent flaps as he came to them.

"No, we're just trying to help," a voice from the
first tent told him.

"Then why are you all hiding in your tents?"

"Are you crazy? There's a hole in the ozone right
over our heads. We're waiting for the sunblock and
aluminum umbrellas to arrive."

"And you are?"

"Environmental Protection Agency. We're here to see if the bug belongs on the endangered species list."

"And if it does?"

"America faces the hardest choice in its history—to protect the thunderbug or feed the starving millions of the world. It's a choice I wouldn't want to have to make."

"Amen," added a voice from the next tent. A sign in front said Federal Radon Testing Administration.

"That's probably why you get paid the big bucks," said Remo, rolling his eyes.

At the next tent, he was asked if he was the press. When he said no, the tent was zipped up in his face, and a whining voice complained, "How are we going to get our federal grant without press?"

Remo got similar answers at almost every tent.

"How do you know which of these people can help us and which cannot?" Chiun asked as they walked along.

"I'll know it when I hear it."

At last they came to one that was sealed. Remo looked for something to knock on and settled for slapping the tent flap hard.

A voice said, "Go away, I'm working in here."

"Bingo," said Remo.

Just then, one of the tent pitchers came over and said, "She's calling for you. Ms. Goodwoman is calling for you, sir."

"Let her call," said Remo.

"She says she has something to show you that will explain everything. I suggest you placate her. She's very powerful."

"Watch this tent," Remo told Chiun.

He followed the man to the newly erected tent and slipped in.

Jane Goodwoman was alone in the tent. It was dark.

Remo's eyes adjusted to the lack of light, got a good look, and decided that darkness was preferable.

"Okay, let's hear it," he said.

"I like you," said Jane Goodwoman in a suddenly husky voice.

"I'm politically incorrect. Honest Injun."

She came closer. "I like a challenge."

"Try mounting a giraffe."

Jane Goodwoman approached with the languorous sway of a net bag crammed with assorted misshapen muskmelons.

She reached behind Remo and zipped the tent flap closed.

"You had something to show me," Remo reminded.

"And here they are!" said Jane Goodwoman, pulling down her blouse front. "Check out these casabas."

"Sorry. I'm not working on the problem of bad silicone implants."

Jane Goodwoman's face sagged almost as much as the rest of her. "Back in Boston, they don't react like that. You're not, you know—"

"Yes. Definitely. Whatever you mean, I'm it."

Jane Goodwoman brightened. "Really? I've always wanted to make it with a gay male."

"Try Rock Hudson. He probably won't even put up a fight. I will."

"I want your lean tigerish body."

"I'm opposed to date rape."

"I insist."

"This is sexual harassment, isn't it?"

"Screw sexual harassment. Take me now or you'll never eat lunch in this town again."

"Lunch in this town is ladybugs, remember?"

"Consider me your ladybug," said Jane Goodwoman, lunging with her arms outstretched and her breasts like twin battering rams.

She was as easy to dodge as a Nerf ball swinging on the end of a string, but Remo preferred not to have the tent come crashing down on his head so he caught Jane Goodwoman by one outstretched wrist and applied enough pressure to lay her flat on the floor, quivering in all directions.

He got out of the tent as fast as he could and almost collided with a pimple-faced teenager carrying a boom mike. He had shiny ears and innocent green eyes.

"There's a woman inside who needs your help," Remo told him.

Moaning came from the tent. "Oh—that was the best—foreplay—I—ever—had!"

The boy hesitated. "What—what do I do?"

"Zip up afterwards," said Remo.

6

The Master of Sinanju was waiting for Remo at the closed tent.

"You are improving," said Chiun.

"Improving how?" asked Remo.

"Once there was a time when you would have rutted with a woman with such udders without respect for yourself or her."

"If I have any respect for Jane Goodwoman, I haven't noticed," said Remo, slapping the tent side again.

"Who's out there?" an annoyed voice demanded.

"Food and Drug Association," called Remo. "Open up."

"You mean Administration."

"Have it your way. Who are you?"

"Centers for Disease Control and I'm busier than a one-armed paperhanger in here."

"How come you're the only one?"

"Because I have a public to protect. Those other idiots are just concerned about turf, ink, and their reputations."

"Then you're exactly the person we want to talk to and we're coming in."

The man was on the rotund side with squinty eyes behind big glasses. He did not look entirely pleased to see them, but after a few moments his more genial side came through.

"I'm Dale Parsons with the CDC," he said.

"Remo Salk."

Parsons blinked. "Any relation?"

"My mother's cousin's father's son," said Remo, who had gotten the name off the ID card.

"So what's the FDA's interest in HELP?" Parsons wondered, eyeing Remo's casual black T-shirt and matching chinos.

"There's a California candy company looking to market chocolate-covered thunderbugs and we gotta approve it as safe."

"Only in America . . ."

There was not much in the way of equipment inside the tent. A folding card table, racks of test tubes and specimen bottles and test equipment Remo did not recognize. Not that there was much in the way of test equipment he would recognize.

There was an array of covered petri dishes on the table, and each of them was dotted with sluggish bugs that reminded Remo of elongated ladybugs, but without the pleasant orange coloration. These bugs were mud-colored.

"Are these the terrible insects of doom?" asked Chiun.

Parsons seemed to notice the Master of Sinanju for the first time.

"Friend of yours?" he asked Remo.

"Japanese beetle expert," said Remo without thinking.

Chiun puffed out his wrinkled cheeks. His eggshell-colored face began turning a smoky red.

"That is, Chiun's an expect on Japanese beetles," Remo said hastily. "Not a Japanese who's a beetle expert. He's very sensitive about that. He's actually Korean."

Parsons's eyebrows lifted. "My father served in Korea."

"So did my father," said Chiun aridly.

That made Parsons laugh and the tension went out of the air.

Parsons said, "If these things are related to Japanese beetles, it's news to me. But I'm not an expert on bugs. I specialize in food-transmitted diseases and this has me stumped."

"What can you tell us?" Remo prompted.

"Well, it's not an autoimmune disease. Whether or not it's a virus, I'm not ready to say. But there are already thirty dead and not much time to get to the bottom of it if this is another AIDS."

"Are you saying it's like AIDS?"

"Well, HELP is like AIDS in that its chief symptom is a wholesale wasting of the victim's body. No question of that. Whether it's a virus, or if it is a virus of the same family as AIDS, is another matter. But it has the potential to be very dangerous."

"Only if people eat bugs, right?"

"If it is *Ingraticus Avalonicus* that's causing it."

"You think it isn't?"

"I can't say either way. I do know that viral infections are hard to get from eating an infected host. Often, the stomach acids destroy a virus before it can be absorbed into the system."

"Then it's not the bug?"

"Well, it could be. These people handle the thunderbugs before they eat them. They could become infected in the food preparation process. Or if they chew the raw bugs while they have a cut or sore in the mouth. It all depends on what my tests determine."

Chiun was examining a petri dish critically. The thunderbugs under the glass stood about like contented buggy sheep.

"They look too lazy to be dangerous," he mumured.

"They don't have a lot of energy, that's for sure."

"Maybe they're sick," said Remo.

"They are the wrong color to be dangerous," Chiun said.

"What do you mean?" asked Parsons.

"Venomous creatures always show their true colors. This bug is neither as green as an adder nor blue as blue cheese."

Dale Parsons cocked an eyebrow. "Blue cheese is venomous?"

The Master of Sinanju waggled a remonstrating finger. "Blue is a color not appropriate for food. Avoid blue cheese as you would the pit viper or the scorpion. No good can come from any of these things."

"You're talking about naturally venomous insects," said Parsons. "This is different. This is a disease the thunderbug may have picked up somewhere and is simply a carrier of, much the way deer ticks carry Lyme disease, which is caused by a spirochete, not a virus, by the way."

"But this bug has no teeth," Chiun pointed out.

"Well, HELP is getting into these PAPA idiots' systems somehow. And this has the potential to be worse than AIDS."

"Yeah?" said Remo.

"Absolutely. With AIDS, you get HIV—Human Immunodeficiency Virus—and then maybe a few years later, it blossoms into full-blown Advanced Immune Deficiency Syndrome, putting the sufferer at risk for contracting fatal cancers or flus. Nobody really dies of AIDS, you know. They die of illnesses they contract because AIDS makes them more susceptible. Here, people get HELP and they're dead in forty-eight hours with no sign of any primary illness or secondary infection."

"But that means they're contagious for only a little while, right?"

"*If* they're contagious. And if they're getting HELP from the bug, and they don't stop eating bugs, it doesn't much matter. More are going to die. And bug-eating is a fad now. Kids are doing it all over the country as a dare."

Remo frowned. "Then we're back to the bugs again."

Parsons shrugged. "A lot of them eat bugs. Only a few have died. As soon as I've got my centrifuge and electron microscope set up, I'm going to talk to the local coroner who performed the first HELP autopsies. I'm a pathologist, but I'm not licensed to autopsy people in this state."

The honking of horns suddenly blared all around them.

"Now what?" muttered Remo, going to the tent flap.

Reporters, both print and electronic, were running hither and yon.

Remo reached out and arrested a running sound man. He lifted him off his feet and his feet kept running. Remo recognized him as the human bone he had thrown to Jane Goodwoman.

"I see you survived," Remo said dryly.

"Is it usually that messy?" the boy asked.

"After Jane Goodwoman, all women are downhill."

"That's a relief."

"Now that I've started you along the road to wisdom, who's coming up the road?"

"Senator Ned J. Clancy."

Remo blinked. "Why? Did someone declare this an open bar zone?"

"I don't know."

Remo dropped the man and his feet got in gear again.

"This place is about to become a zoo," Remo told Chiun.

"It is already a zoo."

"It is about to become the zoo of all time. Let's mosey." Remo stuck his head back in the tent. "We'll catch up with you later."

Dale Parsons didn't look up from his work. "I'll be here."

The rush of press was heading south so Remo and Chiun struck off to the west toward the main PAPA encampment.

Over the sound of feet and the honking of horns they could hear Jane Goodwoman calling frantically, "Where is Senator Clancy? Where is Senator Clancy?"

Remo raised his voice. "Go east about a hundred yards. You can't miss him."

Chiun said, "The one they are rushing to meet is to the south."

Remo grinned. "I know. But the latrine is about a hundred yards to the east. Maybe she'll fall in."

"You are in a mean mood."

"You would be too if she tried to jump your bones."

"My bones would jump back and her bones would be broken," Chiun sniffed.

"I'll count on you to throw yourself between us next time she goes into heat," Remo said wryly.

In the main encampment, they came upon a group of hippie types sitting in the weeds and picking tiny bugs off themselves. They sat under staked umbrellas and buckskin hides stretched over wood frames, presumably to protect them from cancerous ultraviolet rays, Remo decided.

Their approach was noticed, and a bony woman raised a thin hand and waved them to come closer.

"Peace! Come to join the wave of the future?"

"Why not?" said Remo.

"Never," said Chiun.

Remo hissed, "We're supposed to get to the bottom of this. So we're joining these dips."

"We are joining, but I am not eating bugs."

"Fine. Just follow along."

"Are you Snappers or are you Harvesters?" someone asked.

"What are you people?" Remo countered.

"Snappers. Look." And the bony woman plucked one of the tiny bugs off a weed and snapped its head off with the flick of a dirty thumbnail. She put the rest in her mouth and began chewing. She chewed soundlessly for over a minute and finally a smile came over her face. It had been preceded by a tiny crunch. "Got the little bugger."

"They still move after they're decapitated so you have to find them with your teeth," someone said helpfully.

"That's the fun part," added a thin man wearing a Coptic cross and shorts that fought to hold on to his skinny hips.

"How do they taste?" wondered Remo.

"Like lobster."

"No, like Cajun popcorn," a man insisted.

"Like fried rice," said someone else.

"Are you all eating the same bug?" Remo asked.

"We don't call it a bug. It's Miracle Food. You can eat them all day long and never get full, or get tired of them."

"They come in different flavors too."

"Are you not concerned that you will sicken and die?" Chiun demanded.

"Only Harvesters catch HELP."

"Yeah, that's because they're too white and don't cover themselves when they go out into the sun."

Everyone agreed that the Harvester sect of the People Against Protein Assassins caught Human Environmental Liability Paradox. In fact, the Snapper group looked reasonably healthy. A number of them were pretty skinny, but it was diet-skinny, not wasting-away-to-skin-and-bones skinny.

"Then we'd better check out the Harvesters," Remo told Chiun.

A man shucked a handful of thunderbugs off a weed and offered them to Remo.

"Here, man. Take a bunch. It's a long walk."

"Yeah," a young girl said, "and over on the other side of the Schism Line, they cook all the flavor out of the little fellows."

"No thanks," said Remo. "Bug sushi doesn't appeal to me."

"Harvester," the young girl hissed. "If you catch HELP, it'll be your own fault."

They left the Snappers to their snapping and snacking.

The Schism Line proved to be exactly that. Someone had dragged a stick across the vale and there was a wooden sign stuck into it. On the approach side it said SNAPPER TURF. When they passed it, the other side of the sign said HAPPY HARVESTER HUNTING GROUND.

The tepees and wigwams were all clustered on the other side of the Schism Line.

They were arrayed around a campfire that was ringed with stones. There was a pot simmering. As they approached, Remo and Chiun saw people come to ladle in thunderbugs, wait a few moments, and ladle them out again.

There seemed to be a continual procession of PAPA adherents coming to contribute to the communal pot and then return to partake. Nobody looked sick. Nobody looked particularly well fed either. They wore Indian costumes that might have once fit them, but the buckskin and beads now fit loosely, if at all.

Remo walked up to the pot and asked, "How can you tell if they're cooked if you're cooking them all together like that?"

A man looked up. "They cook fast. They're always good. That's why Gitchee Manitou created them."

Remo frowned. "I've heard of the shores of Gitchee Goomie. But who's Gitchee Manitou?"

"The Great Spirit who created the thunderbug and sowed them in the fields with their plump bodies that are good to eat and their tiny legs which cannot run fast so they don't get away. Look, see how they can't wait to be eaten."

Remo and Chiun looked. The lethargic thunderbugs, once they were held over the steaming pot, came to life. They leapt from the ladles and into the

simmering water, where they immediately curled up
in tiny chickpealike balls.

"I never heard of bugs committing mass suicide,"
said Remo.

"It is not suicide. They only want to share themselves with us. When it is our turn to die, we will go
to a place where man is tiny and thunderbugs are
great and we will return the favor by allowing them
to consume our tasty flesh."

"Who fed you this bulldookie?" Remo said.

"Theodore Soars-With-Eagles."

"Where do we find him?"

"Sometimes he is in the wind and cannot be seen,
only felt."

Remo reached down to find the man's neck. He
squeezed. "Can the corn."

"We call it maize."

"I call it bullshit. Where is he now?"

"Sometimes he can be found napping in his tepee,"
the man said through teeth that seemed suddenly
welded together.

"Point us."

The man had only a ladle to point with and he
swept it back around, throwing hot broth and dead
thunderbugs into the parched grass.

When Remo released him, he dived for the bugs
and began popping them into his mouth.

"Welcome, brothers in nature," said Theodore
Soars-With-Eagles when they pushed aside the flap of
his tent. It was made of some slick material that Remo
thought he recognized.

"Naugahyde?" he asked.

Theodore Soars-With-Eagles gathered his chinchilla
cloak about his shoulders. "Gitchee Manitou invented
what the white man came to call Naugahyde. In his
great wisdom he has seen fit not to enforce the patent.
It is called reciprocity."

"The tribal language around here is obviously bull-shit," Remo growled. "You started this cult?"

"There is some disagreement over that. Some say Brother Karl Sagacious, may his noble Greek soul for-ever rest, founded PAPA. Some give me that honor. Some say we were brothers in creation before our unfortunate misunderstanding."

"Some say you had everything to gain from his death," said Remo.

"Such talk slanders the proud name of the People Against Protein Assassins. My ancestors refused to slaughter the proud beefalo for food. How could I harm my fellow man?"

"We just came from the Snappers," said Remo.

Theodore Soars-With-Eagles shook his feathered head sadly. Remo noticed that his bald spot was gone, and his hair moved a half second behind his headdress.

"Poor misguided ones. Gitchee Manitou weeps every time they bite off the head of one of his children."

"According to them, only your side is suffering from HELP."

"A lie. It is only them."

"When we got here, we saw you lead a funeral service."

"The committing of clay to clay. But when one of our number dies we put aside all disagreement and I preside over the ceremony of ashes."

"I didn't see any cremation going on," Remo said.

"We buried three Snappers today. They have been returned to the good earth, never to be seen again. They are ashes."

"They are on their way to your well," said Remo. "Look, we want some straight answers."

"It is only the white skins who speak with false tongues."

"That is a good start," said Chiun, nodding approv-ingly. "Speaking the obvious truth."

"Stay out of this, Little Father."

"When you are in my tepee," Theodore Soars-With-Eagles said indignantly, "you will treat my yellow brother as you would me."

"Listen, you—" Remo started to say.

Just then a girl in braided pigtails poked her head in and said, "Brother Theodore! Senator Clancy has come to Nirvana West!"

Brother Theodore Soars-With-Eagles came off his Navajo blanket, revealing a "Made in Japan" tag.

"Senator Clancy is here? I knew he would come. Whenever there is need, the great senator from Massachusetts arrives on the wings of the Thunderbird."

"I think he came in a limo," growled Remo.

"I must go to him. We will parley. There is much we have in common. We are both men of the people."

"Bring your own booze," said Remo, letting the man go.

They watched him lope off in his buckskin breeches.

"We are getting nowhere," Chiun said thinly.

"That's because we are nowhere," Remo complained. "We're going to have to grab Eagles when there aren't so many people around."

"Long have I dwelt in this land, Remo. There are times when its size and greatness have reminded me of the Rome of the Caesars. We worked for the Caesars and although they were white, they were good to work for."

"America hasn't exactly been shy with its gold," Remo pointed out.

"True, but in the days of Rome only the Caesars were crazy. Here, it is the subjects who are the maddest."

"There I can't disagree, Little Father. With all the beef we have in this country, we've got people who are eating bugs."

A disgusted look came over the Master of Sinanju's face.

"Who would eat the dead meat of cows?" he sniffed. "I mean, with such a wonderful range of good-tasting bugs, who would eat an insignificant thing like this lazy dunderbug?"

Remo stared.

"Of course," Chiun added in a lofty voice, "I do not eat bugs. But if lesser creatures wish to eat bugs, should they not eat the best bugs?"

Someone overheard him and said, "Bugs are the next rice."

"There is only one rice," said Chiun. "And it does not have legs."

Remo noticed that the sun was starting to go down.

"Well, we might as well make the best of it. Maybe we can claim a wigwam."

"I am not staying here."

"Look, we gotta infiltrate this lunatic's reservation. How are we going to do that?"

"I will not sleep among people who eat bugs," Chiun insisted. "People who eat bugs may try to eat my toes while I slumber. We will find a suitable hotel. One which boasts a presidential suite."

"Out here, we'll be lucky to find one without roaches," Remo growled.

"If you wish to stay here for the evening, that is your privilege," Chiun allowed. "I am certain that Jane Goodwoman will make space for you in her personal tent."

"You win," said Remo.

They stepped out of the tepee and gave the bug-eaters a wide berth. They were too busy scooping thunderbugs out of the communal pot to pay Remo and Chiun any attention.

"The way they're going at it," Remo muttered, "it's a miracle they aren't all overweight."

"The way they eat what they eat," Chiun sniffed, "it is a miracle they are not all dead."

7

Senator Ned J. Clancy loved a crowd. He loved people. All people. But especially the half of the human race that wore skirts.

That half of the human race he loved in restaurants, bathroom stalls, sandy beaches—but especially in the backs of limousines.

Most U.S. senators didn't travel by limousine. Most U.S. senators weren't the sole surviving son of a political dynasty that had put its stamp upon American political life for more than a half century now, owing to the fortune the senator's father, Francis X. Clancy, had amassed in the first half of the century, largely through stock manipulation and smut.

So when Senator Ned Clancy traveled, he traveled in style.

These days, Senator Ned J. Clancy no longer entertained teenyboppers in the back of his limousine. Much. He was married now. And as befits a newly married man who is also the senior senator from Massachusetts and who also just turned sixty, he conducted himself as the epitome of probity.

Which didn't mean he couldn't have a little innocent fun now and again.

The white stretch limousine was barreling along at a decorous seventy-five miles an hour along Highway 101 in Mendocino County. The driver was under strict orders never to go any slower and if necessary to force over to the side of the road any blocking vehicle that refused to yield. This was because during a lifetime of public service, irate voters had a distressing habit of shooting innocent Clancys. This had pretty much died down since Ned Clancy had publicly renounced any lingering White House ambitions. But not everybody could be trusted to have gotten the word.

The public renunciation had been a great disappointment to his family and especially to his aged mother, Pearl. But secretly, Ned Clancy was relieved. He never wanted to be President in the first place. He just wanted to draw a government check without having to work too hard for it and enjoy a little nookie when both flesh and spirit were moved. Not unlike his cousins who had remained in the Emerald Isle. Over there, they called it the dole.

Ned Clancy had been married for over a year now and married life was beginning to chafe. He felt like cutting loose.

There was a school bus coming the other way, he noticed.

Talking an asthma atomizer from his pocket, Senator Clancy took two quick hits of vodka—he was officially on the wagon now—and pressed the button that lowered the side window.

"Honk the horn when I tell you," he told the driver.

And Ned Clancy dropped his drawers and jammed his loose cellulite-pocked backside into the open window frame. It was a very tight fit.

"Now!" he shouted.

The driver obeyed. The horn blared.

And the students seated on the left aisle of the bus all turned to look at the speeding pink blob that ejected a blatting sound in their direction. Unfortunately, Ned Clancy wasn't in much of a position to enjoy their expressions, but he imagined they had to be priceless.

Clancy tugged his pants back on and resumed his

seat. He had the back all to himself. No wife this time. She was becoming a ball and chain already.

The backseat telephone buzzed and Clancy picked up the receiver.

"Yeah?"

"This is Nalini," said a musical voice. "Your mother is becoming very agitated, Senator."

Clancy looked back at the trailing limos. There were two, both black.

"She saw it?"

"I am afraid so."

"Did you?"

"Yes."

"What kind of a reaction did I get?"

"They appeared to be schoolgirls, Senator, and their expressions were indescribable."

"Great." He caught himself. "I mean, how unfortunate. I would never do anything to harm the young of our great nation. I thought I was mooning a college football team or something."

"You weren't."

"I feel terrible," said Ned Clancy, taking another vodka spritz. His face, like a snarled old pumpkin with a mossy coating of hair on top, dissolved into an inebriated smile. His tiny eyes seemed to shrink into their fatty sockets until they resembled baby eyes mistakenly set in an old man's face.

"Give Mother my apologies," he said, his consonants blurring.

"Of course, Senator. But she appears very angry."

"Remind her that it's the thought that counts."

Clancy hung up. "I knew dragging that old bat along was a mistake," he snarled.

It was not easy being the elder heir to the greatest political dynasty on earth, mused Ned Clancy. If the truth were to be known, he would have retired from the Senate two or three scandals ago. But the Clancy clan had been growing exponentially even after the deaths of Ned's older brothers, Jimbo and Robbo.

They had sired some thirty offspring between them. Neddo, as he was called in his young carefree days, had sired an equal number on his own, despite not having married until late in life.

Between the need to support the orphan Clancys and the illegitimate Clancys, the family fortune—never wisely invested in the first place—was dwindling fast. And since virtually every Clancy seemed to be chronically unemployable outside of public service, the trust funds were not keeping pace with government payroll salaries.

Ned Clancy took solace in the fact that he would not live to see the family fortune completely squandered. He also took solace in hard liquor. As the capillaries burst in his bulbous nose and the facial mottling of the habitual drunk more and more colored his much-photographed face, he had come to be called—always behind his back—Blotto.

Affectionately, of course. Because everyone loved Blotto Clancy. And Blotto loved them back. In any way he could.

He stopped loving a big group of them—specifically Californians—when his limousine caravan rounded a hill and ran smack into the end of a bumper-to-bumper traffic jam.

"What are these people doing here!" he shouted at the passenger-to-driver intercom.

"They're probably going the same place we are, sir," the limo driver patiently explained. "Nirvana West."

"But they're blocking a U.S. senator. They can't do that. Get on the horn to the State Police and have them all towed. That'll teach them."

"But, Senator, we're not in Massachusetts anymore."

Clancy looked confused. "We aren't?"

"No, this is California."

"Is that a state now?"

"It is, Senator."

"Well, who are their senators? I'll call them and pull rank. Use the old boy network for what it was meant."

"The two senators are women, Senator."

"Do they give head?"

"I wouldn't know, Senator."

"Because I think I might let them do me in return for the favor. It'll give them something to impress their girlfriends with. Just don't tell my wife. Or my mother. Especially my mother. She doesn't understand sex. How she managed to have sixteen kids, beats the hell out of me."

The phone buzzed again and Senator Clancy picked it up.

"Yeah?"

"This is Nalini. Your mother is becoming difficult."

Clancy clutched the phone tightly. "Is she saying anything?"

"You know she hasn't been able to speak since her last stroke. But she is jumping up and down in her seat, and that usually means she's growing impatient."

"Well, change her diaper or something. I have to pull a few strings before I can break this logjam up ahead."

"They are probably the media, Senator. If you step out of your car and present yourself, they might clear the way."

Ned Clancy's beet-red face swelled with pleasure. "They'll also want to interview me. That means ink. And face time. The milk and honey of my racket. Listen, Nalini, ever think of becoming a senator's aide?"

"Your mother needs me more, Senator."

"I need you more than more. Know what I mean? Wink, wink. Nudge, nudge."

"It is time for your mother's medication. Excuse me, Senator Clancy." The line went dead.

"Bitch," muttered Clancy, hanging up. "See if I ever let her stroke my love serpent."

He unbuttoned his blue blazer so that when he emerged he could rebutton it. His handlers told him he always looked more senatorial that way. It also distracted people from noticing his weight problem.

Senator Clancy stepped out. Instantly, the third limo in the caravan popped all its doors and his aides leapt out. They came running, forming a circle around him. This helped to hide his weight problem too. They also made perfect bullet catchers in case of assassins.

"Let's see if we can't break this gridlock," he said, grinning. "That would be a switch, wouldn't it?"

Brother Theodore Soars-With-Eagles ran through the old-growth forest fleet as a deer. His heart was racing. This was it. His first test. If he survived the media spotlight without screwing up, he was home free.

Brother Theodore slowed down and recovered his wind It would not look good foi a pure-blooded Chinchilla to burst on the national scene panting like a hound dog.

When he emerged into the press area, he saw that Senator Ned J. Clancy had already found the podium erected for his own press conference.

"Media hound," Brother Theodore muttered under his breath. Then, straightening his warbonnet and wig, he stepped into the ring of press.

"I have come to palaver with my white brother!" he shouted.

No one heard him.

"I said," he yelled through his cupped hands, "that I have come to speak with the honorable senator from Massachusetts!"

That didn't help any either, so Brother Theodore jumped up and down, trusting his feathers to catch people's attention.

The feathers did the trick. Senator Clancy caught

sight of him and lifted a hand. He said in a solemn voice, "How!"

"Hail, white brother from the eastern land of enlightenment," Brother Theodore called back. He tried to keep his face straight.

At a gesture from Clancy, the crowd parted. Cameras flashed in his face. Videocams whirred.

When Theodore reached the podium, Senator Clancy grinned broadly and threw one arm around him. He said, "Thank you for inviting me to your toupee, blood brother."

"That's tepee," whispered Brother Theodore. For the press, he said, "It is a sign that the Great White Father in Washington takes the promise of the mighty thunderbug seriously that you have come, my brother."

"We will smoke the peace pipe together," Senator Clancy said boisterously. "As a sign that there will be no scalping. But I'm afraid I'll have to pass up the firewater. I'm on the wagon. Witch doctor's orders."

As Senator Clancy took a hit of his asthma inhaler, Brother Theodore thought, *This guy knows less about the Red Man than I do. This is going to be a snap.*

The questions started flying.

"Brother Theodore, what do you have to say about HELP?"

"HELP is a disease of modern civilization. Only those who are attuned to nature will survive the cataclysm that is Human Environmental Liability Paradox."

"What do you mean by attuned to nature?"

"Only by eating the environmentally untainted thunderbug can the white man shield his fragile skin from the deadly rays filtering down from the ozone layer he has wantonly destroyed."

"Then how do you explain the fact that your PAPA followers are dying of HELP?" he was asked.

"Only Snappers are dying. My Harvesters, who cook the thunderbug in a politically and environmentally correct way before eating them, are as healthy as Hekawis. This is the lesson of HELP. Those who wish to see the millennium must live as my ancestors— pure in spirit and politics. I have spoken."

Brother Theodore looked out over the sea of media faces. They appeared to be lapping it all up. It was all going just as he hoped.

Out of one corner of his eye, he noticed the expression on the face of Senator Ned Clancy of Massachusetts. It was an unhappy expression.

"I'm sure Brother Theodore will have more to say after my remarks," Senator Clancy said hastily. Under his breath, he added, "Knowing when to get off the stage is part of the great art of politics, my friend."

And before Theodore Soars-With-Eagles could protest, the senator's aides were pushing him off the podium and Senator Clancy started taking questions.

"Whose press conference is this, anyway?" he muttered. But no one paid him any mind. They were too busy lobbing questions at the senator, whose broad face grew broader as he spoke, like some some elastic human ego feeding on the attention of the media.

8

Getting out of Nirvana West was proving to be difficult.

"Has every nutcase on the planet descended on this ecological disaster area?" Remo was complaining.

The Master of Sinanju shaded his eyes with a thin hand.

"I do not see the President of Vice," he said.

"Maybe he's disguised as a tree," Remo growled.

"If this is so, his head is in dire peril, for there are woodpeckers about."

They had retreated to the hillside from which they had first surveyed Nirvana West. If anything, the press and politicians were thicker than before.

"What's that over there?" Remo said suddenly.

Chiun followed the direction of Remo's pointing finger. The press were gravitating toward a central spot.

"I do not know," he said thinly.

"It looks like one of those nature films—you know, the ones that show honey bees swarming around the queen."

Chiun frowned. "I do not see a queen. Only a fat white in the center talking to other whites."

Remo squinted his eyes. Over the heads of the crowd poked a patch of discolored grayish white hair like bleached seaweed on a reddish rock. Under the bad hair was a bloated face that Remo would have recognized three states away.

"Blotto Clancy," he said unhappily.

"Who?"

"Senator Ned J. Clancy. He's the guy we're trying to avoid, remember?"

"Why do they call him Blotto?"

"Because he's half in the bag all the time."

Chiun's sparse eyebrows lifted. "What bag?"

"The one stamped 'Plastered.' "

"You are making no sense, Remo."

"Remember the Roman emperors who liked to get soused on wine and debauch all day long?" Remo asked.

"Not personally, but their stories are known to me, through the records of my ancestors. Caligula was a good emperor. Domitian was much favored by the House of Sinanju. But Nero was best. His gold took teeth marks exceedingly well."

"Well, down there is the Nero of the twentieth century."

Chiun lifted up on his black sandals and craned his wattled neck. "Really, Remo?"

"He's not President. Never will be. But he gave it his worst shot. He also gave every female that came within grabbing range his worst shot too. If he were ever elected President, the government would be paying child support for a small army of Clancys."

"Perhaps I should meet him," said Chiun, dropping back to his normal height.

"For crying out loud, why?"

Because if he ever becomes Emperor of America, I will want to be on his good side. Emperors of Nero's caliber have notoriously long memories."

"Pass," said Remo.

"Our vehicle is in that direction," Chiun pointed out.

Remo scowled darkly. "Then we gotta go in that direction. But do us both a favor. Let's not get involved. I've seen enough lunatics for one day."

*   *   *

They came down off the hill and joined the rush of PAPA people who had heard of the senator's arrival. For once, they were not noticed.

"He is obviously very popular," said Chiun as they drew near the growing congregation.

"Everybody loves a clown," said Remo.

They worked their way around, sticking to the trees until they were on the other side of the media swarm.

The shouted sounds of press questions came to their ears.

"Senator, why are you here in California?"

"Officially," came the booming voice of Senator Ned J. Clancy, "I've brought my dear mother, Pearl, because I've heard that these wonderful bugs have medicinal properties that might restore her failing faculties."

"You brought your mother here to feed her bugs?"

Clancy looked pained. Obviously, the subject of his mother was a sensitive one.

"No," he said. "But if she takes them off the plate, that of course is her right."

"Is concern for your mother's health the only reason you came to Nirvana West, Senator?"

"While I'm in the Golden State, I thought I'd have a look at the important humanitarian movement called People Against Protein Assassins. In an unofficial capacity, of course."

"Does that mean federal aid?"

"You bet it does," said Remo.

"I never shirk my responsibility to use my political power to help my constituents throughout this great land of ours."

"Senator, your constituency is limited to Massachusetts. Does this mean you are planning another presidential run?"

"Let me say this about that: No."

"What is your opinion on the HELP crisis, Senator?"

"As I told you," Senator Clancy said, his voice

tightening in sympathy with his grimace of a smile, "I'm here unofficially."

"Senator, there are reports that Thrush Limburger is coming here, and that he's prepared to expose HELP as some sort of hoax."

Senator Clancy took up his asthma inhaler and squeezed the canister twice. He immediately began coughing. The thudding of aides' hands on his broad back took several minutes to subside.

"I welcome," Clancy said after his coughing jag abated, "any input into this grave health problem."

"So you think HELP is real?"

"No, I didn't say that."

"Then is it a hoax?"

"That, I cannot say."

"What can you say, Senator?"

"I look forward to Thrush Limburger's arrival here at Nirvana West. Perhaps after he and I have had a chance to chat, I will have more to say on the matter."

The Master of Sinanju said, "That man is a superb politician."

"How's that again?" Remo asked.

"All these people hang on his every word, and he is saying nothing."

"How this guy can have a constituency is beyond me," grumbled Remo. "He can't keep his pants on or his liver dry."

A woman, overhearing that, turned to him and said, "That's an old-fashioned attitude."

"Common decency isn't old-fashioned. Yet."

"I meant that it was true in the old days that we never cared what Senator Clancy did, only what he said. But today we've grown up. We don't care what Neddo says, we only care what he does, and what he does is introduce all our legislation, just the way we write it. What he does in his private hours is his business."

"That's the trouble. None of what he does is private. It's usually all over the front page."

"Regressive," the woman hissed.

"Moron," Remo shot back. He turned to Chiun. "Let's go, Little Father. I've seen enough."

The way to their car was blocked by a clutch of white and black limousines.

"Sorry," a chauffeur said. "You can't pass."

"It's a free country and our car is on the other side of your cars," Remo said tightly.

"We have instructions that no one should pass. Security."

Remo scowled. "Security? Clancy's back there."

"Yeah, but his mother is here."

"And if you keep your voices down, you won't disturb her," Remo pointed out.

Stubby Uzis came up from under the security men's coats.

"We have instructions to shoot potentially hostile persons."

Chiun stepped in front of Remo and said in a plaintive voice, "Please do not hurt my adopted son."

Remo knew Chiun was setting them up for the kill. He hesitated. If any blood was shed, their cover would be blown.

So Remo brought his stiffened fingers up with blurry speed. And before the two guards knew what had happened, their machine pistols were cartwheeling into the underbrush and they were shaking their empty, numbed fingers and sucking air through clenched teeth.

"I didn't know killer bees got this far north," Remo said casually.

Just then a door popped open.

"Is there a problem?" a lilting voice asked.

The woman was slim and the color of a walnut. Her eyes were startlingly large, and so black they might have been constructed of shards of sunglass lenses.

She wore a vivid green sari that shimmered as she approached, topped by a shawl that framed her oval face like a cameo, and all but concealed her lustrous black hair.

The taller guard got control of himself and said, "I don't know who these people are, Miss Nalini, but I told them they can't get close to the cars."

"What is the matter with your fingers?" she asked.

"They sting," the short guard said tightly.

"Killer bees," said Remo. "Maybe they're what's causing HELP. If I were you two, I'd see a doctor."

The two guards just glared. They suspected Remo, but not having seen his hands move, could not accuse him. They recovered their weapons in silence.

"Who are you two, please?" the woman asked.

"It is none of your business," Chiun hissed.

"Little Father," warned Remo. "Let me handle this." He addressed the dusky woman.

"We're with the FDA. We've just been investigating the HELP thing and now we just want to find a decent hotel."

The woman named Nalini looked Remo up and down curiously. Her limpid eyes shone. Then they went to the Master of Sinanju. Their gazes met and locked and a tightness came over each of their faces.

"Allow me to escort you both to your vehicle," she said coolly. She gestured, and the guards lowered their Uzis slightly. They kept their fingers on the triggers.

"Thanks," said Remo.

"It is my pleasure," said the woman. "My name is Nalini."

"We do not care," said Chiun.

"He speaks for himself," said Remo. "I care."

Smiling, the woman lifted slim fingers to take Remo's lean, hard forearm. Remo decided he liked her touch. And her perfume. It was an exotic, musky scent. Usually Remo hated perfume, but this one was both subtle and pleasant. There was none of the flowery excess of manufactured American scents. This had a fruity undersmell to it that reminded Remo of something faraway and unattainable.

"And what is your name?"

"Call me Remo."

Chiun followed with his hands tucked into the sleeves of his kimono and his bearded chin in the air.

"I am the private nurse to Senator Clancy's mother, Pearl," Nalini told Remo.

"I'm surprised she's still alive, after all these years."

"She clings to life. She is a strong woman. Would you like to see her?"

"No," said Chiun.

"We're in a rush," said Remo. "Honest. Another time."

"Another time then."

"How old is she anyway?"

"One hundred and three years old."

Remo called back, "Hear that, Chiun? She's older than even you!"

"I am only eighty," snapped the Master of Sinanju, "and you are embarrassing me in front of my ancestors."

"Your ancestors are lying in the ground and Nalini is just being polite. What's the matter with you?"

Chiun hurried on, skirts flapping, his hands fists.

The sound of a car window humming down caught Remo's attention. He turned his head and a face appeared in the rear window of the limousine from which Nalini had come.

The face was twisted, as if from paralytic stroke, but Remo recognized Pearl Clancy, matriarch of the Clancy clan. Her mouth hung slack-jawed and a tendril of drool leaked out and flowed into one of the webby wrinkle clusters around her mouth, which was grotesque with red lipstick.

"That's her, huh?" asked Remo.

"I will be just a moment, *Adji*," Nalini called. "That means *Grandmother*," she whispered to Remo.

Pearl Clancy seemed not to understand a single word. Staring so hard her eyes seemed to bug out of her head, she brought pale clawlike hands up to her clenched face.

As Remo watched, she made bony fists on either side of her mouth and popped her forefingers out. Then she began wriggling them angrily, as if pointing at Remo. She was bouncing up and down in her seat.

"Come on," said Nalini quickly.

"What was that all about?" Remo asked.

"She's easily upset when left alone. Alzheimer's."

"That's tough. It really is. Bad enough she had to suffer through two of her sons ending up dead and the third a public drunk."

"What did you say your business was, Remo?"

"We're here to look into HELP."

Nalini touched a finger to her mouth. "A terrible thing, all these deaths and no one knows why."

"By the time we're done, everyone will know why. And how. And probably who too."

"You sound very confident."

"When Chiun and I get on something like this," Remo said, surprised at his own boastful words, "we usually bust everything wide open."

"I see," said Nalini in a quiet voice. Remo found himself disappointed in her response. For some reason, he wanted to impress her very much.

Chiun had reached the car when they drew near. His face wore an impatient frown.

"Well, thanks for your help," Remo said.

"I am happy to. Tell me, where are you staying?"

"I don't know yet."

"There is a nice motel three miles beyond Ukiah. You might try that."

"Thanks, I will." Remo hesitated. Normally, he avoided entanglements when on assignment, but there was something about this dusky-skinned woman that caught his interest. "Gonna be here a few days?"

"Yes, I believe so."

"Maybe I'll catch you around."

Nalini's smile was a shy ivory carving beneath the luminous jewels that were her dark eyes.

"Maybe I will allow you to catch me," she murmured.

And Remo smiled back.

He watched her walk away, her slim body swaying in time with the sari, and Remo thought he heard music.

Remo unlocked the door for Chiun and got behind the wheel. The Master of Sinanju's face was a thing carved out of stone.

"What's your problem?" Remo asked after they had started up the road.

"You let that harlot touch you."

"And?"

"She is a Hindu."

"So? She's a nice person. Anyone who would take care of an old dingbat like Pearl Clancy has to have a good heart."

"You did not hear what I said. She is a Hindu."

"I did hear you, and I don't care. I like her."

"Hindus only eat with their right hands."

"So?"

"You know what they do with their left hands."

"No. And knowing you, I don't want to hear."

"They wipe themselves," said Chiun. "Without toilet paper. That is why they do not eat with their left hands. Only their right."

"I knew I didn't want to hear it," said Remo, gunning the engine.

"Now you will need to wash yourself," Chiun sniffed.

"I'm sure Nalini is Americanized."

"Nevertheless, until you have washed the parts of your body that woman has touched, do not touch me."

"Oh brother. Anything else I should know in case I meet her again?"

"I did not like the color of her sari."

"What was wrong with it?"

"It is too vivid."

Remo eyed Chiun's vermilion kimono. "Said the Korean fashion cop."

9

Ukiah was smaller than Remo had expected. A tiny town of probably a thousand or so people. That limited the choice of hotels. There were two. And both had prominent ABSOLUTELY NO VACANCY signs lit up.

"Let's hope the motel Nalini told me about has some space," Remo said as they put the town behind them.

"It is no doubt infested with roaches if it serves Hindus," Chiun sniffed.

"Get off it, will you?"

"Only if you promise not to get on that Hindu."

"No deal."

Remo drove on and three miles up the road came to a little ticky-tacky nest of bungalow duplexes.

"Doesn't look so bad," Remo said.

As Remo pulled into the parking lot, the Master of Sinanju said, "This does not meet my modest standards."

Remo stabbed a finger out his window. "Look, see that sign? VACANCY. We're in luck. It may not look it, but we are."

"It is insufficient for my needs."

"After the press gets all the film and quotes they want, they're going to be descending on every fleabag motel from here to Oregon. We're just lucky they're so hot to get their stories they didn't bother to book their rooms first."

"I will consider it."

"Or you can sleep in the car."

"Only if you sleep in the trunk."

They went in.

The front desk was about the size of a kitchen table and had the same kind of green-flecked formica top. The man behind it was under thirty and had dirty blond hair.

"Greetings, innkeeper," proclaimed the Master of Sinanju. "We seek suitable lodgings."

"He means we want a room," said Remo.

"We will consider engaging a room if your establishment suits our needs," corrected Chiun.

"You run a wonderful establishment," said Remo, sliding a credit card across the formica countertop. "It comes highly recommended. Give us a bungalow."

"We will negotiate once we have interviewed your room service chef," proclaimed Chiun.

The desk clerk looked blank. "Room service chef?"

"You provide room service, of course," said Chiun.

"From time to time, yeah."

Chiun lifted his wide kimono sleeves to the ceiling. "Summon the illustrious purveyor of victuals."

"Purveyor of victuals?" undertoned Remo.

"We are in the West," whispered Chun, "I am speaking western."

"Yippie ti yo-yo," said Remo.

"Do you want a room or don't you?" the desk clerk demanded.

"I do," said Remo. "He's up in the air. Consider us separate clients."

The desk clerk looked unconvinced. "You gonna want room service?" he asked Remo.

"No."

"Good, because I reserve the right to refuse finicky guests. There're a bazillion press guys about two miles down the road and I foresee a long, busy night coming."

"So do I. Where's my key?"

The desk clerk handed Remo a brass key which had a greasy green tag hanging from it with the room number written in faded ink.

"Unit sixteen," he said.

"Thanks," said Remo, signing the credit card slip.

"What about me?" squeaked the Master of Sinanju, his face as tight as a cobweb.

The desk clerk said, "You want room service, I got a night man who'll do a run to the Taco Hell. That's when things are slow. They won't be slow tonight."

"Taco Hell!" huffed Chiun, stamping his feet. "Remo, this is totally unacceptable."

"Not to me. And if I were you, pardner, I'd book a room quick because I feel a cool night coming on and that car looked mighty drafty to me."

"I will take the room adjoining this ingrate," said Chiun quickly. "Be sure to put it on his bill."

The desk clerk eyed Remo. "That okay with you, sir?"

Chiun snapped, "He has no say in these matters."

"Anything that placates him is fine with me," sighed Remo.

"Where does one find true food in these parts?" asked Chiun.

"True . . . ?"

"Rice . . . duck . . . fish."

"There's a Chinese restaurant in Ukiah. Yen Sin's. You might try that."

"Have their best dishes sent to my room and put it in on the white ingrate's bill," said Chiun.

"Sorry, the night man doesn't go into Ukiah. Only to the Taco Hell, which is just up the road."

"I'd have him make an exception in this case," Remo told the desk man.

"I don't see why I should."

The Master of Sinanju reached up and took the charge machine. He eyed it critically. The desk man became nervous.

"Don't drop that, sir."

Chiun looked up. "This contraption is important to you?"

"Definitely. Can't run the business without it."

Chiun nodded. "I will hold it for ransom until I have rice and steamed duck, or unseasoned fish, in my room."

"Sir, you don't want me to come around and take that away from you, do you?"

"I do not care what you do as long as I have proper room service," snapped the Master of Sinanju.

The desk clerk sighed and came out from behind his station.

He took hold of the charge machine before Remo could warn him. Chiun let him hold it long enough to get a good grasp. Then he rammed the heavy embossing slide from one end to the other, catching the desk man's fingers painfully.

His scream was exquisite. He lifted up on tippytoe, found a higher register, and his eyeballs in his upward-pointing face started looking like white grapes being squeezed from wrinkled pink baby fists.

Twenty minutes later, Remo and Chiun were seated on a very clean polyester rug in the middle of Chiun's bungalow room eating rice off fine china supplied by the wife of the desk man, who had been exceedingly grateful to discover that his fingerbones, once he recovered his hand, were miraculously whole.

"Not bad," said Remo.

Chiun made an unhappy face. "The rice has been boiled. I asked for steamed."

"Maybe they don't steam their rice out here."

"Steamed rice is best. Whites insist upon boiling it. Whites and Chinese who try to pass for white."

"Maybe it's the cowboy way of eating rice," Remo suggested airily.

"Do not be ridiculous, Remo," said Chiun, putting the rice aside and attacking his duck. "Cowboys eat cows. That is why they are called cowboys."

Without looking at the clock radio, Remo said, "I'd better call Smith before he leaves Folcroft for the night."

"Leave him be. Smith will not be pleased that we have discovered nothing."

"Smitty will worry if we don't call in. This new President has him antsier than I've seen him in a long time."

Harold Smith picked up on the first ring.

"Remo, what have you to report?"

"Not a heck of a lot. This place is lousy with press and politicians, my two least favorite kinds of people."

"No progress?"

"We seen the bugs, we've seen the bug-eaters and we've seen the bug-eaters eat the bugs. If that's progress, I'm on the wrong planet."

"There may be a break coming."

"Yeah?"

"I was listening to Thrush Limburger today—"

"You too?"

"Everyone listens to Thrush Limburger," said Smith. "At any rate, he is coming to Nirvana West."

"Yeah, I heard," Remo said sourly. "Just what we need—an ex-disk jockey to add to the festivities. All that was missing was a sound track, anyway."

"Limburger claims that on tomorrow's broadcast he will reveal the truth about HELP."

"What's the big deal? People are eating bugs and getting sick from it. The nuns who raised me taught me not to eat bugs when I was five."

"And you minded them?"

"No, I marched right out and ate the first bug I come upon. I think it was a firefly. After I got better, Sister Mary Margaret whacked my knuckles with a ruler and I never ate another bug again. What these dips need is a nun with an unbreakable ruler, and the so-called HELP plague is over."

"The deaths are spreading to the non-PAPA population," Smith said.

"They are?"

"It appears that these bugs are common in many areas of the country. Where they aren't, a black market has sprung up."

"Wait a minute! You mean even though people are dying from eating this bug, they're paying money for the privilege?"

"How is that different from cocaine use, or gourmets who eat wild mushrooms, or puffer fish, which if improperly prepared can kill?"

"I still don't get it."

"That is because you have had a proper upbringing. But the President is very concerned. He has not said so in any specific way, but I believe we and CURE are on probation. As you know, there is talk of folding the CIA into the State Department, which would save five billion taxpayer dollars. Our budget is much greater than that. He is looking at us closely."

"Do tell."

"We must show results, Remo. I am counting on you."

"We'll do our best. Talk to you tomorrow."

Remo hung up and returned to his spot on the rug.

"You heard every word, didn't you?" he asked Chiun.

"I do not eavesdrop."

"You don't have to. You have the ears of a fox."

Chiun raised a correcting finger. "I have the ears of an owl. A fox's ears are ugly."

"Thrush Limburger is definitely coming here. He's supposed to have the whole thing figured out."

"Why are you telling me things I already know?"

"I ask myself that question all the time. Look, I know you're a Limburger fan—God knows why—but remember, we're on a secret mission."

"To save America from its latest vice, bug eating. What would this country do without us to save it from itself?"

"Dry up and blow away like the Roman Empire, I

guess." Remo started for the door, saying, "I'll see you in the morning."

"Remember to shower."

At the door, Remo turned. "Why do you say that?"

"You reek of that woman."

Remo sniffed his arm. The scent of Nalini was on the spot on his arm where she touched him. It brought a smile to his face. "And here I thought it was just her memory haunting me."

"Pah," said Chiun.

In his room, Remo stripped the bed. He couldn't sleep on most beds anymore. At home, a reed mat on the floor was all the bed he needed. This mattress was too lumpy. So he laid the sheet on the rug, stripped to his underwear, and lay down.

He couldn't sleep. He kept thinking of Nalini. He had liked her smile. He thought it was the tantalizing memory keeping him awake, when he remembered the perfume on his arm. That was what was keeping him awake.

Remo washed his arms in soap and hot water, which got rid of most of the scent. But not all of it. He threw up a window which let in cool air and a sound like an adenoidally challenged gander.

Chiun snored in the next room. He had left his window open too.

Remo willed out the sound, then all sounds, and after a last lingering recollection of Nalini's low, musical voice, he fell into a deep sleep.

Somewhere past three A.M., Remo awoke. Something was crawling along his arm and his first thought was *roach*.

Remo gave his arm a shake, and he heard something tick against the wall. He went back to sleep. Ten minutes later, the sensitive hairs on his forearm triggered an alarm, and this time he slapped the insect with his fingers, killing it.

Then he flicked the dead thing off, rolled over, and fell into a slumber that lasted until the break of dawn and the first raucous cries of bluejays.

He dreamed of Nalini. In his dream, he was a teenager again, before CURE, before the electric chair that hadn't worked had catapulted patrolman Remo Williams into his new life as the heir apparent to the House of Sinanju.

He and Nalini were walking down lower Broad Street in Newark, New Jersey, where he had grown up.

They were eating ice cream cones, and even in sleep, Remo tasted his because he had not eaten an ice cream cone or a dairy product or most foods since he had come to Sinanju, the sun source of the martial arts. His cone was cherry vanilla. Nalini's was chocolate fudge. He was looking at her's and wondering if he offered her a taste of his cone, would she return the favor.

They turned a corner and coming up it was Sister Mary Margaret, a wraith in black-and-white. Her eyes were steely. And she was carrying a steel ruler which she flicked. Out snapped a straight razor that was rusty with dried blood.

Remo pulled Nalini back and they got three blocks before the Master of Sinanju appeared, blocking their path.

His yellow hands came out of the sleeves of his bone white kimono and the nails attached to the ends of his fingers were long and curved and also the color of bone.

The Master of Sinanju bared his teeth like an enraged tiger, and from between his tiny white teeth came a sibilant hissing.

Remo woke up tasting cherry ice cream and smelling Nalini's perfume. He found himself looking forward to seeing her again. It had been a long time since he had looked forward to seeing a woman. A long time.

It was one of the downsides of Sinanju that while Remo had through correct breathing, stringent diet, and exercise techniques become absolute master of every cell in his body, and a literal killing machine, the techniques that cover the sexual act were focused on reducing the opposite sex to quivering jelly, which was nice, for the express purpose of fathering children, which was not currently on Remo's agenda. Sinanju sex techniques were so rigid and foolproof that no woman could resist them, and the practitioner, in this case Remo, might as well be wiring up a car stereo for all the pleasure he got out of it.

As a consequence, Remo had more and more come to enjoy sex less and less.

But he found himself humming as he dressed while waiting until Chiun's honking snores softened to a intermittent snuffle, and then knocked on his door.

"Rise and shine, Little Father. It's the beginning of a new day."

"What is good about that?" said Chiun.

"For one thing, Thrush Limburger's coming to town. And he knows when you've been naughty or nice."

"And I know when you have not showered. I am not emerging from this room until you do."

"Damn," said Remo. And the faint scent of Nalini came to his nose again. "Give me ten," he told the Master of Sinanju, ducking back into his room.

Remo hit the bathroom and turned on the shower, preparatory to taking off his clothes.

He got a metallic groan, a driblet of cold water, and the pipe groan resumed, without so much as a drop of water to make up for all the laborious racket.

"Perfect," Remo grumbled.

He called the front desk.

"What happened to my shower?"

"This happens from time to time. It's the drought."

"When will it come back on?"

"We never know," the desk man said.

Remo went out and said to Chiun, "Why didn't you tell me there's no shower water?"

"I had bath water. I took a wonderful bath."

"Well, you took my shower too, because you must have used up the last of the water."

"Now you are blaming me because you smell like a Hindu."

"I do not smell like a Hindu. Look, let's just have breakfast. Maybe there'll be water after we eat."

"I will not be seen in public with one who smells of the Ganges," said Chiun, flouncing off.

Remo let him go. He wasn't that hungry to begin with. He got into his car and drove into Ukiah, thinking he'd look up the local coroner. Maybe he'd have an empty slab and a hose Remo could borrow for a few hours.

Although the more he thought of it, the more Remo liked having Nalini's scent on him. Maybe he'd hold on to it awhile, just to annoy Chiun. Then again, maybe he'd look up Nalini and ask for a booster shot.

10

Remo learned by asking around that the Ukiah coroner was also the local undertaker and that brought him to the town's sole funeral parlor. The name over the door was Esterquest and Son. Remo went in.

A properly funereal-faced man greeted him and said, "I do not believe we are waking anyone today."

"I'm looking for the coroner," said Remo.

"Mr. Esterquest is quite busy."

Remo flashed a CDC ID card and said, "Federal agent. I gotta see him. It's about this HELP problem."

The man exchanged his downcast expression for a glum one. "Could it wait? Mr. Esterquest is in the embalming room."

"I have a strong stomach. We can talk while he works."

The man sucked in his hollow cheeks until the bottom of his face looked like it belonged on a white satin pillow.

"That would hardly be proper," he said.

"Look, just tell him I'm here."

The man went away. He was back less than a minute later, wearing the same hollow expression. His tune was different, however.

"Mr. Esterquest says that he takes no responsibility for any unpleasant thing you may see."

"Fair enough," said Remo, and he followed the

man into the back, past bare wake rooms and an atmosphere that was faintly sweet with flowers, but somehow bitter to breathe.

The double door had a brass plate that said EM-BALMING ROOM, and the man threw it open. Remo entered and immediately cycled his breathing rhythms down so that the strong odor of formaldehyde wouldn't sear his sensitive lung linings.

Esterquest was bent over a body on a slab. The body was of a man, a sheet modestly covering his midsection. He was as gray as a dead picture tube.

He looked up and said, "I thought you were press."

"Center for Disease Control," said Remo.

Esterquest straightened.

"Don't you mean 'Centers'?"

"Who ever heard of something having more than one center?" Remo countered.

"Let me see that ID card of yours."

Remo handed it over. Esterquest was an ordinary-looking man with soft brown hair and no worry lines on his smooth, thirtyish face. He handed the card back with a reddish thumbprint on it.

"Excuse the blood," he said. "You're genuine. Even if you do have a goofy sense of humor. What can I do for you?"

"I'm looking into this HELP business. I hear you autopsied one of the first victims."

"Brother Sagacious. The UCLA professor. He was the only one they didn't dump into a shallow grave, and only because the family insisted upon a proper Southern Baptist burial. Later, I ordered some of the others exhumed for a proper autopsy. Public health regulations, you know. I'm up for reelection next year."

"Find anything?"

"Yes and no."

"Let's hear both sides of it," said Remo.

"The dead all seem to be from the so-called Snapper wing of PAPA."

"I talked to both sides. Each side said only the other side caught the HELP virus."

"What do you expect from people who eat bugs? Well, I did six autopsies before it started getting out of hand. I'm the only coroner for six towns and I have enough of a job autopsying the car accident victims, natural causes deaths, and the like."

"Tough job."

"I said I was overworked, not that I didn't like it. Actually, it's very interesting sometimes. Take this man. Do you see any mark on him?"

Remo looked closer. "No."

"There isn't one. Not that I can find. But they found him behind the wheel of his car, parked at a rest stop, dead as yesterday's corned brisket. Barely forty too."

"Heart attack?"

"He'd be a distinct grayish blue."

"Carbon monoxide poisoning?"

"He'd be an exquisite cherry pink. There's no trauma, edema, no contusions, no cranial concussion. It's a mystery."

Remo grunted.

The man looked up and his face lost its hangdog look. He smiled. A twinkle came into his colorless eyes. "I happen to love a good mystery. You know, a woman's kinda like a mystery."

"Most women are," said Remo, thinking of Nalini.

"They're kinda like a puzzle every man aches to solve. You take your time about it, of course. You have to. Even with the shallowest woman, it takes time to solve the riddle of her ways. If you stay together long enough, finally you do. If you don't, they hang in your memory forever."

"Better to figure them out quick, huh?"

"Oh, I don't know. Once you crack the code, once you figure out what makes them tick—why their moods darken or lighten when they do—they're no longer quite as interesting. Some women, I think, it's better to leave unsolved."

"What good is a mystery if you can't solve it, right?"

"Which brings us back to this gray gentleman," Esterquest said suddenly. "There is no reason for him being dead that I can see."

"Well, he had to die of something," said Remo.

"True, which is why I'm going to spend all of today and as much of tomorrow as I dare, poking about this man's viscera. Because I know they hold the secret and I ache to solve it. Once I do," Esterquest shrugged broadly, "he's just another poor stiff and I'll go plodding on, embalming accident cases and stroke victims until the next tantalizing corpse comes along."

"Corpses don't tantalize me."

"Nor me. As corpses. But mysteries do. And in my job, I see a really meaty one but once in a blue moon. It's the same with the HELP victims."

"You have any ideas about that?"

"No, not yet. But I've been saving all my data, blood and tissue samples. I think HELP can be explained. It's just a matter of time."

"Let's get to the yes of this conversation."

Esterquest smiled easily. "You'll never be a detective, my CDC friend. You don't have the patience. As I was saying, the bodies I saw were all from the Snapper wing. This makes sense if the dreaded thunderbug was transmitting the disease, because the Snappers don't cook their bugs. Cooking would likely kill the viral microorganism, rendering them harmless protein. As you know, a virus is just a bit of genetic material surrounded by a protective protein envelope."

"So it is the bug?"

"Except for one tiny but significant detail. I found no trace of viral infection in the linings of their stomachs, the logical invasion site."

"One federal guy I spoke to thought they could be getting it through mouth sores or cuts."

"A good theory, except that if the bug was carrying a bug, some of the victims surely would show soft-tissue damage in the mouth. And I didn't find any cold sores. Cooties, yes. Periodontal disease, also. But their mouths were clean of viral infection."

"That brings us back to the no-bug theory."

"Except there *is* something killing these people that suggests a virus. If not a virus, perhaps a communicable disease on the order of Lyme disease or a lethal toxin like paralytic shellfish poisoning. Those possibilities are real enough. But I don't know enough about these things to say how they might work or not work inside the body. The HELP agent doesn't appear to be of a type that could kill a full-grown adult inside of forty-eight hours."

"Why not?"

"Because there are no discernible symptoms or effects. The person just becomes very tired one day, and starts wasting until he dies. In order for a virus to kill, there must be physical symptoms, wouldn't you think?"

"I guess," said Remo.

"After all, warts are a symptom of one kind of virus. Chicken pox and mumps have their signature symptoms. Other viral infections settle in major internal organs, such as the heart or the lungs. None of these organs have been affected in any way I can find. HELP victims waste away and they die. But they don't seem to die of the wasting process."

"Kinda like a stealth virus."

"A good way of putting it." Esterquest gestured toward the body on the slab. "You know, I was about to open this man up."

"Be my guest," said Remo.

Esterquest eyed Remo doubtfully. "You have the stomach for seeing me remove this man's stomach?"

"I was in Nam. I've seen everything."

"If you faint, I'm just going to leave you there."

"Don't sweat it," Remo said. "I only faint at election returns."

As Remo watched, Esterquest made a lateral incision from the breastbone down to the pubic bone, without getting anything in the way of blood. He poked around happily.

"Since I see no external signs," he mused, "I'm going to look at this man's major organs. Examine the stomach contents. Perhaps it was something he ate."

"Like thunderbugs?"

"I hear it's a fad now." Esterquest shook his rumpled head in disbelief. "What is this country coming to?"

Remo shrugged. He watched as the dead man's limp liver-colored stomach was excised, sliced open, and the contents removed and set on a stainless steel tray. It was a milky mass that looked like nothing remotely edible.

"If the virus kills after forty-eight hours, will you find any bugs?" Remo asked.

"Probably not. Carapace material is usually impervious to stomach acid, but that damn bug is almost one hundred percent digestible." Esterquest was picking the mass apart and smearing samples on a glass slide. He looked at it through a microscope.

"No bug parts that I can see."

"Then he didn't eat the bugs."

Esterquest looked up and smiled knowingly.

"Oh, there's still the bowel contents to look at, yet."

Remo's face fell. "That part I think I can skip."

"Everyone has their limitations. Myself, I'd prefer to forgo a bowel incision. Even with a face mask, built-up gasses are the worst."

Remo started to go.

Esterquest called, "Oh, there is one other thing."

Remo turned. "Yeah?"

"Even though there was no viral agent in their stomachs, there was something funny in their blood."

"What?"

"I don't know. Never saw anything like it before. And without an electron microscope, and a whole range of testing dyes and the like, I can't pursue it any further."

"Oh," said Remo.

As he started to go, the man called after him, "Next time you're in town, drop by again. Maybe we can compare notes some more. Lord knows an old poison oaker like me could use the company."

Remo noticed the man's colorless eyes flick to a framed picture of a smiling young woman with curly hair.

"Wife?" Remo asked.

Esterquest nodded. "Be gone six years in October."

"Sorry."

"I'm used to death in my business."

"Ever figure her out?"

Esterquest didn't look up. His no was barely audible.

"Catch you around," said Remo, shutting the door after himself. A hissing of released gas came distinctly through the door and Esterquest, his voice once more buoyant, exclaimed, "Gahh! I hate this part. But it'll be worth it if you give up all your secrets, my silent gray friend."

Remo left the funeral parlor in a better mood than when he had gone in. It was good to come upon unexpectedly, someone who was really excited about his work. Even if the nature of that work wasn't always so pleasant. Funny how someone who deals in death all the time should find in that a way to make his life more interesting.

Remo reflected that he and the undertaker were in the same business. Death. Except Remo was more of a manufacturer and the undertaker a packager of the final product.

The town was pretty quiet once Remo got out into the fresh air. There was no sign of the press and Remo wondered if they had simply camped out at Nirvana West. He wasn't looking forward to going back to that clowns' nest.

On the other hand, maybe Nalini would be there.

As Remo started for his car, from down the road came the blare of rock music. It was loud. It was very loud. And it was coming this way fast. It sounded like some idiot teenager had his car stereo cranked up to one-hundred-fifty decibels.

As Remo got his motor going, he saw in his rearview mirror a big RV barreling through town. It was painted red, white, and blue and the too-loud rock was blaring from a loudspeaker mounted on the roof.

"Damn, another politician," muttered Remo, gunning into reverse and peeling out one step ahead of the approaching RV.

On the way back to the motel, Remo spotted the Master of Sinanju walking along, his hands tucked into the sleeves of his sky blue kimono. Remo stopped and rolled down his window.

"Going my way?" he asked cheerfully.

Chiun looked at him with a wrinkling nose and disdainful eyes. "Have you showered?"

"No," Remo admitted.

"Then I am not going your way, unclean one."

"Oh, come on. Don't be that way."

"You smell worse than before," Chiun said pointedly.

"I just attended an autopsy."

"Then it is doubly important that you shower," sniffed the Master of Sinanju, hurrying on.

Remo let him go. He drove past, watching the one who taught him Sinanju in his rearview mirror with unhappy eyes.

"Every time I meet somebody I like, he's gotta pull this tired old crap," muttered Remo.

11

The conventional wisdom was that Thrush Limburger would end up like Morton Downey. His ego is too big, they said. He's growing too fast. People listen to him just to laugh at him, others insisted. Just you watch, once his ratings start to fall, they'll find that windbag in some airport men's room stall, his head shaved, Mirrors of Venus—the symbol for womankind—lipsticked all over his dazed face, babbling that the "Feminasties" are out to get him.

They said that in his first year. They said it in his second. When he jumped to television, they claimed it would be the kiss of death. Thrush Limburger. He's so "hot" he's on TV. Ha-ha-ha.

The conventional wisdom said that when a trend or movement or whatever hit the tube, that meant it was on its way out, if not already dead.

Everybody knew it. Everybody except Thrush Limburger, that is. He was already hard at work on his next bestseller, *I Told You So,* as his red, white, and blue remote broadcast RV rolled into the town of Ukiah, the proud letters TTT NETWORK emblazoned on the side.

"As I speak to you from the rolling hills of Mendocino County," Thrush boomed into the microphone, simultaneously typing on his portable computer, whose keys were padded so he could write and broadcast simultaneously, "I am struck by how gullible large segments of the American people have become in our electronic age. Let's take Theodore Soars-With-Beagles—I mean Eagles. Now the press is reporting that he's a full-blooded Chinchilla Indian. My friends, I have combed every encyclopedia, spoken to noted anthropologists and ethnologists, and they all tell me that there is no such being as a Chinchilla Indian. Now I admit even I had to look this up. I couldn't be certain. Sure, it sounded funny, but I suppose it's possible for there to be such a thing. After all, there's a tribe calling itself the Pontiacs, and they have nothing to do with the auto industry. So let me share something with you."

Abruptly, Limburger gave his jowly right cheek a slap with his fleshy right hand. The sound was like raw pork chops colliding.

His audience accepted the mushy sound without a qualm. They understood that Thrush Limburger was an excitable fellow. He often drummed his fingers, stamped his feet, and fluttered faxes and newspaper clippings into the open mike. It was part of his on-air persona, he boasted. What he neglected to mention was that Thrush Limburger suffered from a mild form of Tourette's Syndrome.

Thrush was also on a self-improvement program where if he found himself using a mushy word on the air, he would stop and slap himself in the face as an ungentle reminder that he had committed an inappropriate public utterance.

In this case, the mushy word was "share."

"Now Theodore Soars-With-Eagles calls himself a Chinchilla Indian," Thrush continued. "And that is his God-given right. He can call himself a springbok if it so pleases him. But here's a flash. There are no Chinchillas, except the furry ones women wrap around their necks. At great peril to their well-being, by the way, thanks to the animal rights crowd. For the benefit of the adherents of PAPA and Mr. Theodore Soars-With-Eagles, if you can hear me, my fine feathered friend, the correct tribal name is Chowchilla. Not *Chin* chilla. *Chow* chilla. Now I ask you, listeners, how seriously can we take the pronouncements of a self-appointed Indian spokesman *if he can't even get the name of his own tribe right*?"

Thrush chuckled throatily, a good-natured sound, even amplified by sound systems all across the nation. "I'll be back, after this message from our sponsor, Tipple."

Limburger popped a cassette into the rack, and as his deep orator's voice extolled the virtues of his favorite soft drink, his haberdasher, and the very loud ties he wore, he hit the intercom button and asked his assistant, "Where are we, Custer?"

"Approaching Ukiah, Thrush."

"Hot damn. You call that coroner?"

"He says he'll see you. But not on the air."

"Why not? Doesn't he know Thrush Limburger is on three-hundred-thirty stations here and in Canada, one for every blessed pound in his generously proportioned body?"

"Maybe he doesn't like the press."

"Press? I'm not the press. I'm the antipress. I'm the truth."

"He won't budge, Thrush."

"Okay, I'm a reasonable man. We'll do it his way. What we'll do is a bunch of packaged stuff. Feminasty Report. Furry Friends Update. Liberal Valhalla. The whole works. That should give me time to talk to him, and the audience won't even miss me—because I won't ever have stopped talking."

"You got it, Thrush."

When the RV pulled up before the Esterquest and Son funeral parlor, the rear door popped open and Thrush Limburger lumbered out, the sound of his own canned voice following him in.

He was inside not ten minutes. He came out like a rogue elephant, jumping to the driver's side window and bouncing happily. The entire van rocked on its heavy-duty shocks.

"I got it!" he chortled. "I figured it out! This is perfect. This is amazing. Only Thrush Limburger could just roll into a town and crack open something that has stumped official Washington."

"You always say official Washington is made up of lukewarm chowderheads," said his assistant, behind the wheel.

"I was right then and I'm right now, Custer. Let's get on to Nirvana West, pronto. I want to bust this thing wide open from the environmentalist whackjob ground zero. Damn, am I good."

The red, white, and blue RV roared out of Ukiah trailing a long coil of carbon monoxide.

And all across American, the voice of Thrush Limburger proclaimed, "My faithful listeners, you are about to be rewarded for your loyalty to this show. In the months to come, you people are going to be able to boast that you were among the discerning multitudes who heard Thrush Limburger debunk the HELP crisis for all time. That's right, while you were listening to my Democratic Hall of Shame via the magic of audiotape, your tireless servant was lifting up rocks and digging up the unpleasant muck under them. And guess what I found? What I always find. What you expect me to find. Dramatic pause here." Thrush cleared his throat with a sound like a steamroller grumbling and lowered his voice, knowing that millions of Americans, already on the edge of their seats, would lean closer to their radios. "I found . . . the truth. *And it shall set you free!*"

With that, Thrush Limburger popped in an ad cassette and leaned back in his chair, his pudgy hands folding over his ample belly. A self-satisfied smile crossed his broad, open features.

Cody Custer was Thrush Limburger's chief of staff, gofer, and when necessity arose, his personal driver.

Thrush Limburger did not drive. He liked to say that he had been too busy to stop and learn how. But the truth was, at three-hundred-thirty pounds, getting behind the wheel of even a Lincoln Continental was an effort for Thrush Limburger. Besides, the steering wheel always left a red crease in the rolls of fat surrounding his navel.

So he didn't drive. Cody Custer drove for him.

Two minutes out of Ukiah, a tape cassette came through a slot that connected the driver's cab with the RV body, and Thrush Limburger's voice said, "When we get there, put this out over the PA speaker. That ought to atttact a huge crowd."

"Right, Thrush."

As he piloted the TTT Network RV to Nirvana West, Cody Custer wondered how even his brilliant boss could pierce the veil of media fog that surrounded Human Environmental Liability Paradox. Sure, Thrush was a genius in his way, part philosopher, part showman. And his book had been number one on the bestseller list for three months, except for that black period when Madonna's overhyped nonbook had knocked it to the number two slot. But Thrush hadn't been inside that funeral parlor for more than ten minutes. Less.

Cody Custer's musings were interrupted when, coming around a sharp bend in the road, he was confronted with a set of California Highway Patrol saw horses.

He started compressing the brake pedal. The big RV began to slow. Rubber smoked and squealed.

There was a CHP black-and-white unit and a motorcycle, he saw, parked off on the shoulder of the highway.

Three CHP officers in suntan khaki and calf-high black boots approached. They looked grim behind their mirror shades.

Cody Custer returned their grimness with a polite

tone. "Hi. This is the Thrush Limburger mobile broadcast van. Is there a problem?"

"Going to Nirvana West, sir?" one officer asked.

"That's right."

"We're warning all traffic going into the area that there is a chance this HELP plague is getting contagious."

"My boss will laugh at that. He says there's no such virus."

"It's our duty to warn you of the dangers of proceeding, sir. This is the only roadblock between here and Nirvana West."

"We'll go ahead."

"I'm sorry. I have to apprise every motorist individually of the risks involved. Health Department regs."

Now they are taking this too far, Custer thought. Aloud, he said, "My boss is in back, but he's broadcasting."

"We won't take but a minute of his time."

"Okay, go ahead and knock. But don't be surprised if you wind up explaining yourself on the air. Thrush loves this kind of weak-kneed stuff."

The California Highway Patrol officer touched the bill of his uniform cap, and two of them went around to the rear of the RV.

Custer watched them in his rearview mirror while the third officer watched him with unreadable eyes. Those eyes kept Custer from grinning noticeably. One of the cops had a ponytail tucked up under his cap. Only in California, he thought.

The two officers were not gone long. But they did get in. Custer could tell by the creaking of the RV springs, caused by the shifting of weight in back. Every time Thrush moved around, the springs complained.

Only one of the troopers came back. "You're all set."

"Did he give you a hard time?"

"No, sir. He was very cooperative."

"Guess he is in a good mood."

The sawhorses were set aside and Custer drove on.

The Tell the Truth mobile broadcast RV lumbered into Nirvana West like a red, white, and blue amphibious vehicle. The loudspeaker was blaring Fed Leppar, known to be Thrush Limburger's favorite rock band.

That was enough to get the attention of the swarm of press people who were jostling one another for the rapidly dwindling supply of lobster salad sandwiches being handed out at the food service truck. They were eating them as if it were the last food on earth.

The music stopped when the RV did. Behind the wheel, the driver popped the music cassette and inserted another.

Fanfare blared. Minicams were rushed to the site. A white limousine arrived and out squeezed Senator Ned J. Clancy, looking worried and working his asthma inhaler often. His aides, seeing this, pressed close in case he started to list.

And from the loudspeaker, came a hearty baritone.

"Ladies and Gentlemen. This is Thrush Limburger. I have promised that I would come and now I have. You have been yanked. That is, you have been deceived. I have brought you the truth, and it shall set you free."

The fanfare returned. It was brassy, triumphal, attention-getting.

And everyone who could, got around to the back of the RV where they expected Thrush Limburger to emerge. Those who had sandwiches brought them.

But the door did not open. His voice did not come again.

Behind the wheel, Cody Custer looked at his watch.

Someone shouted, "What's keeping him?"

"Probably in the john," Cody thought to himself. "But he picked a hell of a time for it." He turned on his radio. From the local station normally broadcasting *The Thrush Limburger Show,* there was only low static.

He cued up the announcement cassette again, louder this time, and leaned close to the radio speaker to see if Thrush's mike picked it up. It didn't.

They gave Thrush Limburger three more minutes, then someone walked up and knocked on the door.

There was no answer.

Finally, Cody Custer came out with the key to the door. He unlocked it, threw it open, and climbed in.

There was the miniature soundproof broadcasting booth. There was Limburger's microphone, his personal computer, his size fifty-seven coat draped over his big chair.

But there was no Thrush Limburger.

He was not in the john or in his sleeping cubicle or kitchenette.

He wasn't anywhere.

Cody Custer didn't have time to be shocked or frantic or anything. He poked his head out of the door and cameras clicked and mikes were thrust in his face.

"Thrush Limburger is missing!" he shouted. "Somebody call the police."

Pandemonium broke loose. Everyone wanted a shot at the empty microphone.

"I knew this would happen," a reporter crowed. "That bag of wind finally broke open and nothing came out."

There was a scramble for cellular phones.

From under his coat, Senator Ned J. Clancy pulled one of his own. It had been hanging from a hook sewn into the double-strength lining of his coat. He spoke in low careful phrases. When he was finished, he restored the unit to its hook, exactly where a pistol would be hidden in a shoulder holster.

"I have an important announcement to make," he bellowed.

"Senator Clancy has an announcement," repeated his chief aide.

"Senator Clancy is giving a press conference right now," added another.

The word spread fast. It passed from mouth to mouth.

And suddenly Senator Ned J. Clancy was exactly where he wanted to be—in the calm eye of a media hurricane.

"I have just been in consultation with my aides in Washington," he said, his voice steady as a rock, "who have just drafted in my name a bill that I will personally introduce into the Senate that will mandate research into the causes of, and provide free medical care for sufferers of Human Environmental Liability Paradox, a terrible scourge that threatens all humanity, possibly the worst health threat ever faced by middle-class America. I know my colleagues on both sides of the aisle will join me in supporting this important legislation."

"What caused you to change your mind, Senator?" a reporter demanded.

"I did not change my mind, I have been working quietly toward this end for some weeks now, and only wished to announce it at the proper moment."

"How are you going to fund the HELP bill, Senator?" Jane Goodwoman called out.

Clancy smiled boozily. "With a value-added tax on the sale of condoms."

Some reporters actually tucked their mikes and notepads under their arms and broke out into polite applause. They would have cheered, but their mouths were full of lobster salad.

"What do you have to say about the disappearance of Thrush Limburger, Senator?"

"My heart goes out to his family—if he has one."

And so the disappearance of Thrush Limburger became an instant page three item. Senator Clancy's proposed HELP bill led the evening newscasts and was destined to be tomorrow's headline.

At the edge of the swarm of reporters, Cody Custer tried to tell any reporter who would listen, "I think he was kidnapped. I think Thrush was abducted by his political enemies."

He was ignored. He was laughed at. Except by those who sneered.

"Everybody knew Limburger would pull something like this once his ratings started to fall," Jane Goodwoman spat, lobster salad fragments spraying from her rubbery mouth.

And even Cody Custer began to wonder if the conventional wisdom had been right all along.

There was no other reasonable explanation.

12

Remo stopped by the front desk before returning to his bungalow.

"Water back on?" he asked the desk clerk, who held his red and tender fingers in the air as if afraid to touch hard objects with them.

"Not yet."

"Damn."

"Sorry."

"Not as sorry as you will be if I don't shower soon," Remo said.

"The drought is out of our control, sir."

"Remember my friend with the fast fingers?"

The desk clerk dropped his tender hand under the counter where it would be safe. "Indelibly."

"He wants me to shower more than anything in the world."

"More than he wants rice?"

Remo nodded soberly. "More than rice."

"I might be able to scare up enough water for a bath."

"Start scaring."

"It'll take a while for the ice to melt, though."

"I'll be in my room counting the minutes," said Remo, stepping out into the cool California air. He glanced up the road, but the Master of Sinanju was nowhere in sight.

"Let him play games if he wants to," muttered Remo, going in and turning on the TV.

He got the top of the hour CNN News.

"In Peoria, Illinois, authorities have just announced that Dr. Mordaunt Gregorian, self-styled thanatologist, has just assisted in his twenty-eighth suicide. The victim, forty-seven-year-old Penelope Grimm, was suffering from a severe vaginal yeast infection easily cured with an over-the-counter prescription. Unfortunately, the woman's Christian Scientist beliefs forbid their use. Asked to comment on his latest foray into medicide, as the practice of doctor-assisted suicide has come to be called, Dr. Gregorian said, 'This is a gigantic step forward for the medical community and for women, who no longer need to be terminally ill in order to end their suffering. My toll-free death-line number is—' "

"Damn," said Remo, grabbing up the telephone. He thumbed the 1 button. Relays clicked.

Harold Smith answered, "Yes?"

"It's me and I have a problem."

Smith's voice tensed up. "What is it?"

"I'm stuck in California when I should be in Peoria."

"What is happening in Peoria?"

"Dr. Doom just executed another sick woman. This time, she wasn't even terminal."

"I have heard that report. It is very disturbing. This man seems determined to test the euthanasia laws in every state in the union."

"It's sick, and I should be doing something about it, except I'm stuck here, dodging press and politicians and wasting my freaking time."

"One moment, Remo. I seem to have left the radio on."

In the background, Remo heard a hiss of static. It went away. Smith's voice returned, sounding faintly perturbed.

"Something must have happened to the feed for the Thrush Limburger radio show."

"Maybe that hippo sat on it," Remo growled.

"Remo, why are you in such a foul mood?"

"From the top, I can't shower because there's no freaking water; because I can't shower, Chiun won't have anything to do with me; and I can't do my job because Nirvana West is crawling with political free-loaders and media dips."

"You have made no progress?"

"I talked to the local coroner. One of the few sane people I've come across out here. He can't make any sense of it, either."

"Then you've learned nothing?"

"No." Remo was looking at the TV and said, "Hold the phone." He grabbed the remote and brought up the sound.

"What is it, Remo?"

"CNN just flashed Thrush Limburger's fat face."

"Thrush Limburger," the newscaster was saying, "had no sooner pulled into Nirvana West when it was discovered that the popular radio and TV personality was no longer on board his broadcast van. When questioned, his driver and personal assistant, Cody Custer, claimed that Limburger had been abducted en route by members of the California Highway Patrol."

"Oh, sure," Remo said skeptically.

"That may explain the static," Smith mused.

"Publicity stunt," said Remo.

"Perhaps not," Smith said thoughtfully. "Remo, I was listening to the Limburger show when you called. He claimed he was about to crack this thing wide open."

"He also got the last presidential election dead wrong," Remo said sourly.

The newscast continued. A clip of Senator Ned Clancy was thrown up on the screen. The newscaster was saying, "Shortly after the alleged disappearance of Thrush Limburger, Senator Ned J. Clancy of Massachusetts announced that he would sponsor a bill calling for a four-billion-dollar research program to combat the growing HELP crisis, entirely funded by a value-added tax on condom sales nationwide."

"It is my hope that the bulk of these revenues can go to ending this scourge, whatever it may be," he said in his broad Massachusetts accent.

Remo turned off the sound.

"You hear that, Smitty?"

"Yes."

"This is awful fishy."

"How so?"

"Yesterday, Clancy was ducking the question of HELP like crazy. You could tell he was worried about what Limburger was going to say and do. Now Limburger's vanished and all of a sudden there's a giant bill in the Senate."

"It is almost as if Clancy knows Limburger isn't coming back," Smith said slowly. His voice grew sharp. "Remo, can you get to Clancy?"

"As a matter of fact, I'm in good with his mother's nurse. I can talk to her."

"Do so," said Smith.

"I'll get back with you, Smitty," said Remo suddenly, hanging up.

Remo had spotted the Master of Sinanju through a bungalow window. He threw open the door.

"Hey, Little Father! I'm headed for Nirvana West. You coming?"

"Have you showered?" Chiun called back.

"The ice hasn't melted yet. But before you say no, Thrush Limburger just disappeared."

"The fiends!" shrieked Chiun, rushing forward, his wide kimono sleeves flapping like the wings of some ungainly bird.

"What fiends?" asked Remo, going out to meet him.

"Whichever ones abducted Thrush the Vocal. They must be depraved to commit such a heinous act."

"They also must be able to bench press elephants if they carried him off themselves. Come on. We gotta talk to Nalini."

The Master of Sinanju froze as Remo threw open the car door for him.

"Why must you do that?" he asked coolly.

"Clancy just pulled a flip-flop. He's sponsoring a bill to fight HELP. Could be he knows what happened to Limburger."

"Then we will rend his dissipated flesh from his treasonous bones," cried Chiun.

"Nothing doing. He's a U.S. senator. We don't mess with him without authorization from Smith. You know how he is about hitting politicians, especially if they're ours."

"I do not understand. What are assassins for but to do away with nettlesome rivals?"

"Look, Clancy belongs to a famous political family. I know they're mostly jerks, you know they're mostly jerks, and Smith knows they're mostly jerks. Could be he's more than a jerk. Could be he's pulling a scam for some reason."

"So?"

"So, he belongs to the same party as the new President."

"Ah." Chiun's eyes narrowed. "This new President, he is not to Emperor Smith's liking?"

"Every time Smith calls him, he's gotta remind the President to turn down the radio."

"The new President is an adherent of Thrush too?"

"Not Thrush. Elvis."

"The dead one whose restless spirit haunts supermarkets and post offices throughout this land?"

"That's the only Elvis I know about."

The Master of Sinanju's visage tightened in thought. "Perhaps after this assignment the opportunity I have been waiting for will come," he said thoughtfully.

"What opportunity?"

"To unseat the President and place Harold Smith

on the Eagle Throne where he rightfully belongs and where he will be in a position to handsomely reward our loyalty."

"Never happen."

"Smith has secretly ruled this great nation for three decades. Is it not proper that he should come out of hiding?"

"Smith isn't in hiding. He's undercover. That's how he operates. Do us both a favor, don't bring this up."

"Why not?"

"Smith might be tempted this time."

Chiun smiled as he stepped into the car and allowed his penitent pupil to close the door for him.

They couldn't get anywhere near Nirvana West by car. Traffic was backed up. A half mile from the place, Remo eased the rented car up onto the soft shoulder of the road.

"Keep an eye out for anyone who might recognize us," Remo warned.

"I am not afraid of Ned Doppler and his ilk."

"Maybe not. But last time out an awful lot of TV anchors bought the farm. Smitty would be upset if you wasted any more."

"I only killed two. One by mistake."

"That was a hell of a big mistake."

"He was easily replaced," sniffed Chiun.

"Just be careful."

They slipped into the woods and made no sound as they worked their way to Nirvana West. Roosting birds were not disturbed by their passing.

"I guess we can scout the situation from that hill," Remo muttered.

They passed through an area of evergreens that had rubbery leaves instead of needles. Their scent was fresh and clean.

Something dropped from a branch onto Remo's shoulder.

He reached up and brushed it off. It scuttled away.

Further along, another sprang onto his head. Remo shook his dark hair and a brownish-red insect jumped off like a grasshopper to vanish amid the parched grass.

Chiun paused. "What is it, Remo?"

"Ant, dammit."

"Why are you so annoyed by a mere ant?"

"Because that's the second one that dropped on me since we got here."

Chiun shrugged. "Since you are an American, you should not complain when food offers itself to you."

They resumed walking. Remo had not gone six paces when another ant leaped onto his bare left forearm. This time, he lifted his arm to take a look at it. It was a rusty red and had the strangest head Remo had ever seen. It looked like a ram's head at the end of a long pipestem neck.

He shook it off, saying, "How come these pesky ants are after me and not you?"

"Because they are wise ants," replied the Master of Sinanju.

"Huh?"

"They understand the fate that awaits them if they intrude upon the Master of Sinanju."

"Ants aren't that smart."

"Nor are you, who cannot walk under a tree branch without acquiring passengers."

"Har de har har," said Remo.

Further ahead, they heard sounds. The noise of a car's suspension getting a workout, but no accompanying engine rumble.

"Better let me take point," said Remo, moving ahead.

Beyond a copse of trees with bark as smooth and shiny as watermelon rind, they came upon a long black limousine parked in the shade.

"We're in luck," Remo whispered. "That's Clancy's car."

"Leave him to me," said Chiun, leaping ahead.

The car was bouncing wildly now, Remo saw.

"Wait a minute, Chiun," he cautioned.

Before Remo could overhaul the Master of Sinanju, he had leaped to the right rear door and flung it open.

"Step into the light, pretender to the throne!" he cried. "For you have much to explain."

No one stepped out, so Chiun peered in. The limo had stopped bouncing on its springs.

Abruptly, the Master of Sinanju jerked back. He turned, his prim features shocked, his hazel eyes wide.

Remo looked in.

Blotto Clancy was sprawled on the spacious backseat, looking like a nude Jabba the Hut. He was sprawled over an equally naked woman.

The woman lifted her head to see over Clancy's cyst pimpled shoulder. Her eyes went wide behind the eyeholes. The rest of her face was masked by a large fuzzy blue circle that seemed to be made out of cotton candy.

"Can't you see I'm interviewing Senator Clancy," the unmistakable voice of Jane Goodwoman snapped.

"I'm not Senator Clancy. I'm one of his aides," puffed Senator Clancy.

"If this is an interview, what's that blue thing on your face?" demanded Remo.

"Legal requirement," puffed Clancy.

"You told me you couldn't get it up unless I wore one," Jane Goodwoman complained.

"I can't—since my cousin's statutory rape trial."

Remo slammed the door and the limo resumed bouncing.

"What did I tell you?" Remo told Chiun as he led the Master of Sinanju away from the struggling limousine. "Nero would have been proud."

"Nero," said Chiun in a stiff voice, "would have had better taste in females."

"At least, it gets Jane Goodwoman off my back for a while. Let's see if we can't hunt up Nalini."

"Yes. By all means hunt up that other harlot. Perhaps Clancy will allow you two the use of his chariot when he is done."

"Blow it out your butt, Chiun," said Remo, walking away.

Coming to the base of a low hill, Remo started up the gentle slope. From the summit, he could see the rustic sprawl of Nirvana West, not much changed since the day before.

This time, the press had not gathered around Senator Ned Clancy. Instead, they were listening to Theodore Soars-With-Eagles.

He was trying to explain that Thrush Limburger had been spirited away by old-growth forest devils, angered that he insulted the proud Chinchilla tribe.

"Limburger said the tribe called themselves Chowchillas," a reporter shouted back.

"That was another tribe," Theodore retorted. "Our poor relations. We do not speak of them. I am a Chinchilla, from the soles of my chinchilla moccasins to the shoulders of my chinchilla cloak."

"There's no Chinchilla tribe registered with the Bureau of Indian Affairs."

"That is because my Chinchilla ancestors refused to register with the oppressive white man, so their braves would not be drafted into unjust foreign wars against other oppressed peoples. Because they were unregistered, they were denied food until their numbers dwindled until this day, in which I stand before you all—the last of the Chinchillas."

The press wrote down every word and asked no more questions.

The Master of Sinanju joined his pupil and said in a sere voice, "Yours is a cruel race."

"Oh, come off it. He's making it up as he goes along."

"Then why are the scribes not doubting him?"

"Because it's easier to copy than research." Remo frowned. "It's a sure bet we won't be able to get near Theodore any time soon. Damn. How are we going to investigate this mess with all this press milling around?"

"Perhaps by investigating Thrush Limburger."

"Good idea. Maybe we can locate the van he was supposed to have vanished from."

A change in the direction of the wind brought a familiar scent to Remo's nostrils.

"Hold the phone," he said.

"What phone?"

"Change in plan. I smell Nalini."

Chiun sniffed the air—or pretended to.

"I smell no such thing," he said thinly.

"Well, I do."

"Then you are smelling yourself."

Remo didn't answer. His dark eyes were raking the panorama below.

"There's her limo," Remo said, starting down the hillside.

Chiun called after him. "Remo, you are going the wrong way."

"Nice try, Chiun. But no sale."

Remo moved between the thick trees, stopping every so often to shake off the ants that seemed to like to drop off tree limbs and into his hair like hyperactive fleas.

He came out close to the black limousine that carried Senator Clancy's mother. The same security guards stood watch.

The back door was open and Mrs. Clancy sat inside, her paralysis-twisted features looking like something out of an old Creature Feature.

Her eyes happened to be looking in Remo's direction, so he thought what the hell and stepped into view.

Mrs. Clancy's eyes popped in their sockets and she began bouncing in her seat, obviously agitated. She brought her hands up to her mouth and her forefingers began gesturing crazily.

Nalini's voice called, "What is it, *Adji?* What is wrong?"

"It's just me," said Remo.

The guards snapped to attention and pulled Uzis from under their coats.

"It is okay," Nalini cried, stepping out from the other side of the limo. "It is okay! This man is not an enemy."

Reluctantly, the Uzis were lowered—but not reholstered.

Remo started for the limo.

Mrs. Clancy wriggled her fingers even more crazily.

One of the rusty ants leaped up from the ground and landed on Remo's bare wrist. Another came off a tree. Remo flicked them away without thinking.

Nalini ducked her head into the back of the limo and bulged her eyes out, bringing her fingers up to her mouth. She made the same crazy finger wriggling, and Mrs. Clancy settled down.

Her face tight, Nalini came to greet Remo.

Remo smiled. Nalini did not.

"Hi!" he said.

"What are you doing here, Remo?"

"Investigating. Nice job of humoring the old dingbat."

"Please do not call her that. She is *Adji.* I call her that because she is like a grandmother to me since I come to this country."

"Sorry," said Remo.

"And what you call crazy, is a form of signing."

"Signing?"

"You have heard of sign language? The deaf use it."

"She's deaf too?"

Nalini shook her covered head. "No. But she cannot speak and so must communicate some of her thoughts with her fingers."

"Right," said Remo. "Listen, I've been looking for you."

"And I, you."

"Want to have dinner later?"

"That would be nice."

"Good. Because after today, I have a feeling I'm going to need some R&R."

Nalini looked blank, then confused. Her face actually darkened in what Remo took for a blush.

"That means rest and recreation," he said quickly.

"Oh."

"Where can I meet you?" Remo asked.

Nalini reached up and drew him off to one side, her fruity perfume filling Remo's nostrils pleasantly.

"We are staying at Ukiah, but it would be better that I meet you at your motel. Are you staying at the little place of bungalows as I suggested?"

"Yeah. Unit sixteen. How's eight sound?"

"Eight o'clock will be fine. Now I must go. *Adji* does not enjoy being left alone."

"Catch you later," said Remo, fading back into the trees. He paused, took a look at Nalini as she slipped into the back of the limousine, and closed the door shut. Remo moved on.

He spotted Chiun floating away, a wraith of sky blue silk.

When Remo caught up, Chiun spat, "You smell worse than before."

Remo smiled. "Oh, I kinda disagree."

"You allowed her to touch you?"

"Don't sweat it. She used her right hand."

"You are a fool that goes wherever his aroused manhood points. It is a wonder you have not walked off a cliff to your doom before this."

"Aw, come off it. I just put up with your mooning over Cheeta Ching for what seemed like forever, and here I meet someone nice and you act like I caught leprosy."

"It is too early to tell if you have caught leprosy or not. The fingers do not fall off right away."

"You should have seen her, Chiun. That old bat

Pearl Clancy was acting like a lunatic and Nalini settled her right down. You know how?"

"By acting like another lunatic," spat Chiun.

"Yeah—no. I mean, she tried to talk back in her own language. Some kinda sign language. It seemed to work."

"Lunatics understand one another and you are impressed."

"We got a date tonight."

"Wear a condom. If you can find one that fits over your empty head."

They walked along. Remo kept his eyes peeled for more of the flealike ants.

He spotted one on a branch, seemingly staring at him with two eyes like black spots set in front of its ramlike head.

It jumped. Remo faded back and the ant went sailing by. It landed on a leaf with a dry skittering sound.

Moving on, Remo brushed away a single strand of spiderweb draped between two trees and encountered no more of the ants.

They came upon a group of print journalists and Remo asked one of them, "I'm looking for Thrush Limburger's people."

"The Tell the Truth RV is around here somewhere. It's the red, white, and blue one."

"Thanks," said Remo.

Rejoining the Master of Sinanju, he said, "Limburger's van is red, white, and blue. It shouldn't be hard to find."

It wasn't. They found it parked at the north entrance to Nirvana West, a young man sitting on the rear bumper, looking miserable.

Remo stepped up to him.

"You belong to Thrush Limburger?"

The man jumped up. "Are you press?"

Remo offered a card and said, "Remo Zimbalist, Jr., FBI."

"He's disappeared!"

"So we heard."

"No, he really, really disappeared," the man said excitedly. "I keep telling people this, but these so-called journalists refuse to believe me."

"Start from the top," said Remo, trying to sound official.

"I'm Cody Custer, Thrush's chief of staff." He blinked. "Aren't you going to take notes?"

"Photographic memory," said Remo.

"And who's he?" Custer asked, indicating Chiun.

"That's my Korean crime-scene photographer."

"Where's his camera?"

"He's got a photographic memory too. Let's hear your story."

"We pulled into town about ten o'clock. Thrush stopped in at the local funeral parlor."

"Esterquest and Son?"

"Yeah, that was the name. He went in and talked to him a while and came out all excited. Thrush said he had the whole thing figured out, and told me to drive straight here."

"Then what?"

"On the way, we were stopped by the California Highway Patrol. They said they were quarantining the area, but we could go through once they explained the risk."

"Yeah?"

"I told them I was okay with it, and they went in back and talked with Thrush. Not more than a minute or two. I drove on, pulled into here, ran Thrush's ballyhoo tape like he told me to. But he never came out."

"Okay, let's look at this logically. You sure he got back on in town?"

"Positive. When Thrush gets on or off this thing, believe me, you know it. We gotta replace the shocks every six months."

"And you didn't stop except for the police?"

"Yeah. It's the only way it could have happened."

"What is?"

"The highway patrol kidnapped Thrush Limburger. They must have."

"You know how that sounds?"

"Yeah, but I think they weren't really police. One of them had a ponytail tucked up under his cap."

Remo looked to the Master of Sinanju. The Master of Sinanju stepped up to Cody Custer and looked him straight in the eye with hazel orbs like cold lasers.

Custer looked at Remo and asked, "What's he doing?"

"Taking your picture. Just hold still."

"He is telling the truth, Remo," said Chiun, stepping back.

Remo frowned. "Great. As if we don't have enough to do, we've got a kidnapping. Maybe we'd better talk to the coroner."

"That's what I kept telling the press. Talk to the coroner. But all they're interested in is food service trucks and bug-eaters. In that order."

13

There was a crowd outside the Esterquest and Son funeral parlor. Police cars were pulled up before the door and an ambulance stood waiting, its rear doors open.

There was also a contingent of press. Minicams and print journalists jostled one another for position.

"I don't see anyone who might recognize us," Remo said, easing the car into a parking slot.

"Something is wrong," said Chiun. "I smell death in the air."

"I just hope it's not what I think it is."

They got out and sauntered up to the edge of the waiting crowd. A sheet-wrapped body was being carried out. The electronic press crushed close as if the anonymous body on the gurney were the most important figure on earth.

"Don't they normally take bodies *into* a funeral parlor?" Remo said, loud enough for anyone to hear.

"Not when the body is the owner," a print journalist said.

Remo winced. "Esterquest?"

"That *is* the name over the door."

"What killed him?" Remo asked.

"No one knows the what, but the police have a pretty good idea of the who."

"Who?"

"Thrush Limburger. He paid the guy a visit less than an hour ago, and now he's croaked."

"Yeah, and Limburger's missing," added another reporter.

"Which proves he's guilty," said a third.

"How does one thing prove another?" asked Remo.

"It ain't coincidence."

"Yeah," echoed the first reporter. "The only question is where Limburger went to."

"My guess is Argentina," yet another reporter ventured.

"Argentina?"

"Yeah." The man chuckled. "Argentina has a lot of beef and at three-hundred odd pounds, it's a cinch Limburger isn't about to hide out in a country where he has to eat bugs."

"Can I quote you on that?" the first reporter wondered.

The other shrugged. "Sure, just don't use my name."

The first reporter raised his voice and looked around. "Anyone else hear that Limburger took off for Argentina?"

A sharp-faced woman perked up and said, "Yeah. Just now."

The first reporter scribbled something on his notepad. "Good. That gives me two sources. My editor won't squawk."

"Wait a minute!" Remo said. "He just floated that rumor and now you're going to print it?"

"Now, it's rumor. After they print it, it will be news. Don't you know how this game works?"

"I'm getting an education," Remo growled. "Listen, while you're in the rumor-mongering business, I caught Senator Ned Clancy porking Jane Goodwoman in the back of Clancy's limo."

The reporter made a disgusted face.

"We can't print that!" he exploded.

"Why not?" asked Remo.

"It's unsubstantiated."

Remo cocked a thumb at Chiun. "My friend here also saw it."

"Yes, it is true," said Chiun. "The pig Clancy was porking the other pig Goodwoman."

"That makes two of us," said Remo. "And Clancy's a married man now, isn't he?"

The reporter made a face. "That's a character thing. We don't do character issue stories. They're no fun anymore."

"I give up," said Remo. He searched for a pay phone and finally found one. It was an old-fashioned glass booth, which meant he could call Harold Smith with a modicum of privacy.

"Smitty? Remo. This isn't getting any better. Everywhere Chiun and I go, we meet a face from our past. Remember that coroner I mentioned? He just turned up dead. And get this, before he disappeared, Thrush Limburger dropped in on him too. According to Limburger's assistant, he came out all excited, claiming he'd figured out HELP."

"It is possible," Smith said slowly.

"Maybe. But get this: I saw Limburger's van rolling in when I was pulling away from the coroner's place. I thought it was another politician, at the time."

Smith's voice grew concerned. "Obviously, Limburger spoke with the man just after you did."

"Yeah, but when I left him, Esterquest didn't have a thing. The way I figure the timing, Limburger couldn't have spent ten minutes with the guy—and he has HELP all figured out?"

Smith's dry voice grew doubtful. "Odd. For all his showmanship, Limburger has a reputation for telling the truth."

"Why? Because he calls his network Tell the Truth? Isn't that like a used car salesman calling himself Honest John?"

"This is very odd," Smith said. "Perhaps Limburger is not what he seems, after all."

"Well, Limburger's assistant seems to be telling the truth that Limburger was kidnapped, if the press's reputation for missing the real story still holds. But here's another flash: the assistant claims a California Highway Patrol roadblock stopped Limburger's van just before he turned up missing."

"He suspects them?"

"According to him, one of the cops had a ponytail tucked up under his uniform cap."

"California Highway Patrol officers must adhere to a strict grooming code," Smith mused.

"That's what I figured."

Across three thousand miles, Smith seemed to lean closer. "Remo, this whole affair is becoming very strange."

"Yeah. Any minute now I might start believing that Nirvana West is under a hole in the ozone, myself."

"Unlikely," said Smith. "But there is another thing you should know."

"What's that?" Remo asked.

"Before he went off the air, Thrush Limburger pointed out that there is no such thing as a Chinchilla Indian. The tribe is actually called the Chowchillas. Theodore Soars-With-Eagles is a fraud."

"That part I already figured out," Remo said dryly.

"Remo, I have looked into his background. His real name is Theodore Magarac."

"Doesn't sound very Chowchilla to me."

"It is Latvian. Magarac is Latvian on both sides of his family. It is strange that the press hasn't uncovered this fact, given the intensity with which they are covering this event."

"Nothing the press does or doesn't do is strange," said Remo, eyeing the reporters filming the departing ambulance. "Chiun and I will deal with Magarac—if we can get close to him."

"Any who stand in our path will die!" the Master of Sinanju cried in a loud voice.

"For God's sake, Remo. Do not let Chiun kill any more network anchormen!"

"I only dispatched two," Chiun cried. "I was referring to certain politically incorrect pretenders to the Eagle Throne."

"He means Clancy," Remo interjected.

"Remo, under no circumstances are you to molest Clancy in any way."

"No problem, there. He's not the molestee type anyway."

"Stay in close contact, Remo." And Smith disconnected.

Remo came out of the phone booth and said, "For your information, Clancy is politically correct."

"He is?"

"Uh-huh. At all times."

Chiun's parchment face gathered its wrinkles into a tighter web.

"If Clancy is a political enemy of Harold Smith, and Harold Smith runs this country, how can Clancy be correct?"

"Because being politically correct is incorrect and vice versa," explained Remo.

Chiun's hazel eyes thinned to steely slits. "Is this like cultimulcherism?"

"Multiculturism," Remo corrected. "And no. But if it will help you understand then I take it back. The answer is yes."

"Are we then politically correct, you and I?"

"No. But we are correct."

"Why is that?"

"Because we're the good guys and the good guys are always correct."

They began walking back to the car.

"I'll explain it on the way," said Remo.

"And if you cannot?"

"You can ask Theodore Magarac. I'm sure he'll give you any answer you want—once we promise not to scalp him when the cameras are on."

14

Theodore Soars-With-Eagles Magarac squatted on his "Made in Japan" Navajo blanket in the center of his Naugahyde faux Chinchilla tepee, which when purchased had been advertised as a Hopi wigwam, and meditated.

It was happening. It was finally happening. He was on the threshold of the scam of his life. And all because he happened to overhear a restaurant conversation between Brother Karl Sagacious and his earliest adherents. And was quick to jump in the pool.

At first, Theodore Magarac had been content to grab for a piece of an emerging cult, gather together a few suckers, feed them bugs, fleece them when they least expected it, and blow town.

But when the first adherents of PAPA began dying of Human Environmental Liability Paradox, Magarac began packing. He had been eating the bugs all along too. Not exclusively, like the others. He couldn't go very long without prime rib and lobster—although the thunderbug was a good cheap lobster substitute.

In fact, once the PAPA angle had been milked to death, Magarac had envisioned marketing the thunderbug as minced lobster salad. He had read somewhere that a fast food chain was able to legally sell octopus and squid as crabmeat, just by adding a small percent of real crab into the meal and paying off a congressman or two to get the legalities squared away.

And he had written the first chapter of *The Authentic Chinchilla Thunderbug Cookbook,* which he hoped to sell to a New York publisher.

But HELP changed all that. At first for the worse. But then as only the members of the Snapper wing of PAPA began dying, he began to see fresh angles to the scam.

When some blamed HELP on the thunderbug, Theodore Magarac stood up and pronounced it the work of a new hole in the ozone layer. It was the biggest scare in the news that week and inasmuch as some were calling HELP the next AIDS, he knew he would need a bigger scare to offset the AIDS insinuations.

And it worked. Official Washington stampeded to stick its oar in and the next thing he knew, bug-eating was the top talk show topic and everyone wanted a taste. The more people who dared to eat thunderbugs, especially live on TV, the bigger PAPA was becoming.

And best of all, Washington had sent an army of bureaucrats to look into everything. Theodore Magarac, through some dummy catering company, had set up the food concession, and was raking it in. The press idiots never dreamed the lobster salad they were wolfing down was actually mashed thunderbug.

Now it was just a matter of moving to the next phase.

Theodore Magarac knew how the game was played. Senator Clancy had announced sponsorship of a bill to fund HELP research. He had asked Theodore Soars-With-Eagles for his support, and Theodore had been only too happy to give it, in return for an eight-by-ten of Magarac shaking hands with the senator. That alone would be worth its weight in gold once HELP took him to the next plateau.

There was only one fly in the ointment.

"What the hell was killing the Snappers? And why only them?"

In his mind, Theodore Magarac had assumed it was

because they ate the bugs raw. But if that was so, why didn't they all die? Why was it only certain ones?

"Something's gotta be killing these Snappers," he muttered. "But what?"

A feminine voice he had never heard before said, "I know the answer to that question, Theodore Soars-With-Eagles."

"Hello? Who's out there?"

"Do not come out of your tent, Theodore Soars-With-Eagles. It is not permitted to see me."

"Why not?"

"Because I am the Eldress."

"Eldress?"

"Had Brother Karl never mentioned me?"

"He did sometimes babble about someone he called She."

"I am that She. It was my voice that drew Brother Karl to discover the bug which will nourish the world."

"Is that so?" said Theodore Soars-With-Eagles.

Surreptitiously, he crawled to a peephole in the Naugahyde tepee front. He peered out. He saw nothing. No one.

"So that crafty old Egyptian wasn't lying after all," he said after retreating to his blanket.

"No," said the female voice. It was thin and reedy, like the wind in the parched grass. "I bestowed the gift of the Miracle Food upon him and yet he proved unworthy of the boon. Thus, I was forced to harvest his soul."

"Sagacious died of HELP. He got weak, and two days later he was dead as an Egyptian mummy."

"The gift you call HELP is a tool, by which the Eldress claims her own when their rightful time comes—or punishes them for infractions against her will."

"You killed Sagacious?"

"I took what became mine at the moment he knelt in the grass and consumed my bounty."

"Why toast him—I mean, why claim him?"

"Because I saw in you greater purity. He claimed to be things he was not, but you possess a pure spirit. I knew with Brother Karl's return to the earth you would lift the thunderbug to greater world consciousness. And I have been proven correct."

"You got that right," said Theodore Soars-With-Eagles, trying to keep the suspicion out of his voice. If this Eldress is whatever she's claiming to be, how come she doesn't know I'm a Latvian from Pittsburgh? he wondered.

"Anything I can do for you, Eldress?" he asked, just to test the waters.

"I have given you the thunderbug and you have done well with it. Now I have something greater to bequeath upon you."

"Yeah? What's that?"

"I hold it in my hand in a small box of ivory and rosewood and I give it to you freely, for what is in the box means wealth and power beyond measure."

"You want me to come out and get it?"

"No, but I will pass it in to you. But you must close your eyes, for to behold the Eldress is to have one's eyes shrivel as the grass beneath my feet."

"You're responsible for this drought too?"

"No. But if it were my wish, the rains would come in plenty."

"Hey. California is parched. I do a mean rain dance. We could clean up."

"Are your eyes closed?"

"Yes," lied Theodore Soars-With-Eagles.

The flap of the tepee shook and a hand came in. The hand was dark. There was enough light coming in for him to see it clearly. It was a thin woman's hand, with tapering nails. And the fingers clutched a small box, not much bigger than a matchbox, and covered with decorative ivory inlays.

Theodore took the box. The hand withdrew.

"Open the box," commanded the thin voice.

Theodore did. The lid lifted and in the dimness of the tepee he saw a dark shape against the white velvet that lined the box interior. He had a penlight and used it.

He saw what appeared to be an ant. Rusty red with a weird bulbous head set at the end of a long bristly neck. It reminded him of a wooden match.

"What is this?" he muttered.

"A gift to mankind greater than what you call the thunderbug," promised the Eldress.

And as he watched, the bulbous head of the strange insect split in two from tip to neck. And like matched straight razors, curving black thorns unfolded from each half.

15

"Basically," Remo was saying as he drove back to Nirvana West, "the people who call themselves politically correct are down on American culture."

Chiun frowned at the twisting road ahead. "And what is wrong with that? American culture is junk."

"Not all of it."

"It's true the so-called soap operas this nation once produced soared to magnificent heights. But in recent years they have sunk to abysmal depths of perversion. Now all your culture is junk."

"Western culture, I mean. They're down on Western culture."

"It is not as good as Eastern culture," Chiun allowed, "specifically Korean culture, but it is not as bad as French culture, which celebrates eating snails and imbecilic actors like Larry Jewish."

"I think you mean Jerry Lewis, Little Father, and for your information, French culture is part of Western culture."

"It is not. Even their language is debased. It is to Latin what the patois the black people of your magnificent ghettos speak is to English."

Remo looked doubtful. "Magnificent ghettos?"

"Show me a Somali who would not give all he owns to live in the worst of them."

"Show me a Somali who owns anything."

Chiun beamed. "My point is proven."

Remo rolled his eyes.

"Look," he said, "let's table this until after we've talked to Magarac."

"Not that all Eastern culture is good," Chiun went on as if his pupil had not spoken. "Hindus are considered Eastern by some and they eat with one hand because the other is perpetually unclean. Have I told you why that is, Remo?"

"Only once, but believe me the memory is going to be hard to shake."

"Even the women do this. Alluring as they may seem to innocent white eyes, they are no more clean than Hindu men."

"Leave Nalini out of this. We have a date for tonight."

Chiun frowned darkly and pretended to rearrange his kimono skirts. "You will need five condoms, then."

"Five?"

"One for each of the fingers of her unclean left hand and one for the unsanitary thumb. This is, if I correctly understand the purpose of this date."

"Which is?"

"To hold hands long into the night, so as to judge the suitability of this woman for matrimony."

"We might hold hands, yeah," said Remo. "On the other hand, we could just skip preliminaries and go all the way."

Chiun's wrinkled cheeks ballooned in anger. "You would not stoop to kiss a Hindu harlot!" he hissed.

"No, I would not. I'd stand on my own two feet, and *then* kiss her."

"Paughh! I do not wish to think of you touching that daughter of the Ganges."

"Nalini is very nice."

"She eats her rice with curry," Chiun spat. "As if rice is not perfect as it is. Heed my words, Remo. A woman who would soil good rice with curry would stoop to anything—including eating bugs."

"Nalini doesn't strike me as the bug-eater type."

"Bug-eating is a sickness. I have no doubt that curry is at the root of this plague. Curry and vile hygiene."

"I guess political correctness isn't limited to the West," muttered Remo.

And Chiun looked at him with the blank expression of a Buddhist monk who had stumbled upon a voodoo ceremony.

It was almost noon, so naturally, the lunch buffet had been laid out. Remo noticed a sign that read LOB-STER SALAD and said, "Whoever the caterer is, he has expensive tastes. Lobster isn't cheap."

He drove past the press enclave and found a spot to pull over. They worked their way in and found that the press had been pretty much congregated around the food.

Remo grinned. "Great. We get a break at last."

They slipped into the evergreens.

Immediately, the ants once again began dropping on Remo.

He flicked them off and watched the tree branches closely for others. He spotted one. It lifted its rusty hammer of a head and seemed to regard him with flat black eyespots.

"Watch out, Little Father, that bug is about to jump you."

"He would not dare," retorted Chiun.

Chiun passed under the branch. The ant stayed where it was.

But as Remo approached, it sprang toward him. Seeing it coming, Remo ducked. It shot over his head and landed on the ground. Remo stepped on it, and that was the end of the ant.

Remo caught up with the Master of Sinanju and asked, "Why the hell don't they jump on you?"

"I told you why. Ants respect the Master of Sinanju."

"That, I don't buy."

There was another ant on a tree trunk. They passed it on the right, which meant Chiun walked between it and Remo.

As they drew near, the ant sprang across their path to light on another tree. Then it jumped at Remo.

Remo caught it with the back of his hand and batted it away. It went ticking through the evergreen leaves.

"These guys definitely have it in for me," he muttered.

They came to the Snapper's pasture.

Chiun halted abruptly. He began tasting the air with his tiny nose, his mouth tightening into a concerned knot.

"What is it, Little Father?"

"I smell death."

Remo tasted the air. It was there. The gases of decomposition, the stale stink of sweat and stagnant blood.

They advanced, making absolutely no sound despite the dry underbrush. It was as if their feet knew exactly where to plant themselves.

And in the dry weeds, they found the first dead Snappers. They seemed to have died seated in the weeds, where they had been contentedly eating thunderbugs, and simply fell backward, their legs still folded. They wore pleasant smiles on their gaunt faces.

"Looks like they died happy," Remo muttered, kneeling to feel their flesh. Warm, but cooling. "And they didn't die all that long ago," he added.

Chiun nudged a body with a sandled toe. "They died of the dunderbug disease?"

"Sure looks that way to me," said Remo. "Come on."

They found more bodies further along. They too had died sitting in the weeds eating to their heart's content.

"I guess that cinches it," Remo decided. "You eat the bugs raw and you die. It just takes a little longer to get some people."

They crossed the Schism Line to the Happy Harvester Hunting Grounds. There, the Harvesters were gathering thunderbugs, of which there seemed an inexhaustible supply, and dropping them into the simmering communal pot.

"Anybody know where Theodore is?" Remo called.

"Sometimes he flies with the eagles, and can be seen wheeling in the sky above," a buckskin-clad blond girl called back.

Chiun looked up and said, "I see only crows."

"Theodore Soars-With-Eagles would not be caught dead flying with crows," the blonde said unconcernedly.

"That was my guess," said Remo.

"Therefore, he must be in his wigwam, thinking wise thoughts," she added.

"I'd bet on the former, but I have doubts about the latter."

They found Theodore Soars-With-Eagles in his tepee, his warbonnet and toupee askew. They seemed to be of one piece. He had collapsed in a seated position, and only the tepee wall kept his balding head from slipping to the grass floor.

His eyes were rolled up in his head, and the whites were blue.

"Remo!" squeaked Chiun. "Look at his eyes!"

"I see them. They're all blue."

"This man is not yet dead."

"Yet?"

"He is dying."

Remo knelt and shook the man.

"Magarac, can you hear me?"

Theodore Magarac stared sightlessly at nothing. His thin lips began to writhe. "She came . . ."

Remo knelt to catch the dying man's words. "Who is she?" he asked.

"Eldress. She . . . did . . . this . . ."

"What did she look like?"

"Didn't . . . see . . . her."

Then he died. He had been breathing in and out shallowly. Then the air began coming out of his mouth and nose in a long, slow exhalation, like a balloon slowly deflating. Ten seconds after his lungs went flat, Remo and Chiun heard his heart skip a beat, then stop beating altogether.

"Gone," said Remo, coming to his feet. "And I don't see a mark on him."

The Master of Sinanju began looking around the inside of the tepee. They found a modest cache of junk food, three back copies of *The Girls of Penthouse,* and not much else.

Remo heard a crunching sound and lifted a foot.

"What did I step on?" he asked.

Chiun looked at a mushy spot on the rug.

"A bug."

"Musta been a loose snack," Remo said. "I don't see much here." He stepped out of the tepee and looked around.

The Harvesters were busily cooking thunderbugs. They seemed oblivious to the death of their leader. In fact, they seemed oblivious to everything but thunderbugs.

Grabbing a passing Harvester, Remo asked, "Anybody visit Theodore lately?"

The man frowned and brushed back his pigtails before speaking. "There was a woman at the tepee."

"How long ago?"

"Ten or fifteen minutes."

"See what she looked liked?"

"I only saw her back."

"How was she dressed?"

"Like an Indian."

Remo looked around at the Harvesters dressed in their buckskins and growled, "That narrows it down a heap."

Remo returned to the tepee.

"Guy says there was a squaw hanging around not fifteen minutes ago," he told Chiun.

The Master of Sinanju lifted a wizened claw. "Look what I found in the man's hand, Remo."

Remo looked. It was a carved rosewood box covered with ivory inlays and lined with white velvet. Otherwise it was empty.

"He clutched this as he died," said Chiun.

"Mean anything?"

"I do not know . . ."

"Well, someone murdered this guy."

"I see no marks on him," said Chiun.

"Yeah. But he's not wasted enough to be a HELP victim. Besides, he wasn't sick when we saw him yesterday."

"We will extract the truth from the others."

The Harvesters were only too happy to answer their questions, even with their mouths full. They couldn't seem to stop eating thunderbugs.

"Yeah, I saw her too," a youth in a mohawk haircut admitted. "But only from the back. She had on a nice dress."

"Ever see her before?" Remo asked.

"I don't think so," he said, picking black bug meat from between his teeth with a toothpick. "She's probably a Snapper."

"What makes you say that?"

"I don't know. It was just a feeling. But she wasn't a Harvester."

"That's right. She wasn't one of us."

"I got news for you," Remo told them. "The only difference between you and the Snappers is that they're dead from eating bugs and you're not. Yet."

"Only Snappers catch HELP. And if they are dead, it is because Gitchee Manitou had decreed it. We will give them a proper burial once we are full of his children."

Remo asked, "If only Snappers catch HELP, what killed Theodore Magarac?"

"Who?"

"The Latvian Chinchilla. We just found him keeled over in his wigwam, scalped."

Assorted confused expressions crawled over the faces of the Harvesters. Disbelief won out in the end.

"Theodore Soars-With-Eagles is eternal," one shouted.

"Yes. Gitchee Manitou would not take him from us on the eve of a Chinchilla rebirth," insisted another.

"It can't hurt to look," prompted Remo.

The blonde in buckskin did look. She pulled aside the tepee flap and let out a screech.

"Brother Theodore is dead!" she cried.

Between mouthfuls, others took up the cry. "Oh, this is terrible!"

"Woe, we are leaderless!"

"The last of the proud Chinchillas has gone to the Happy Hunting Ground. It is the end of an era."

Through their plaintive cries, they kept stuffing bugs into their mouths.

"It might be a good idea to lay off the bugs until we know exactly what killed him," Remo suggested.

"We know what killed him."

"Yes, it is the hole in the ozone layer, created by the white man's inhuman progress."

"What if it was the bug?" Remo countered.

"Heresy. Don't let Gitchee Manitou hear you slander his powerful but humble creatures."

Remo looked at the thunderbugs as they were dropped into the boiling pot water. They immediately curled their inch-long bodies into tight brown balls, as if death relieved the tedium of their mundane existence.

"One last question," he said. "Ever hear of someone called the Eldress?"

No one had. Then someone remembered that in the days before the Great Schism, Brother Karl Sagacious spoke of the prophet he referred to as She.

"She?" said Chiun.

"That is the only name Brother Karl gave to her.

We think it is one of the goddesses of his Greek ancestors."

"Sagacious was no more a Greek than I am," Remo said.

"You are too pale to be a Greek."

"Greeks were as pale as Americans," said Chiun.

"Pale as African-Americans, you mean."

The Master of Sinanju turned to Remo and undertoned, "These people are demented, Remo."

"Must be something they ate," Remo said, eyeing the contentedly boiling thunderbugs.

No one appeared to be lying—their pulse rates and respiration cycles were audible to both Remo and Chiun, and neither betrayed telltale nervousness—so there was no point in extracting any more information by force. Remo took Chiun aside and said, "Something's going on here. First the Snappers keel over, and now Magarac."

"These ones do not appear ill. Only hungry. Do they never stop eating?"

"What I want to know is how they stay so thin when all they do is eat bugs by the carload?"

"I do not know."

"Maybe they're bulimic."

Chiun's sparse eyebrows crept up his forehead. "What tribe is that?"

"Bulimic means they eat like pigs, throw up, eat some more, and throw up again so they can keep eating. It's called binging. Or purging. Maybe both."

"It sounds very Roman," Chiun mused. "Romans would often eat and drink until their stomachs rebelled. Once emptied, they would resume eating. Between you and I, Remo, I think there was something in the water that made them demented."

"The Romans or the PAPAs?"

"Whatever," Chiun said vaguely.

Remo looked around. He saw no one throwing up. Just gorging. "We'd smell vomit if they were bulimics," he decided aloud.

"I would gladly inhale vomit if it would mean I no longer had to endure the stench that woman has attached to you."

Remo lifted his arm. He sniffed. "It's practically gone now." But a contented smile quirked his thin mouth.

Chiun made a disgusted face. "You reek and you do not even care. All my training, it was for naught. I have given a white man the sun source, and alas, he is still white."

"Forget it. Let's see, Brother Karl Sagacious is dead. The coroner is on ice. The Snappers have snapped their last. Theodore Magarac is now Theodore Worm-Food. And Thrush Limburger is nowhere to be found. It's gotta be Limburger behind this."

"Ridiculous," sniffed Chiun.

"Who's left?"

"We are. And as long as we remain upright while others recline, it will be recorded that we were the victorious ones."

"I mean who's left that could be behind this?"

Chiun looked skyward. His eyes tightened. "Perhaps there is a hole is the sky after all."

Remo threw up his hands. "I give up."

"But I do not," said Chiun, starting off.

Remo followed. As they passed from the Harvester area to Snapper turf, he noticed the parched grasses were springing up and down and he saw the rust red ants bounding from weed to weed just like grasshoppers. And like locusts on the march, they were hopping in their direction.

"Let's cut around," Remo said quickly. "Call me a fraidy cat, but I don't like the way those ants coming our way keep looking at me."

"Fraidy cat," said Chiun. "Had you bathed, you would have nothing to fear."

"What makes you say that?" asked Remo as they floated into a stand of evergreens.

"It is obvious that your unappetizing odor is attracting them."

"Oh," said Remo, suddenly realizing the Master of Sinanju was probably right.

When they got into the trees, Remo watched for lurking ants. There were none. Looking back, he saw the dozens of them leaping from weed to weed, and even the lethargic thunderbugs were compelled to get out of their way. The slow ones—which was most of them—were pounced upon.

Remo didn't wait to see what happened next. He was sick of bugs by now.

16

Dale Parsons was puzzled.

They had brought the body of the Ukiah coroner Lee Esterquest to him because they feared he had died of HELP.

As a federal pathologist, Parsons was not licensed to autopsy people in Mendocino County. Drawing blood was another matter. He had done that, taken tissue samples, and was looking at them under the electron microscope powered by a portable gasoline generator. The generator whine was enough to permanently injure his hearing, but Parsons was so deep in his work he was barely aware of the racket.

He almost didn't hear the impatient slapping on his tent flap either.

"Go away," he snapped. "I'm working."

The flap was swept aside and a familiar face poked in.

"Remember me?"

"Salk. FDA, right?"

"You got it."

Parsons grunted. "Whoever named this virus got it exactly right too."

Remo Salk stepped in, followed by the Korean Japanese beetle expert. The old man simply stood there, stony and wordless, his long-nailed fingers clapped over his tiny ears.

"Paradox?" asked Remo.

"Here, take a look."

Noticing the draped form, Remo asked, "Dead Snapper?"

"No. That's the local coroner, Esterquest."

Remo's face grew sad. "I met him. He was a nice guy. Took a lot of pride in his work."

Parsons nodded. "I'm kicking myself for not talking to him before this. He tell you anything about the autopsies?"

"Just that he couldn't make heads or tails of it. But he found something strange in the bloodstream."

"He did? Now that's very interesting. Take a look through this microscope."

Remo put his eye to the eyepiece. Parsons said, "What you're looking at is a blood sample magnified ten thousand times. See those spindle-shaped things inside the blobs?"

"Yeah?"

"Protein particles, embedded in the cytoplasm of white blood cells. Dead matter that has lodged into the bloodstream after doing its work."

Remo looked away from the lens. "That what's been killing people?"

"Probably. But those aren't virus particles."

"What are they?"

"I don't know, but here comes the paradox. They match nothing I find in the thunderbugs I've autopsied."

"You autopsied bugs? With what—safety pins?"

"Very funny. What I found in the bug is interesting. An enzyme harmless to people. It's not poison, it's digestible and excretable. But it does have an interesting property."

"What?"

"Remember that the thunderbug is high in protein, nutrients, and carbohydrates, is easily digested, and even causes people to lose weight the more they keep eating them."

"Yeah?"

"Well, apparently this enzyme chemically bonds with receptors in the small colon, blocking them from absorbing the nutrients and proteins and carbohydrates."

"You can tell that from cutting open a little bug?"

"Actually, I couldn't make heads or tails of the enzyme itself. But I was walking around this place and happened upon the latrine. I noticed the awful smell."

"It's hard not to," Remo said dryly.

"When I looked in, I noticed almost all the stools were yellow and greasy-looking. A sure sign of steatorrhea—undigested fat in the stools. I took a few stool samples back and ran some tests."

"You're a braver man than me if you climbed into that mess."

Parsons nodded unhappily. "It's a gross job, but someone had to do it. My tests showed that not only was fat passing through the PAPA people's intestines unabsorbed, but so were carbohydrates and proteins. The way it works was the chemical receptors would latch on to these enzymes, thinking they were real food, and they'd get clogged up like the wrong key stuck in a lock. The poor proteins and carbohydrates would go marching past untouched. The human body extracts the value of food through the intestines, not the stomach."

"In other words, they were getting nothing out of eating?"

Parsons nodded. "You can eat thunderbugs all day long, and none of the nutrients are going to get into your system. You might as well be eating cardboard. Hell, cardboard would be a step up from thunderbugs."

The old Korean approached, his hands coming off his ears. "What is this you are saying?"

"Those people out there gorging themselves? They think they're eating well, but they're not. They're actually starving themselves. That's why they keep eating and why they keep wasting away. They're fooling their stomachs into thinking they're eating but their bodies keep demanding more and more nourishment. Not getting it from their diet, the body draws it from stored fat and muscle tissue. If they go on long enough, they end up looking like Somalis."

"So that's what's killing them, huh?" said Remo.

"No. Eventually, maybe. But none of the PAPAs ever reached the point of starvation. Yet they die. Before they starve."

"Of what?"

"I have absolutely no idea. But the same particles I found in the HELP victims are in Esterquest's bloodstream."

"If he ate any thunderbug," Remo said, "so will I."

"Reenter, the paradox. And here's another thing—the stuff in their blood doesn't seem connected with the thunderbug enzyme. More blood to test will verify that, but right now I'm leaning toward that theory."

"Well," said Remo, "you have a lot more of blood to draw."

"What makes you say that?"

"We just came from Snapper land. They're all dead."

"All?"

"Every finger-flicking one of them. But the Harvesters are still munching away. Except for Theodore Soars-With-Eagles. He's dead too. We found him in his tepee with the whites of his eyes all blue."

"Blue?"

"Robin's egg blue. Mean anything to you?"

Parsons pointed to the sheeted figure. "Yes. This man's eyes were blue when he was discovered in his embalming room, dying. But look—"

Parsons lifted the sheet and digitally opened the dead man's eyes. The whites were perfectly white.

"It's the only pathological clue and it goes away within minutes of death," he said.

"I've never heard of the eyeballs turning blue," Remo said after the sheet had been restored.

"In liver disease patients you can get a really striking yellow. But blue sclera—which is what it's called—is rare. Usually, it means osteoporosis—bone disease, which I can definitely rule out."

"So what's it mean?"

"If I find out, I'll let you know. Meanwhile, I'd better take a look at those Snappers you say are dead."

"Watch out for ants."

"Ants?"

"They're really active this time of year. They'll jump anything that goes near them."

"Except me," added the old Korean.

Parsons's brow furrowed. "Ants don't jump."

"These ones do," said Remo.

Shaking his head, Dale Parsons left the strange pair.

17

Outside the tent, where he could hear himself think, Remo said, "As soon as word of the dead Snappers spreads, we're going to be in white water, media sharkwise."

"You are speaking Imbecile," said Chiun. "Speak English."

"We'd better clear out."

"It will grow dark soon, we will not be seen if we do not wish to be seen."

"I need a shower, remember?"

The Master of Sinanju's eyes narrowed suspiciously. "You need a cold shower, for you have lust in your eyes."

"Don't let's get started, Chiun. Come on."

They found their car and drove back to the motel in silence.

"You have any ideas about what's going on?" Remo asked after a while.

"Only the brilliant Thrush Limburger can explain it, but where is he?"

"One thing's for sure, he's not anywhere around here. He's too fat to hide inside anything smaller than the Goodyear blimp."

"He is not hiding. He has been spirited away by the secret fiends who are at work in these woods."

"Well, secret fiends or not," Remo said, looking around, "someone or something killed Theodore and that coroner. Something that turns their eyeballs blue temporarily."

"Poison."

"Huh?"

"Poison," repeated Chiun. "That is what the word virus means: poison."

"No, it doesn't. A virus is a bug."

"A bug is a bug."

"A virus is kinda like a microscopic bug. If it gets into your system, it reproduces and takes it over until nothing works. Kinda like congressmen."

"In Latin, a language that is good despite the fact that it is no longer spoken," said Chiun, "the word virus means poison."

Remo looked thoughtful. "I had some Latin when I was a kid. A lot of English words come from Latin, but they don't always mean the same thing as they did to the old Romans."

"You were taught Latin by pagans," Chiun sniffed.

"Those nuns at St. Theresa's taught me a lot."

"Trivia," Chiun sniffed. "They filled your empty head with trivia and superstition. I taught you everything that matters."

"I remember it a little different, Little Father." Remo suddenly remembered something. "Want me to drop you off at the Chinese restaurant?"

Chiun stroked his wispy beard. "Not unless you are going to eat too."

"I figure I'll eat later," said Remo.

"Then I prefer to starve. I am no better than a bug-eater if you prefer the company of that curry-mongering woman to that of the one who raised you from the muck and ignorance of the nunnery."

Remo sighed. He pulled into the bungalow just as it grew dark.

"Look," he said, getting out. "Eat or don't eat. Just don't lay any guilt trip on me because I want to enjoy a little female companionship once in a while."

"You are welcome to females by the score. As long as they are appropriately colored."

"You mean white?"

"No. Korean. Have I ever told you that the Korean woman is the fairest flower of them all?"

"Yes, and I can dig up my own female companionship, thank you."

"I am going to my room," said Chiun. He eyed his pupil for a reaction.

"Okay by me," said Remo in an unconcerned voice.

"To sleep," added Chiun.

"Pleasant dreams," said Remo.

"If my slumber is troubled by the sound of rutting, I will make myself heard."

"You make yourself heard every night with that goose-honking of yours."

Chiun drew himself up to his full five-foot height. "Slanderer! I do not snore!"

"And I tell no lies."

The Master of Sinanju flounced into his bungalow, slamming the door after him. Remo slammed his door too.

But a few minutes later, Remo was humming. He had hot water and it felt good coursing soapily down his lean, hard body. He was going on a date. He had not had a date—a real date—in years. Women he had had. Dates, no. It was nice to think he could still date, have a good time and get away from work. Especially this assignment.

By the time the knocking came at the door, Remo was whistling.

His whistle trailed off into a startled squawk when he threw open the door.

For there stood Jane Goodwoman, stark naked. More stark than naked, although she was totally naked. She was very stark.

"What are you doing here?" Remo demanded.

Jane Goodwoman smiled as wide as a Cadillac grille. "I got your note, lover!" She threw out her arms and her breasts wobbled like mismatched pink jello molds, setting her hoop earrings jangling.

"What note?"

"The one you sent to my hotel that said 'I love you madly.' "

"I hate you absolutely," said Remo. "Therefore, I sent no mash notes."

Jane Goodwoman gathered up her E-cup breasts, shoved them into Remo's face and demanded, "How can you hate these?"

Looking at the mass of flesh slopping over Jane Goodwoman's clutching hands, Remo remarked, "I didn't know tits could have thyroid problems."

Jane Goodwoman turned red and threw her hand back to slap Remo in the face. Remo was too quick. He slammed the door. The slam and the smack of her hand hitting the door blended into a single short, sharp sound.

"This despicable harassment will be in tomorrow's *Blade*!" she called through the quivering door.

"Get stuffed. Just be sure you spell my name right. It's Salk. S-A-L-K. With the FDA. And it *is* Association."

"Bastard!"

"At least I had *one* parent who owned up to having me."

The sound of a car going away was a relief. It was almost eight. Nalini was due any minute. Remo went over to the connecting wall with Chiun's duplex and slammed it hard enough to loosen plaster.

"Nice try, Little Father, but you blew it. She couldn't wait till eight."

The sound of snoring came loudly. It was not the usual goose-honking, so Remo knew Chiun was faking it, surrendering dignity in return for avoidance of blame.

When she came, Nalini entered the room like a balmy breeze. Her sari was a livid pink and clung to her willowy body like ocean foam. Framed by her shawl, her dusky face was like some dark-hearted lotus blossoming.

"Hello, Remo," she said, lowering her big luminous eyes coyly.

Remo couldn't suppress a grin. "You're right on time. Wanna eat?"

"Certainly."

She took his arm and her perfume flavored the walk to the car.

At the Chinese restaurant, they talked over their meal. Remo was surprised at how he hung on Nalini's every word. He found her fascinating, in a mysterious way. He was halfway through dinner before he remembered he needed to pump her too.

"Clancy still hanging around?" he asked.

"Yes. He is very determined to save mankind from this terrible HELP. It has been his burden since the death of his brothers. Those poor men, Remo. Dying of overwork because they cared about helping people too much to rest themselves properly."

"You don't buy that crap?"

Nalini shrugged languidly. "I am a simple nurse from a foreign land. What do I know of such things? Some say there is a hole in the sky and others a disease in the air. I do not know. Others wiser than I will tell me what is truth."

"I heard that Jimbo and Robbo Clancy both died of syphilis."

Nalini's dark eyes flared. "That is not true!"

"How do you know it isn't?"

"I hear all the secrets of the Clancy family and I have never heard such a thing said. Why do you ask me these things, Remo?"

"I told you. I'm looking into HELP, and Clancy's been acting strange since he got here. I'm trying to figure out where he fits in."

Nalini looked at him closely. She leaned across the

table and said, "You are not with the FDA. Who are you? You can tell me. I am good with secrets."

"Then here's one you'll appreciate. The thunderbug isn't giving people HELP. It isn't helping them either. It's worthless as food, despite what people are saying. Those PAPA crazies are starving with every bite."

"I do not believe that," Nalini said doubtfully. "You are making fun of me because I am different from you."

"There's a pathologist with the CDC who figured it out. He's going to blow the thunderbug part of the scam apart once he finds a reporter with a working brain."

Eyes darkening, Nalini said, "These things are beyond a poor foreign girl like me."

"Where are you from originally?" asked Remo, changing the subject quickly.

Nalini leaned back and toyed with her curried rice dish. "Ceylon," she said, her voice a pout. "It was called Ceylon when I was a girl. It is Sri Lanka now."

"So you're not Indian?"

"I am a Tamil, a Hindu. It is not so very different to Western eyes. I left my country to escape the strife."

Looking into her large black eyes, Remo felt he had known Nalini a long time, or in some past life. He kept forgetting his food. He kept forgetting everything except those alluring eyes and the perfume that made him feel pleasantly restless. His steamed rice had grown cold and the duck greasy. He had barely touched them.

Before he knew it, they were driving back to his bungalow and she was sitting close to him, her fruity perfume filling his head. He could feel the heat of her body. It was pleasant too. It also made him anxious to get to his destination.

Remo didn't have to invite her in. Nalini entered as if the invitation need not be spoken, and it was not long before they were kissing experimentally. Remo led Nalini to the bed and she smiled unabashedly as he tried to figure out how to remove her sari.

Laughing, she reached down and took it up by one trailing bit of silk. Then, coming up on one foot, she spun in place—unwrapping herself for him. To his surprise, she wore no undergarments.

Her body was a supple brown masterpiece with nipples as dark as her eyes. They seemed to stare at him.

She bent to turn off the light beside the bed. In the darkness, her smile was a thousand silent invitations to pleasure. They began exploring each other's bodies. Remo found her skin silky smooth.

Remo pushed everything he had ever learned about Sinanju sexual technique to the back of his mind and took her the way he would have in the carefree days before he had come to Sinanju.

Nalini was no coy maiden, for all her demureness. She knew sex, and she knew men.

What followed was rough and wild and Remo lost himself in her perfect, responsive body.

After Remo had rolled off her, Nalini surprised him by mounting him. Before, she had been warm and delicious. Now she became a tigress, moving up and down, making tiny, inarticulate sounds of pleasure that built into a crescendo so acute she closed her eyes and bit her lips as if suddenly ashamed to give voice to her passion.

The last thing Remo remembered was her dark breasts bouncing before his eyes, her nipples, so close to his face, like flat, alien eyes. They reminded him of something, but he was suddenly too busy responding to her rhythms to care what.

They came together, and then sleep came.

Sometime in the hours past midnight, Remo woke up with Nalini's scent still in his lungs and a relaxed feeling that he had not felt in many years. His bones felt loose and easy in his skin and his muscles were completely devoid of tension.

Then, a wrench turned something in his stomach.

He was instantly aware that he was alone. No warmth came from the empty spot on the bed beside him.

He was naked, the covers down around the foot of the bed.

And on his stomach something crawled.

Remo lifted his head carefully. Eyes adjusting to the darkness, he spied a long grotesque shape where his navel was.

Even in the gloom, he could see the flat alien eye-spots. And he remembered what Nalini's nipples had reminded him of.

And before Remo could react, the longhead opened like a scissors, and from the inner edges of each separate bulb, long pincerlike mandibles unfolded like biological straight razors.

His Sinanju-trained nervous system kicked in and Remo's hand was moving before he willed it to move.

He slapped the hideous thing off his belly and across the room, where it struck the wall with a dry but final sound.

Remo rolled off the bed, hit the lights, and knelt to see exactly what he had killed.

It was dead, its legs already curling up.

The head was in two parts. Long fangs lay revealed.

It was one of the rust-colored ants that had been such a nuisance. Definitely. Only now it looked less like an ant than something else. Remo didn't know what.

Then he felt something on his back.

Remo whirled, and the sensation was abruptly gone. He heard the sound of something tiny slapping into a window curtain.

He looked at the rug under the curtain. Scrambling to find its legs was another of the ant things. Remo dropped a telephone book on it, and that was that.

More came. He brushed one off his shoulder,

crushed it under a bare heel. It was like stepping on dry prickly twigs.

They were coming from the window. It had been closed. Now it was open a crack.

Remo slammed the sash down, crushing at least three. Their separating heads wilted, fangs not quite in open position.

He made a sweep of the room and found one more. He killed it with a shoe.

Then Remo lay down on the bed and willed the wrench in his stomach to loosen whatever emotional bolt had been tightened.

When he got his emotions under control, he felt very cold. And angry.

In the darkness, Remo whispered a single soft word. "Nalini."

18

In the morning, after Remo had explained it all, the Master of Sinanju did not say, "I told you so." His eyes said it, but his mouth only whispered, "I did not know." His tone was strange.

"Know what?" wondered Remo.

"That they still lived."

"Who does?"

Chiun shook away the clouds in his hazel eyes. They cleared. "I have never told you of the Spider Divas," he said solemnly.

"Spider Divas?"

"They were great rivals of ours in the days of the Mogul emperors."

"In India?"

"Yes."

"Nalini told me she was from Sri Lanka."

"Which was once known as Ceylon. The Spider Divas came from the island of Ceylon."

"Why are they called Spider Divas?" asked Remo.

"Because it is said that they could speak the language of the spiders and make them do their wicked bidding."

"Spiders don't speak."

"And ants do not hop. Yet we have seen ants do just that."

They were in Remo's room. The Master of Sinanju was examining the crushed bodies of the dead antlike things. Remo had flushed most of them down the toilet. One or two mashed dry corpses remained.

"They look like ants to me," Remo said.

Chiun frowned. "I can make nothing of them, but it is possible it is true."

"What's true?"

"Although the Spider Divas were seen, their assassins were not. That was the mystery Master Sambari failed to fathom."

"I detect a legend coming on."

Chiun pointed to a spot on the rug. "Sit."

Obediently, Remo sat, first checking the rug for vermin.

The Master of Sinanju sat too. They faced one another, their legs tucked in the classic lotus position.

"Master Sambari," Chiun said, "is a Master of whom I never before spoke."

"Another black sheep?"

Chiun's tiny nose wrinkled slightly. "No. I tell you these stories of my ancestors so that you may learn. The lesson of Sambari was never necessary for you to learn because Sambari vanquished the last of the Spider Divas in the days of the Mogul emperors."

"So how come we have them in this country? Sambari was before Columbus, right?"

"Who is to know?" Chiun said dismissively. "When we return home, I will have to revise the scrolls that extoll Sambari's achievement. The man was a bungler. He let one get away."

"Nalini looked a little young to be this Eldress," Remo pointed out. "Or a long-lost Spider Diva."

"She is obviously a descendant of that unclean clan. There can be no doubt that it was she who dispatched Theodore Soars-With-Eagles, possibly by sending one of her spiders to his toupee."

"Tepee," said Remo absently. "Still, the Harvesters *did* say that a strange Indian girl had been hanging around Magarac's tent."

Chiun's face gathered up in annoyance. "Indian! You told me a squaw."

"I know I did," Remo said heatedly. "I was told Indian. I thought that meant squaw, not East Indian."

"If you had repeated to me the word *Indian,* I would have guessed the truth instantly!"

"You'd only have jumped to a conclusion."

"A correct conclusion. One that would have spared you the terror of this night."

Remo folded his arms stubbornly. "So what's the story?"

The Master of Sinanju's bony fingers found their opposite wrists and his kimono sleeves came together, hiding them from sight.

"The Spider Divas were assassins," he said. "Exceedingly cunning temptresses who seduced their victims and left them to sleep the sleep of eternity with their unclean creatures. This is known."

"You're losing me."

"You almost lost yourself through ignorance and lust. I will begin at the beginning."

Chiun looked down at his ivory white sleeping kimono and began speaking. His squeaky voice grew stern in timbre.

"The days of which I speak were the days of the Mogul Emperor Aurangzeb. These were glorious days, although not as glorious as the days of the Egyptians or the Romans or especially the Persians. Still, the Mogul emperors of India had much to offer Sinanju, for they presided over a fractious empire, in which Hindus and Sikhs and unimportant others were persecuted. For the Mogul emperors of India followed the Prophet Mohammed."

"Lotsa enemies to be killed, huh?"

Chiun shrugged. "Enemies exist to be crushed. Aurangzeb knew this and so offered good gold to insure that the House of Sinanju stood by his throne. In time, his enemies waned. But a foe is often more dangerous when his power wanes, for when he recognizes

his fate approaching, he often lashes out with no regard for his own life. It was so here, Remo.

"Now one of the more tenacious foes were the Raj-
puts, who were Hindus. They revolted often. They
were in truth revolting inasmuch as they ate with their
right hands only. They did this because—"

"Can it, and move on."

"As you wish," Chiun said thinly. "Now the Raj-
puts sent to the island of Ceylon for one to succor
them. They knew they could not harm the Mogul emperor, for he was shielded by the awesome hand of
Sinanju, through Sambari the Careless, formerly
known as Sambari the Protector."

"How fast they fall from grace once the truth leaks
out," Remo said wryly.

The Master of Sinanju frowned primly and spoke
on.

"Now in Ceylon lived a people called the Tamils.
Although they were not Indians, they were Hindus.
And among them lived a clutch of females known as
the Spider Divas, who lived without men, taking
mates but once in their lives, and then only to reproduce, as is proper. After that, they ate them."

"They *ate* their husbands?" Remo exclaimed.

"The lucky ones, yes."

"What about the unlucky ones?"

"Slaves. For the Spider Divas were said to possess
charms beyond those of mortal woman. No one knew
what these were. They were temptresses and were said
to converse with spiders, thus impelling them to do
their deadly bidding. For the Spider Divas, having ill
luck with their menfolk, made their way through the
world by hiring themselves out as assassins. This is a
terrible thing, Remo."

"Competition always is, to the one being competed
against."

"I meant that women would take on honorable
work rightly belonging to men. In Korea, women
stand on pedestals of honor."

"So they don't catch on how unimportant they are. Let's get back to the Spider Divas."

"These base females stole the very food from the mouths of the babes of Sinanju, whom my ancestors fed."

"Let's just skip the part about the starving babies," Remo said impatiently. "What happened next?"

"Now in these days, the Spider Divas were in decline. They had suffered greatly whenever they challenged the hand of Sinanju. Their numbers were few. And they were having difficulty finding willing men."

"No kidding," Remo said dryly.

"People had begun to talk."

"Imagine."

Chiun leaned forward to whisper, "It is rumored, Remo, they had had been reduced to harlotry."

"No!"

Chiun nodded wisely. "At this time, it was known that only three Spider Divas still lived in seclusion. But when they made their appearance in the city of Ahmadnagar, where the Mogul Emperor held forth, persecuting his subjects prudently and with wisdom, all knew of their purpose. For they were known for their great dark eyes, and the bright harlot colors of their saris.

"Hearing this, Master Sambari sought out the Spider Divas. The first, he killed in her sleep. The second he surprised when the harlot was dallying with one of the dandy soldiers of the Mogul Emperor, for knowing their lord was protected by the House of Sinanju, they had grown soft in their ways. Sambari dispatched both with a single blow and jellied their loins as they copulated, unwitting."

"At least they died happy," said Remo.

Chiun made a face, then went on.

"But the third Spider Diva, whose name comes down to us as Padmini, proved elusive. Master Sambari hunted her high and low, finally learning that she had slipped out of the city, in rightful fear of her life."

The Master of Sinanju closed his eyes and began rocking to and fro, as if reliving the events of centuries gone by.

"Sambari followed her, and in a forest whose name is unimportant, otherwise he would have mentioned it in his scrolls, Sambari came upon Padmini, the last Spider Diva.

"She slept by the firelight, her perfect face peaceful as that of a child. The wind toyed with her apricot sari. And for a moment Sambari took delight in her aspects."

"Nice tits, huh?"

"You are cavalier for one who has been seduced and abandoned," Chiun scolded, eyes remaining shut.

Remo scowled darkly. "Don't remind me."

"It is my job to remind you, lustful one."

And when his pupil had no reply to that, the Master of Sinanju went on. "Sambari looked upon this sleeping vision and grew intrigued by this creature. He wondered about stories he had heard as a boy of the Spider Divas. For strange tales were told by men who had seen them naked, Remo."

"Yeah?" said Remo, recalling Nalini's smooth brown body. "Like what?"

"That under their saris, they possessed the ugly bristled limbs of spiders."

"Nalini wasn't like that."

"In the dark, all women are alike," said Chiun in a careless tone. "As the Spider Diva Padmini slept, Master Sambari reached down to expose her nakedness so as to satisfy his curiosity. The silk came away and he saw that the Spider Diva did not sleep alone. Crouching in the moist warm spots of her body, under her arms and in back of her knees were dark shapes. They were decorated with eyes, Remo. Black unwinking eyes. They peered from everywhere, from even the less wholesome hollows of her alluring form.

"Frightened, Sambari restored the cloth and slew the hideous sleeping creature with a single blow to her forehead. Then he ran. Not in an unseemly fashion, of course, but in a prudent one."

"Of course."

Chiun's hazel eyes snapped open. His voice resumed its normal squeaky tones.

"No more was ever heard of the Spider Divas after that," he said.

"So it was a happy ending," said Remo.

"Not exactly. For upon returning to Ahmadnagar, Sambari discovered that the Mogul Emperor Aurangzeb had died in his sleep."

"A spider got him?"

Chiun shrugged elaborately. "There was no mark, no sign, and as the Mogul Emperor had achieved the age of eighty-nine—old for him but young for Sinanju—death was credited to his advanced years. Except for one thing Sambari wrote in his scrolls but told no one else."

"What's that?" asked Remo.

"There was a scent clinging to the dead emperor and he died with a contented smile on his face. The scent was a scent Sambari had smelled when in the presence of the Spider Divas, Remo."

"So they got him despite Sambari?"

Chiun shrugged. "No one knew this, so Sambari was properly compensated for his work and no blame attached itself to him—until now."

Remo snapped his fingers suddenly. "The ants! Maybe they're not ants, after all."

"Perhaps they are spiders," agreed Chiun.

"It would explain why the spiders were never seen. These things look like ugly ants, but when they strike, their heads split open and these pincers pop out."

"Poison. That has been what has been killing the bug-eaters. Poison spiders, not dunderbugs. Just as I foretold."

"That doesn't explain HELP. People who catch it take forty-eight hours to die. Magarac died instantly."

"Details," sniffed Chiun.

Remo snapped his fingers in the air. "Hey! There was an army of these things moving in on the Harvesters when we left Nirvana West."

"No doubt they have all succumbed."

"Why do you say that?"

"The wicked ones are through with their tools and wish to be rid of them."

"Nalini, you mean?"

"And Clancy the clown."

"No way, Chiun. The guy's plastered most of the time."

"Who else then?"

"Maybe Thrush Limburger. Maybe Jane Goodwoman. Hey, she was here before Nalini. Maybe she left the spiders, not Nalini."

"You are a fool who has been blinded by the irresistible scent of the Spider Divas, which still clings to your self-indulgent body."

"Yeah, well, I saw Jane Goodwoman naked, and if there was ever a Spider Diva, she wins the blue ribbon. Her legs belonged on a tarantula."

"Then why did the Tamil harlot steal away in the night? What woman, when she encounters the power of Sinanju, can abandon the bed in which she was pleasured beyond her wildest imaginings?"

"You got a point there," said Remo, reaching for the phone. "We'd better call Smith."

"Emperor Smith will be pleased at our progress."

"He's going to strangle us when we tell him the guy behind HELP may be a U.S. Senator. You know how he is about domestic political messiness."

19

In his office overlooking Long Island Sound, Harold W. Smith listened in silence, the color going out of his pinched patrician face. There was not much color in it to begin with. It was a gray face. Smith was a gray man. After he had listened to Remo's report, his face was the color of ashes, in which the gray color of his eyes resembled dark stones.

"These ants," he croaked. "How many legs do they possess?"

"What does that have to do with anything?" Remo wondered.

Smith fingered the too-tight knot of his hunter green Dartmouth tie. "Please."

Remo went away and came back.

"Eight legs," he reported.

"It is not an ant. They are called hexapoda because they possess six legs. Spiders, which are arachnids, possess eight. What you have there is some exotic form of arachnid capable of mimicking an ant."

"Never heard of such a thing."

"One moment, Remo."

Smith went to his computer. He punched in some key words, and moments later he was scanning an on-line encyclopedia with wireframe illustrations. The illustration showed a many-segmented antlike insect whose bulbous nose could separate and reveal extremely vicious curved fangs.

Smith picked up the receiver again. "Remo, I have it."

"You do?"

"Yes. It is called *Myrmarachne plataleoides*. It is a species of jumping spider, indigenous to Sri Lanka. They do not dwell in webs, but in trees from which they leap upon their prey, trailing a thin strand of silk which enables them to ease themselves to the ground with their catch."

"That's gotta be it."

"Except that my information is that they are not poisonous," said Smith.

"It's a sure bet this one is," said Remo. "But what about the real problem, Clancy?"

"We have no proof Senator Clancy is behind this. The finger of guilt clearly points to his mother's nurse, Nalini, who must be this mysterious Eldress."

"But what would a nurse be doing orchestrating a fake viral plague?"

"What would Clancy get out of it?" countered Smith. "He is at the pinnacle of his political career right now. In fact, it is widely rumored that Clancy is contemplating retirement after his current term in office expires."

"Who knows?"

"Remo, proceed with your investigation, but tread carefully. Make no moves that might expose you or endanger Clancy."

"You got it."

Smith disconnected. He looked to the dialless red telephone that was the dedicated line to the White House. He would not apprise the President of these facts. The situation was still fluid. All might not be as it seemed. It might not even be necessary to order his agents to quietly terminate a United States senator.

But if it was, Harold Smith was capable of giving the order. It was his job.

20

Senator Ned J. Clancy heard the sound of the ringing telephone through a fuzzy alcoholic haze.

"Answer the phone," he mumbled, rolling over in the big hotel bed. The spring groaned in complaint.

A muffled voice he mistook for his wife's mumbled something he couldn't quite make out.

"I said, answer the telephone," Clancy repeated.

The phone kept ringing. The muffled voice kept trying to say something, and between the two sounds, Ned Clancy surfaced from sleep like a submarine breaking the surface.

He blinked blearily at the motel room ceiling. He knew it was the ceiling because it was white. If it had been another color, it would have been the floor. Clancy had awakened with his burst-capillaried nose pressed into many a hotel room rug in his long lifetime of public service. Once, he had awakened in a standing position, his face against a wall. Naked.

The phone was still ringing and he flopped an arm to the night table, knocking the receiver loose. Over the muffled voice he mistook for his wife, he distinctly heard the dial tone hum.

And the phone rang again.

It was then Clancy realized it was not the motel room phone summoning him, and he found his motivation. He rolled over on the horribly lumpy mattress and the muffled voice suddenly broke into clearly audible gasps.

Clancy looked over his pimpled shoulder.

And there on the bed—the bed which his bloated body had completely dominated—lay a spread-eagled woman whose flattened breasts resembled giant pink sunnyside-up fried eggs. Her breathing came in spasmodic gulps.

"I thought I was going to suffocate," she wheezed.

"You're not my wife! Who are you?"

The woman bolted up. "You bastard! Don't you remember?"

"No," admitted Ned Clancy, reaching over to yank off the fuzzy blue ball she wore over her head.

"I still don't recognize you," he muttered.

"I'm Jane Goodwoman, you sexist swine!"

"Oink. Oink. Didn't I pork you once before this?"

"You don't remember!"

"All women look alike to me—above the neck."

Jane Goodwoman grabbed up her clothes and stumbled into the bathroom. She slammed the door after her and Ned Clancy rolled off the bed and onto his jacket, which he had hung up for the night by dropping on the carpet. He fumbled for the cellular phone clipped to the lining.

"Hello?" he undertoned, one eye on the closed bathroom door.

A thin female voice he knew well said, "This is the Eldress, Senator Clancy."

"Keep it low. I'm not alone."

"It is time."

"What is?"

"Clear your brain, fool. If you go to Nirvana West, you will find the Harvesters have departed this mortal vale. Go there. Make a speech. Blame their deaths on Human Environmental Liability Paradox and swear an oath to get to the bottom of it all."

"What about the growing hole in the ozone layer?"

"There is no hole."

Clancy drywashed his bloated face. "You mean the whale was right?"

"Never mind him," the thin voice snapped. "After your speech, fly home."

"Home Cape Cod or home Washington?"

"To Washington. You must ram the HELP bill through the Senate, and increase your prestige."

"Why?"

"That is not for you to know. But go quickly. There is no time to lose."

"You're not my wife, are you?"

"I am not your wife. You would know your wife's voice, would you not?

"Just checking. Sometimes I'm not even sure you're a woman."

"Why do you say that?"

"You got too much balls to be a woman."

"I will take that as a compliment," said the voice of the Eldress. "Your plane is waiting for you at San Francisco International Airport. Everything is in readiness."

"What about, you know who?"

"The whale?"

"Yeah. Him."

"The whale has been beached. His ultimate fate is for the Eldress to decide, not you. You are only a pawn in the great plan."

"Now you remind me of my father—pushing. Always pushing. He never let me have any fun."

"I am not your father, Senator Clancy. And if you do not do as I say, I will release to the media the tape recording of your drunken confession. The girl was only fifteen. Remember?"

"Not clearly," Ned Clancy said honestly.

"She never saw sixteen. She never saw the age of consent. Do you recall the day you confided the indescretion to your father? It broke his heart. After that, he would not eat. You were the last politically viable son he had. After that day, he allowed himself to slowly starve to death."

Senator Ned J. Clancy shuddered uncontrollably.

"My mother will kill me if it all comes out," he croaked.

"Obey, then. Obey the Eldress. I am your truth."

The line went dead and Ned Clancy tried to pull his clothes on in a way that made it clear he didn't quite recognize them.

From one wall of the motel room, the hard sound of a cane rapping against plaster came insistently.

"Coming, Mother!" Ned Clancy called.

From the bathroom, Jane Goodwoman snapped, "I'm not your damn mother!"

"My mother had nicer tits," mumbled Ned Clancy, deciding not to wear underwear since he wouldn't be in town much longer. His second pair was pretty gamey already.

The sacrifices he made to keep the family name from being tarnished. No wonder Jimbo and Robbo died so young.

21

CDC pathologist Dale Parsons awoke with the dawn.

It had been a busy night. He had supervised the removal of the bodies from the Snapper wing of the People Against Protein Assassins.

With the local coroner dead, there was no one to do it on an official basis. It had to be done and Parsons had shouldered the burden because no one else wanted to touch it.

At the Harvester wing, the survivors were too distraught over the death of their leader, Theodore Soars-With-Eagles, to care. They refused to abandon their encampment.

"Only Snappers catch HELP," they repeated.

"What about Eagles? He's dead too."

"Brother Theodore Soars-With-Eagles will never die. When we breathe the good clean air, we inhale his protective spirit."

There was no reasoning with these dimwits, Dale Parsons had concluded. He had left them there. There was paperwork still to be done.

The only good thing was the press had gotten bored with Nirvana West and had gone to town for the night.

Now with the red sun peeping over the ponderosa pines, Dale Parsons set out to ask the Harvesters some questions.

He found instead only silence.

The Harvesters had passed the night in their tepees

and wigwams and somewhere in the night, they had died there.

Parsons hurried from tent to tent, examining the bodies.

"Damn! What hit these people?"

At one tent he came upon a woman with some life still in her.

"Can you hear me, miss?"

The woman could manage only subvocal murmurings. Parsons knelt and lifted her eyelids. The whites of her eyes were a distinctive blue. Not the light blue of osteoporosis, but a livid blue.

The woman's pupils relaxed first, then the rest of her, and the air coming out of her lungs came slow and final.

Parsons straightened and finished his rounds.

There was no question. Every Harvester was dead. It was not HELP. They had not seemed ill the day before. In fact, they had been carrying on something awful when he had last seen them.

When he brought the word to the arriving news media, there was a mad rush for the Harvester encampment.

"Hey!" he called after them. "We don't know what killed them! It may be dangerous to go into the death zone."

"It was HELP, right?"

"I don't think so," Parsons said.

"Then maybe the ozone hole cracked wide open."

A number of photographers pointed their cameras skyward to catch the gaping hole they imagined was up there.

"I see it! It's pink!" one shouted.

Parsons said, "That's the sun coming up. You couldn't see the hole if there was one. Ozone is invisible."

"Just in case," a TV news producer said, "record every square inch of that sky."

Disgusted, Dale Parsons trudged back to his tent.

He came upon a food service truck, where two young men in white were spooning mayonnaise into great steel pots. He noticed that with every spoonful, they were sprinkling in tiny brown things that could only be thunderbugs.

"What are you making?" he called.

"Lobster salad," said one.

"For the press," added the other. They both wore guilty expressions.

"Since when are bugs part of lobster salad?"

"There's no bugs in here. Only shredded lobster."

"Guess I was mistaken," said Parsons, going on. "Something's sure fishy in Nirvana West," he told himself.

Returning to his tent, he discovered the flap was open. He had closed it. Rushing in, he was relieved to find all his equipment present and intact. He wouldn't have put it past those sneaks from the National Institutes for Health to have liberated his centrifuge.

Then he noticed the rosewood box on his workbench. There was a note attached to it. It read:

"ENCLOSED YOU WILL FIND THE SECRET OF HELP. TELL THE WORLD."

He opened the box. Inside, he was surprised to see a red ant. He grunted, looked closer.

For an ant, it was pretty strange-looking. And as he watched, it lifted its grotesque, many-segmented body up on its rear legs. Two eyespots at the end of its head seemed to glare at him.

Then Parsons noticed the thing had lifted itself up on four rear legs, and was waving four more in the air threateningly.

"An eight-legged ant?"

He squeezed his eyes shut. When he opened them, the picture was the same. It was not a hallucination caused by lack of sleep.

Then Parsons noticed the other set of black eyes

dotting the second segment. He counted six eyes. Two great big ones and at least four smaller satellite eyes.

"If you aren't a spider, I'm an embalmer," he muttered, reaching for a pair of tweezers to hold the thing still while he got it under a lens.

He turned his head aside for only a second. He missed the switchblade action of the thing's separating head. When it sprang for him, fangs extended, it was already too late.

22

Traffic was backed up between the town of Ukiah and Nirvana West. It wound between the piney hills like a torpid blacksnake and reminded Remo of the first time he had come here—except now they were north of Nirvana West instead of south.

Remo got out and walked up to the next car in line.

"What's the holdup?" he asked the driver.

"They're dying at Nirvana West," the man said excitedly. "It's the story of the decade!"

"The Snappers?"

"The Snappers and Harvesters, and even some of the feds."

"Feds?"

He nodded his head. "They're dropping like flies. People are saying the ozone hole is cracking wide open."

"If it is, wouldn't it make sense to be going the other way?"

"You crazy? The other way is Ukiah."

"Nobody's dying in Ukiah," Remo pointed out.

"There's no story in Ukiah. It's all happening in Nirvana West. This is going to be great!"

And the man leaned on his horn so hard Remo gave up trying to talk to him. He retreated to his car.

"What news?" asked Chiun.

"They're dropping like flies," said Remo, climbing

in. "And it's not just the Snappers. It's the Harvesters too. Just like we figured."

Chiun regarded the line of cars visible through the windshield with doubtful eyes. "Then why are these people so anxious to go to the place of death?"

Remo shrugged. "I guess they wanna drop like flies too."

"We will walk," said Chiun, stepping out.

Remo started to get out and almost lost his door to a speeding line of limousines that came flying up the other lane, going in the wrong direction. He ducked back behind the wheel, pulling the door after him.

There were three limos. A white one trailed by two black town cars.

"Damn! That's gotta be Clancy," Remo said, getting out. "Get back in, Little Father. If he can go that way, so can we."

They piled back in and Remo pulled into the other lane.

The press had the same idea. They started pulling into the other lane too, blocking Remo's rental car.

Instead of one blocked lane, now there were two. And nobody was going anywhere fast. Horns started honking again.

"I'll bet Nalini was in one of those limos," Remo said bitterly. "We could have nailed her right here."

"We will walk," said Chiun. "And then we will nail her."

So they walked.

Twenty minutes later, they reached Nirvana West, where Senator Ned Clancy had seized the podium that was still there from the day before.

"I vow on the sacred memory of my dear departed brothers," Clancy was saying, his voice ringing with righteous indignation, "to do all I can to rid the world of the curse of Human Environmental Liability Paradox in our lifetime. No price is too high to pay. No cost too burdensome. No—"

"—tax too outrageous," grumbled Remo, watching from the shelter of some evergreens. "I don't see Nalini anywhere," he added.

"I do not see the other limousines," said Chiun, his hazel eyes raking the jam of still-arriving press vehicles. "Only the white chariot of Clancy."

"We gotta get close without being seen," Remo said, starting off.

They moved in on a pair of cameramen who were filming establishing shots from a distance, and as if their plan had been worked out beforehand, Remo and Chiun slipped up behind them and found nerves in the back of unwary necks with their fingers.

Both cameramen buckled at the knees, and after they had collapsed on the ground, their equipment was in Remo and Chiun's hands.

"How do you operate these contraptions?" asked the Master of Sinanju.

"Just carry them on your shoulder and close to your face," said Remo. "That way no one is liable to recognize us who shouldn't."

Cameras high, they advanced toward the media circle, and gravitated to its outer edges.

Clancy continued speaking.

"I have come to believe that there is no hole in the ozone," he was saying. "My dear departed blood brother, Theodore Eagle-That-Soars, the great Mohair Indian warrior, was wrong in his assumptions. Whatever is visiting the HELP virus on innocent, environmentally aware Americans, it will be unmasked for what it is. Whatever it is."

On the other side of the gathering, Remo came upon a chauffeur trying to get his feet untangled from a knot of remote cables on the ground.

"We're looking for Senator Clancy's mother," he said.

"She went on ahead," the chauffeur said, without looking up.

"Ahead where?"

"To the SF Airport."

"Damn!"

Remo rejoined the Master of Sinanju.

"We missed her, Little Father."

Chiun's face darkened. "What do we do now? We are forbidden from harming Clancy the clown."

Remo looked around. "I dunno, but follow me."

They worked their way from the press conference, toward the area where federal agencies had set up operations—such as they were. Not much was going on. Except breakfast.

The federals were eating, of all things, lobster salad sandwiches and packing them away as if there were no tomorrow.

"These people are pigs," Chiun observed.

"They're acting like PAPAs, all right," muttered Remo.

Abruptly, the Master of Sinanju flitted to the nearby food service wagon. He disappeared behind it. Frowning, Remo hurried to catch up with him.

He found the Master of Sinanju squeezing the earlobe of a man in cook's whites. The man was dropping to one knee and he would have howled for his life, but the pain was already too intense. Remo knew that there was a nerve cluster in the earlobe that Chiun had trained him to find.

"What's the problem?" Remo asked Chiun.

"This man has been collecting dunderbugs."

"So? It's a fad."

"And feeding them to the unwary," Chiun added.

Remo blinked. He noticed then the stainless steel pot that was filled with mayonnaise. There were thunderbugs in the mix. They moved their hairlike legs sluggishly as if enjoying the prospect of becoming food.

"Whose idea was this?" Remo demanded.

Chiun eased up on the pressure so the man could speak.

"That Chinchilla," the man gasped. "He set up the food concession. We're just hired hands."

"Food concession?"

"After this, we were going to go national. We'd have cleaned up."

"Probably would have too," Remo muttered. "Okay, forget him. He's small potatoes."

Chiun gave the man's lobe a final squeeze and the pain was obviously too much because he fainted dead away.

Back at the press conference, Senator Clancy was still going strong.

"And if it should turn out that the thunderbug, the Miracle Food of our age, should harbor the HELP virus, I pledge to you my fellow Americans to lift any rock, to move any mountain, to find some way to allow Mankind to consume this wonder bug in complete safety."

Remo lifted his voice.

"You better hope it's not the bug because you've all been eating it."

Clancy tried to locate the voice in the sea of media faces. "Who is that? Who is speaking?"

Keeping his minicam up to his face so no one would see his mouth move, Remo added, "Those lobster salad sandwiches you've been wolfing down? It only tastes like lobster. It's thunderbug."

"What!"

"If eating thunderbug gives you HELP," Remo went on, "you're all overdue for a dose."

At that, the food service truck's engine started and began backing out toward the highway.

Its erratic behavior was not lost on the press, some of whom clutched lobster salad sandwiches.

A few brave souls ventured toward the spot where the truck had been set up and came upon the stainless steel mixing pot and its wallowing thunderbugs.

"It's true!" *Nightmirror* correspondent Ned Doppler cried. 'We've been eating the bug all along!"

"But it tastes exactly like lobster!" MBC News anchor Tim Macaw screamed.

"Thunderbug is supposed to taste exactly like lobster," Remo shouted, after shifting position.

"How do we tell?" a voice wondered.

Just then, a woman came stumbling back from the far side of Nirvana West. Her chest bounced with every halting step. It was Jane Goodwoman. Her face was as white as a sheet.

"I think I'm dying!" she moaned. "I think I'm dying!"

Jane Goodwoman was immediately surrounded by whirring videocams. "Why do you say that?" a reporter asked.

"Because the others are dying too, you idiot!" she snapped, dropping to her knees.

"What others?"

"The other reporters. We went to look over the Harvester encampment, and they started to drop in their tracks."

"The Harvesters?"

"No. They're already dead. Other journalists! It was awful. It was as if their cameras and press credentials couldn't protect them."

The woman's eyes suddenly rolled up in her head and everyone noticed that the whites were turning blue. Jane Goodwoman slumped forward on her face.

Another reporter started to ask, "How does it feel to know you're dying from HELP, Ms. Goodwoman?"

There was no response, so a line producer gave the body a push so the camera could film the columnist's dying face.

"What does it mean?" someone asked.

And not far from Remo and Chiun, Tim Macaw intruded his boyish face between his cameraman's lens and the scene being recorded.

"What does it mean? This is the question of the hour as America asks itself if dying Americans is too high a price to pay in return for a chance to eradicate the specter of world starvation."

The dying columnist was asked, "Did you eat any of the lobster salad sandwiches?"

"Yeah . . . ," she gasped. "They were . . . delicious."

"They weren't lobster," Remo called out. "They were thunderbug."

"The . . . sign . . . said . . . lobster. . . ."

Then, all over the place, reporters, cameramen, and other journalists inserted fingers down their gullets and started retching.

"Our cue to exit, Little Father," said Remo.

That seemed to be Ned Clancy's idea too. Without concluding his remarks, he allowed his press aides to hustle him into the waiting white limousine.

"Let's find Parsons," Remo said.

They found Parsons in his tent. It was the Master of Sinanju who discovered his inert, blue-eyed body. Remo came up in response to Chiun's call.

Remo saw the man's dead face and said, "It got him too?"

"Alas, yes," said Chiun sadly.

"Now there's nobody credible to tell these people the truth about the thunderbugs."

Chiun looked over to the press, who were now in full flight.

"They would not listen to him or anyone," he said thinly. "Not even to the illustrious Thrush Limburger."

"What's that?" Remo said suddenly.

The Master of Sinanju went to the ornate rosewood box on the bench.

"This is the same box that the false Indian clutched," he intoned. "And here is a note, promising the secret of the dunderbug disease if one opens the box. The Eldress murdered this poor man."

"Damn!" said Remo.

"What?"

"Last night over dinner, I let slip to Nalini that Parsons figured out the thunderbug was harmless."

"And she slipped away to silence him."

Remo was looking around the floor, his face tight. In a corner, something skittered. He stepped on it, hard.

"That's what I'm going to do to whoever killed Parsons," he promised.

"We will see," the Master of Sinanju said thinly.

When they emerged from the tent, Nirvana West was a ghost town. All that remained were the dead.

Remo and Chiun were sweeping the area when Remo noticed something red moving on the branch of a tree.

"Hey! There's one of the spider things."

"I see it," said Chiun, edging closer.

"Notice something?"

"Yes, it is very ugly, even for a spider."

"No. It isn't trying to jump me."

"Perhaps it has heard how you slew its brethren."

"Not likely." Remo stepped closer. The reddish spider lifted up on its rear legs and waved its long bulbous nose at Remo. The nose split and out unfolded the dark fangs that were so deadly.

Remo set himself to dodge, but the thing remained on the branch where it sat.

"Why isn't it trying to jump me?" he muttered.

Chiun regarded the thing curiously. It shifted slightly, waving its fangs at him. Its black eyes stared with an alien malevolence.

The Master of Sinanju lifted his right hand. The spider shifted again, prepared to defend itself. And a single curved fingernail sliced both poison fangs off. The spider leapt away, and because they were looking for it, Remo and Chiun both saw the thin strand of spider silk spinning out behind it.

Chiun dismembered the spider with fingernails too fast to be seen. It fell in three sections.

Chiun stroked his wispy beard thoughtfully. "Perhaps it did not attack because you no longer smell of the Ganges."

"Huh?"

"The scent that Hindu harlot placed upon you. You have washed it off?"

"Yeah. I showered before we left the motel."

Chiun nodded sagely. "That is how it was done. The Spider Divas would place their scent on their intended victims so their tools would know whom to bite."

"There was no scent on Magarac when we found him."

"He was in a confined place with no place to hide. No doubt the spider that was his end fell upon him the very moment he opened the box that contained death."

"And the other HELP victims didn't smell either," added Remo. "Parsons too."

"Perhaps there is more to this than meets the eye, Remo, but it is clear now how the Spider Divas worked their wicked will in days gone by."

"Makes sense," Remo admitted. "Sort of. But I still can't figure out how some people buy it as soon as they're bitten and others take forty-eight hours to go out."

Harold W. Smith could not understand it either, when they reached him by phone. He listened in tight-lipped silence to Remo's report.

"Much of what you have told me has come over the airwaves, Remo," Smith said. "However, the death of Dale Parsons is a serious setback. He is the only one who could prove the thunderbug is not the source of HELP."

"So what do we do now?"

"One moment," said Smith.

Remo heard the clicking of computer keys as he waited. They had commandeered a cellular phone at another federal tent. In the distance, sirens wailed.

Ambulances and other official vehicles had been summoned from surrounding towns. There were a lot of dead. The ambulances had been coming and going for the last hour.

Finally, Smith said, "I have accessed the airline reservation computer system, Remo. Senator Clancy appears headed back to Washington. His mother and a woman identified here as Nalini Toshi were due to arrive in Boston's Logan Airport in five hours, with connections to the Hayannis Airport."

"We go after her?"

The line hummed in the silence that followed.

"Remo, this is a very sensitive matter. But yes, go to the Clancy Compound, locate and interrogate this woman. Do it quietly. There is no telling where this could lead."

"What about Clancy?"

"If the trail leads to the senator, it leads to him and that bridge will be crossed if and when necessary."

"We're on our way."

"First, there is something you must do."

"What's that?"

"Eradicate those infernal spiders before more people die."

And Smith hung up.

"Guess who just pulled extermination detail?" Remo told Chiun.

23

The spiders that resembled ants were very easy to kill. And because they were a distinctive rusty red, they were easy to locate too.

The trouble was, there were tons of them. And the press was starting to creep back into Nirvana West.

Remo caught up with the Master of Sinanju and said, "This could take all day."

"Then it will take all day," said Chiun. "It is our assignment."

Remo lowered his voice. "We might not get them all, you know."

"We are Sinanju. We will get them all if you have to get down on your hands and knees and pursue them into their very lairs."

"Thanks for volunteering me," Remo said dryly. "But I have a better idea."

Chiun looked doubtful. "Yes?"

Remo stepped on a patch of dry grass and weeds with his shoe. The underbrush crackled.

"One match would get rid of all the bugs and this ecological sinkhole too."

Chiun gasped. "We are assassins, not arsonists. Would you shame the art?"

"Would you rather chase spiders into next Tuesday?" Remo countered.

The Master of Sinanju stroked his wispy beard thoughtfully.

"I will turn my back. What you do or do not do shames your ancestors, not mine."

Remo grinned broadly. "Fine with me. I don't even know my ancestors."

Remo picked up a dry twig, found another, and knelt in a particularly dry patch of brush. He tried the old Boy Scout trick of starting a fire. After ten minutes, he had a hole in the ground on two well-worn twigs.

He found a piece of hard rock and held one in the brush. With the edge of his other hand, he began chipping off pieces. Sparks flew. One started smoldering in the grass and Remo blew on it until he got fire.

He stood up and stepped back.

"I think I did it," he called over to Chiun.

"I am not looking," replied the Master of Sinanju. "To look is to accede. I am ignorant of any disgraceful behavior."

The fire was going good now. It leapt and spread outward. Spiders scurried. They were fast. The flames were faster.

"Okay, let's get out of here," said Remo.

It took two or three hours, but Nirvana West was a conflagration, kept from enveloping the surrounding hills by fire trucks and helicopters dropping orange fire retardant chemicals.

Surveying the scene from a nearby hill, Remo and Chiun were confident they had gotten them all.

"I think we're leaving Nirvana West in better shape than we found it," Remo said happily.

Chiun cast his eyes skyward. "I know nothing of what this uncontrollable white is saying," he informed his ancestors.

They were walking back to their car, which they had parked in a secluded area, away from everything, when a black hearse pulled up.

A desiccated voice asked, "Is this Nirvana West?"

"What's left of it," Remo said.

"Where are the dying?"

"There aren't any."

The hearse door popped open and the last person Remo expected to see in Nirvana West emerged. He wore black. His round-brimmed hat was black. As was his string tie. He was a tall, hollow-cheeked cadaver of a man, with dry skin and quarrelsome birdlike eyes.

"I have come a long way to assist them in their final agony," said the disconsolate voice of Dr. Mordaunt Gregorian.

"You know," said Remo, his eyes going hard, "I've been hoping to meet up with you for a long, long time."

Dr. Mordaunt Gregorian shifted his quick black eyes from Remo to the Master of Sinanju.

"You do not look well," he told Chiun.

Chiun lifted his chin proudly.

"I have the strength of a lion and the heart of an eagle."

Dr. Gregorian looked back at Remo and said, "Alzheimer's. Very sad. I will be happy to ease him to the other side. For a modest one thousand dollars. Less than the cost of a common vasectomy."

And Chiun gasped like a startled old maid.

Remo moved then. He grabbed the man's shoulder and squeezed. Instantly. Dr. Gregorian's eyes popped out in his gaunt face and he went down on his knobby knees.

"This is for all the little old ladies you keep snuffing," Remo growled, lifting his hand.

A thin wrist blocked the blow before it could begin. Chiun's.

"He's mine," said Remo.

"He is not!" snapped Chiun. "He is not to be killed."

"We've had this argument before. He's a ghoul."

"I'm a licensed pathologist," gasped Gregorian, his eyes closed in pain. "Retired."

"He performs a service," said Chiun.

Remo glowered. "Not good enough, Chiun."

"And he is not an assignment."

"So? He's a freebie."

"If the House of Sinanju performs service without proper compensation, then word will get out and no gold will be offered to us."

"Take it up with Smith."

"Remo, do not be an amateur."

Remo hesitated. There was cold fire in the Master of Sinanju's eyes.

And because he respected his teacher above all others, Remo gave Dr. Mordaunt Gregorian a final squeeze that left him squirming in a spreading pool of a bodily fluid that was not blood.

"Some day," Remo vowed, walking away, "I'm going to get to waste him."

"And if Emperor Smith so decrees it, I will be the one to dispatch that ignoramus," Chiun spat.

Remo looked surprised. "What changed your mind?"

"I do not care that he eases the suffering of those who choose to hire his services, vile as they may be. But did you hear the pitiful price he quoted for my life? One thousand dollars, Remo. Paper money. Not even gold. The man obviously has no idea who he wished to snuff."

And despite himself, Remo laughed as he started up the car.

24

Harold W. Smith sat before his computer screen. On it he had typed the names of the key players in the problem of Human Environmental Liability Paradox. His analytical mind found working with tables very productive as a focusing tool.

He went down the list.

It had all begun with Brother Karl Sagacious, now deceased. He appeared to be a fool who stumbled across fool's gold.

Theodore Magarac, alias Brother Theodore Soars-With-Eagles, was now deceased too. It no longer appeared to be likely that Magarac had done away with Sagacious. But someone had murdered him, Lee Esterquest, and all the remaining members of People Against Protein Assassins at Nirvana West. But who?

Jane Goodwoman, also dead, was never much of a suspect, despite Remo's suspicions.

The loss of Dale Parsons, the CDC pathologist, was more troublesome. Even if Smith could somehow get out the word of the truth behind the HELP scare, without a credible spokesman wielding hard evidence there was no turning back the thunderbug mania. All over the country, teenagers and people seeking to lose weight without going on starvation diets were eating thunderbugs. It was ridiculous. And here was a United States senator, attended by a pack of media hounds, vowing to expend unguessed sums of taxpayer moneys just so people could go on eating an unsafe bug, instead of counseling against the cheaper and more reasonable solution of not eating the thunderbug in the first place.

Where was everyone's common sense?

Now that Smith knew the truth—that *Ingraticus Avalonicus* was not the source of HELP—it was just as important that the facts come out. Those people were slowly starving themselves by eating a worthless nugget of undigestible protein.

Which brought Smith back to the central problem. Who was behind HELP?

Senator Ned J. Clancy remained the top suspect. There was no doubt that he was tied into it all. His mother's nurse, Nalini Toshi, clearly controlled the exotic but venomous spiders that were—or seemed to be—responsible for the actual HELP, in reality not a virus, or a disease at all. But a subtle toxin, administered by a spider.

Was Nalini the mastermind? If so, what was her motive?

Was she a tool of Senator Clancy? If so, what could his motive be?

And there was the missing Thrush Limburger. He had been as quick as Clancy to leap on the HELP bandwagon. Except that he had been out to expose it. Or so he had claimed until his bizarre and puzzling disappearance.

Had Limburger discovered the truth? If so, who had abducted him? And where was he now? Was he even alive?

Harold Smith preferred not to think the worst. That Thrush Limburger was in fact the author of the Human Environmental Liability Paradox, and had engineered this entire scenario as a way to boost his already meteoric ratings.

Still, in some way, it was preferable to the only other probability.

Namely, that Senator Ned J. Clancy was orchestrating everything and had from the very beginning.

There remained one unknown. The Eldress. Theodore Magarac had spoken of her in his dying moments. Who was she? There was ample evidence that she was Nalini Toshi, who although young, seemed to be the last survivor of an ancient cult of assassins who killed via venomous spiders.

There was no one else left on the board.

His computer beeped, and Smith froze his on-screen table and shrank it into a corner of the screen. An incoming news bulletin, siphoned off the wire services, was appearing.

It was a report of a speech Senator Ned J. Clancy was giving upon his arrival at Washington National Airport. It was about HELP.

Smith read the text through rimless eyeglasses and muttered, "The man sounds like he has begun his re-election campaign early."

And then it hit Harold W. Smith.

A motive. There was a motive for scaring the nation with a plague that defied analysis. A virus that did not exist in the first place. Smith knew that in the history of the human race, no cure had ever been found for a virus. The common cold, a virus so simple it killed no one but the very infirm, had never been cured despite intense medical research.

But if the virus was a fraud, a fraudulent cure could be made to appear to succeed.

And the man or woman who cured that virus would be a national hero. He would be lauded and lionized and there would be no stopping him.

Even if he chose to ride his fame to the highest office in the land.

And in that flash of realization, Harold W. Smith got his first inkling of who the Eldress was and why she had set into motion the events that were now culminating in CURE's enforcement arm about to infiltrate the Clancy family compound.

Harold W. Smith removed his glasses and, closing his tired eyes, he murmured a heartfelt prayer.

In his heart, he knew he had sent his enforcement arm after the wrong target. He only hoped they realized the truth in time. . . .

25

Darkness had fallen when Remo piloted his car over the Sagamore Bridge to Cape Cod, Massachusetts.

They had flown to Boston, stopping to change clothes in their condominium castle. Chiun had taken the time to excavate a scroll from one of the many steamer trunks, which he immediately began to write on.

"We don't have time for this," Remo had said impatiently.

"It is important that the truth be recorded about Master Sambari and the Spider Divas," returned Chiun, setting up his ink stone and weighing down the four corners of the peeling scroll with polished sapphires.

"Why?"

"Because if we fail, future generations must know that the Spider Divas employed a certain perfume to mark their intended victims." He inscribed slashing strokes on the scroll.

Remo blinked. "What future generations? There's only you and me."

"If I perish, I know you will be too lazy to record this important truth. I am only protecting your future pupil. Besides, your Hangul characters are atrocious. No one can read them."

"If we don't get a move on," Remo warned, "we're going to blow this mission and we'll be out of a job."

"I am nearly finished. And for what we must do, darkness will be our friend."

Now they were driving through the Cape Cod darkness, past slant-roofed capes with their weathered cedar shingles. The Atlantic rushed and roared in the near distance. The moon was an ivory coin low on the horizon. As it rose in the sky, it seemed to grow in size.

It was probably for the best, Remo had decided as they neared the Clancy compound, the tension going out of his body. Darkness would help them. Chiun had changed into a night black stalking kimino, with a slightly shorter skirt and high sleeves. Remo wore the traditional two-piece fighting outfit of the night tigers of Sinanju's early days.

Chiun, noticing Remo's slow relaxing, said, "You have no qualms about facing the temptress Nalini?"

"I owe her for what she tried to do to me," said Remo, not taking his eyes off the road. "And for murdering Parsons."

"You care for her still?"

Remo frowned. "I hardly got to know her. A one-night stand. Big deal."

"Your words mask your hurt."

Remo was silent a long time.

"She's mine."

"If you will have her."

"I have no problem taking out somebody who tried to dump me in the boneyard," Reno said tightly.

"You will be able to prove this very shortly," the Master of Sinanju said in a warning tone.

Remo said nothing. His flat dark eyes, fixed on the road ahead, were as unreadable as obsidian chips.

On either side of the road, Cape Cod saltbox cottages whisked by like mausoleums.

26

Seamus O'Toole was head of security for the Clancy family.

He was of solid, Irish-Catholic stock, born and bred in South Boston. For twenty years he had walked a beat on Broadway, from the quiet days of the early 1960s through the tumultuous events of the busing crisis to the day they found his police cruiser parked behind the Gillette factory, with Seamus slumped over the wheel, two quarts of good Irish whiskey burning in his belly.

He had not responded to the officer down radio call and because of his dereliction of duty, a gut-shot rookie had bled to death. At the hearing, he was thrown off the force without so much as a by-your-leave. After twenty good years. And for what? The one who had died was only an Italian.

But a fondness for the bottle was not looked upon as a weakness in the Clancy compound, and when his brother, a ward heeler of the old school, told his cousin, who in turn passed word to an aide to Senator Ned Clancy, a spot was made for Seamus O'Toole on the security staff of the Clancy compound.

They only had to fire one Polack to make the spot too.

In the decade following, O'Toole had risen to the exalted position of head of Clancy security, which was not so exalted in these days of dwindling elder Clancys and rambunctious younger Clancys. One by one, all the others had been laid off and only O'Toole remained, in charge of electronic gadgets he didn't understand. What was the world coming too?

Thank goodness, he reflected as he made the round of the walled compound before shutting the electric gate for the night, that the young rambunctious ones took their highjinks down to Florida and other such warm climates. Seamus O'Toole could abide with high-spirited drinking and ravishing a semiwilling girl or two, but it was getting out of hand, what with the rape trials and the accidental drownings and the like.

Seamus liked to keep his conscience as clear as possible. The fewer trips to the confession box the better for him. His knees were so bad it was all he could do to properly kneel during the Communion service.

The last of the bushes checked, O'Toole wandered back to the electric gate. The elder Mrs. Clancy and her entourage had returned to the compound and were now safely bedded down for the night.

There was no reason to leave the gate open any longer, and so he went to the guard box and tripped the red switch. The gates closed with the well-oiled silence that only the finest security system money could buy could guarantee.

Then he flipped the black, green, and blue switches that activated the motion sensors, video cameras, and other, more exotic devices.

Then, confident that his charges were as safe as in the Virgin's arms, Seamus O'Toole stripped the paper wrapping off the fresh jug of Gallo cream sherry and settled down to a long, comfortable evening's diversion.

He needed it after lugging that huge steamer trunk into the cellar. It felt like it was stuffed with baby elephants.

27

Remo parked the car within sight of the high brick wall of the Hyannisport compound where three generations of Clancys had retreated when they wished to escape the glare of the press—or the consequences of their actions.

The place was a sprawling white monstrosity that looked like someone with too much money and not enough taste had taken a simple Victorian house and added wings and gables until he had finally run out of money or land or both. Its yellow-lit windows peered over the barbed wire and jagged glass of the compound wall like a crouching octopus in fear of the encroaching sea. Waves crashed against stone jetties down by the private beach.

"This place has probably got more security than the White House," Remo warned Chiun.

The Master of Sinanju shrugged his frail shoulders in the darkness.

"A fortress is a fortress," he sniffed. "If there are ways out, there are ways in. We will discover the one that affords us the greatest element of surprise."

"What's the best way in?" Remo asked.

Chiun looked up. "Why do you ask me?"

"You're the teacher."

"And you are the pupil. Therefore, you must find your own way if you are to learn."

"You think I can't?" Remo said tightly.

"I am willing to accept the possibility," Chiun said thinly.

"Fine. We'll split up then."

Chiun regarded his pupil coolly. "If we split up, the first to come upon the Spider Diva will have the privilege of vanquishing her."

Remo thought about that a moment. "I'll take my chances."

Chiun bowed. "Then we will split up."

Remo looked back to the walled compound. He saw vague movement in one of the lighted windows, but even his trained eyes could make out nothing more than an unrecognizable shape.

Remo turned back to the Master of Sinanju. "I say the best way in would be—"

But Chiun was no longer there. The Master of Sinanju had disappeared like a shadow in the greater darkness.

"Damn," said Remo. And he started for the walled compound himself. Chiun was trying to beat him in. Maybe he figured Remo wasn't up to the job. Remo planned to prove him wrong.

Remo went up the wall like a climbing spider, a black shape against a blacker sky. Below, the grassy grounds were lit here and there with spotlights and monitored by motion sensor detectors. The zones didn't overlap perfectly. A mistake.

Taking the coil of barbed wire in his hands, Remo felt along it until he found a weak spot. It snapped when he tugged it apart.

Then he rolled off and dropped to the ground in a pool of shadow.

A Plexiglas guard shack was not far away. The guard was hard at work emptying a green jug. He had his eyes on a TV monitor. He would not be a factor, Remo decided.

Moving with an economy of motion that would not attract the human eye or show up on a video screen, Remo eased along the inner wall until he came upon one of the gaps in the sensor zone. He dropped to his stomach and began to crawl on elbows and knees. He could feel the weak outer edges of the ultrasonic motion-detecting field on his exposed skin. He kept from intruding on its integrity.

There was enough light to show him up if anyone happened to stare into the patch of darkness, so Remo wasted no time. He gained the wide veranda, slipped up the rail, and dropped onto the porch.

So far, so good. He wondered how the Master of Sinanju was doing. There had been no sign of him.

The Master of Sinanju dismissed the idea of scaling the wall as too obvious. Any amateur could scale a wall. The best approach to a fortress, he knew, was to employ the fortress's own secrets against itself.

And no fortress built by man existed without a secret escape tunnel for the convenience of the owner. He went in search of it.

There was a saltbox home situated on a dune well back of the beach, within line of sight of the sprawling Clancy compound, but beyond its walls. It was the only such place within practical tunnel-digging distance, so he went to it.

The door was padlocked. The padlock surrendered to a single chopping blow and the door opened but a crack. The crack was sufficient to swallow the Master of Sinanju, unseen.

Furnishings were sparse, but there was a single decorative rug. With a sandaled toe, he eased this from its accustomed place, revealing a not very cunning trapdoor and a rusty steel ring. Bending, he lifted the ring from its circular socket and the trap opened upward.

It was a concrete-lined tunnel, which meant there would be no unpleasant vermin to contend with.

Chiun dropped into the space, his black skirts billowing and his hazel eyes adjusting to the utter blackness.

Moving in no particular hurry because he knew he would not be expected, the Master of Sinanju wondered if his pupil had yet succeeded in breeching the wall.

There were alarm wires on the door and windows Remo was able to check, so he slipped along the veranda that dominated the white Victorian house along two sides.

He went up a round supporting column, gained the porch roof, and lay flat among the shadows. Through the columns would be transmitted any sounds of warning.

There were none. Footsteps came and went, unhurried and unimportant. No buzzers buzzed. He had tripped no alarms.

Remo got up enough to creep along and no more. He went to a darkened window.

There were foil strips attached to the other side of the glass. An alarm system.

So he stood up under a gable, reached high to grasp some decorative gingerbread, and pulled himself up onto the central roof, like a coiling snake.

Remo had a wide menu of chimneys to choose from. The wings must have been added in the days before central heating, because each wing had its own chimney.

The main chimney was the largest, so he went to that.

Remo peered down and saw darkness. No crackling of a fire came to his ears. Grinning, he climbed in, and used the spaces between the crumbling bricks to descend. They might as well have left out a ladder for his convenience.

His frown vanished when his feet encountered a stubborn obstruction.

It was solid enough to take his weight so he dropped on it. It was the flue, down in closed position.

Remo leaned his hands against one chimney wall

and walked his feet back until his heels found the
opposite side. He kept walking backward until his
body was horizontal and he was suspended by the
pressure of hands and feet pushing in opposite
directions.

One hand reached down and he pulled up the flue.
It barely creaked.

He dropped into the fireplace, paused to wipe soot
onto his face and spread the rest on his hands, and
peered out.

The room—a big spacious New England parlor with
overstuffed chairs and antique armoires—was empty
of people.

Remo slipped out and straightened up.

Almost immediately, he heard the whining of something mechanical coming his way.

The Master of Sinanju followed the concrete tunnel
that was inexplicably littered with women's undergarments until he came to a set of crude wood steps. He
mounted these in silence. There was a trapdoor above
his head and he placed one ear to it.

No sounds reached his ears, so he placed his hands
against the trap and straightened his pipestem arms.

The trap lifted into a room filled with darkness.

The Master of Sinanju, like a furtive moth, stood
in the darkness a moment, swiveling his head from
side to side, ears hunting for sounds.

He heard none.

He began walking to a pair of doors that lay open.

And a strange sound came to his ears.

It was a low, whining sound, and it was approaching
rapidly.

Chiun faded back, disappearing behind a curtain
from which he could safely view the strange threat
before deciding to attack or retreat.

Into the room scooted a thing no bigger than a
punch bowl. In fact, it very much resembled an
upside-down bowl moving on tiny tires close to the

floor. It was blue and black and an orange light blinked on its chrome face.

It paused and circled as if sniffing the air like a curious dog. The orange light blinked silently.

The Master of Sinanju remained still.

The round thing continued to circle the room. Then, apparently deciding the room was empty, it abruptly backed up and disappeared up a long corridor.

When the sound of its rubber wheels was far distant, the Master of Sinanju detached himself from the curtain and followed its path.

He did not know what the thing was, but he knew it was but a machine of some sort and therefore no threat to a Master of Sinanju. Perhaps it would be something for Remo to play with.

Remo crouched in the fireplace as the whining grew closer.

He began to recognize the sound for what it was and was not surprised when Pearl Clancy entered the room in a motorized wheelchair.

She was seated in the wheelchair like a corpse that had been left there to dry up and shrivel. One gnarled hand clutched the control stick, a silver pen in a universal socket.

Her eyes, like two wicked buttons, swept the room.

Seeing nothing, her hands fumbled for a button on the armrest and the overhead lights came on.

Remo kept still. He was still in shadow.

Then her gaze fell on him and her mouth made a grimace of surprise.

Remo came out of the fireplace too fast for a healthy person to react, never mind a stroke-debilitated old woman. Pearl Clancy's hand was on its way to the control stick when Remo intercepted it. He detached the stick and tossed it out of reach.

"Sorry," he said softly. "Can't have you causing

problems." And Remo reached around for the battery cables. He pulled them. The electric motor cut off.

"Remind me to plug you back in on my way out," he whispered.

Pearl Clancy only bugged her eyes out at him. She seemed to be trying to stare him to death. Lifting her forefingers to her slack mouth, she began making animated wriggling motions.

"Crazy as a bedbug," said Remo, closing the door behind him.

He eased up a long corridor whose walls were decorated with oil portraits of previous generations of Clancys. Remo could tell he was starting at the older end because the further along he moved, the more bloated and dissolute the Clancy clan faces became.

At Senator Ned J. Clancy's portrait, he took a left without thinking. It was as if he were being drawn toward a specific goal.

There was something in the air. He recognized it. It was Nalini's scent. The fruity smell was coming from somewhere in the corridor ahead.

Remo found himself quickening his pace without realizing it. He paused at each door. The scent wasn't coming from any of them. He moved unerringly toward the end of the corridor door.

The scent was definitely coming from the other side of the door now. His heart started beating faster. He willed it to calm down. What was wrong with him? Was he afraid of what he had to do?

Remo took the knob and with infinite slowness, turned it. The lock tongue coming out of its groove made no sound. He eased the door in. The hinges were quiet. He expected that. It was an old house but well maintained.

The room was dark except for a slice of moonlight slanting in through a curtained window, and Remo slipped in, closing the door behind him.

Eyes and ears alert, he oriented himself. The fruity scent was all around him. And he zeroed in on it.

It was coming from a big four-poster bed in the center of the room.

Remo moved to it, walking on the outsides of his soles. He made no more sound than the curtains waving in the open window.

Nalini slept under a quilt coverlet, her dark hair a spray of ebony on the big white pillow. She breathed through her open mouth, and her lips were as red as when Remo had last seen her. Moonlight gleamed on the hard edges of her perfect white teeth.

And as Remo watched, he was overcome by the urge to lift the covers and see her perfect brown body one last time. Before he took her out.

Remo's hand drifted out. He snagged the hem of the quilt. Nalini slept with one hand tucked under the pillow and the other resting on the exposed sheet. She would not feel the quilt move.

Remo, surprised at his own curiosity, drew away the quilt.

He saw her perfect body lying there, rounded breasts rising and falling with her breathing, dark nipples like flat unseeing eyes. He noticed something he had not noticed before—a wealth of thick black hair under each armpit. They seemed to stir.

And the hairs on the back of his neck lifted.

Crouched in the shadowy hollows of Nalini's exquisite body, dark shapes crawled and squirmed. And all at once, myriad black eyes winked open.

There were fumblings coming from the main section of the house. The Master of Sinanju crept in that direction.

Surprisingly, there were no guards. Once, he encountered a clod-footed man making the floorboards creak under his feet as he passed through the darkened house, his breath reeking of alcohol.

The Master of Sinanju eluded him easily. It was less trouble to fell him with a blow to the back of his neck and leave him where he fell than to concern himself about where to hide the overweight carcass.

The fumbling sound came from a door that was closed. There was a keyhole and Chiun bent to put his eye to it.

He recognized the seated figure of Pearl Clancy, her arms flopping in her wheelchair, as if trying to goad it into life.

The Master of Sinanju saw the soot-smeared severed battery cables and the fireplace beyond, and deduced how his pupil had gained entry.

Chiun nodded to himself. It was a serviceable approach. There was little art in it, but the Master of Sinanju expected no art from his adopted son, who although practiced, was white and therefore congenitally graceless.

He left the woman to her helplessness. She was not important.

He walked along, seeking the familiar scent he knew would lead his unfailing senses to the last Spider Diva—and a reckoning that was long overdue. There was no hurry. Remo had had time to find the Hindu harlot by this time—and face a test of his ability to meet the difficult demands of a Master of Sinanju in training.

The jumping spiders began leaping at him from the moist hollow places in Nalini Toshi's brown body.

Remo used his hands to fend them off. There were too many of them for him to do otherwise. They leaped for his face, his hair, and his arms.

And encountered an invisible barrier that was Remo's flashing hands. They bounced back, not always whole.

The jumping spiders struck walls, bedclothes, and Nalini herself.

Her eyes snapped open. They fixed on Remo, and on the shattered, squirming rust-red body segments accumulating on the white sheet.

"My children!" she shrieked.

Immediately, she hugged her nakedness, trying to locate still-living spiders on her person. She seemed to find none.

"Who are you?" she demanded.

Remo batted away the last two attackers and said, "Forget me already?"

"Remo!"

Her voice was dull with shock.

"Surprised?"

She pulled the sheet over her breasts. "What—what do you do here?"

"I came for answers."

"To—to what?"

"To why you tried to kill me. To why you're killing people with spiders and blaming a virus that doesn't exist."

"I—I harm no one. . . ."

"Can it. I know everything. How you murdered Magarac, Parsons, and for all I know Lee Esterquest."

Nalini's eyes became wary slits. "If you know so much, you would not come seeking answers to questions."

"I know about the Spider Divas," Remo said.

Nalini just stared. "Who are you?"

"Not who. What. I am Sinanju."

And Nalini hissed like a cat in the darkness. Her eyes became hot. She flung off her sheet to reveal her splendid body anew. "If you are truly Sinanju, then I am helpless before you," she said submissively.

A cool, musty breeze was coming from under the door. The Master of Sinanju detected other smells mixed in with the mustiness. Sweat. Fear. He opened the door and descended unpainted steps.

A heartbeat in the cool darkness, muffled and sluggish. Great lungs labored for air. The Master of Sinanju sought those sounds.

There was a steamer trunk standing on end near

the cold furnace. He went to it, knowing the sounds of life came from within.

The trunk was closed with padlocks but they surrendered to fingers that understood their strengths and weaknesses.

The Master of Sinanju pushed the halves of the trunk apart, and a great form rolled out and stopped at his feet.

"Roger, Thrush," said the Master of Sinanju.

Nalini was saying, "Please do not harm me, Man of Sinanju. I am but a poor servant who cannot harm you." Her voice was pitiful. Her heart was beating wildly.

Remo hesitated. Her fruity scent was in his nostrils, tickling them.

"Straight talk," he said.

Nalini gathered herself up, her liquid eyes steady on Remo's towering form.

"What do you wish to know?" she murmured.

"There's no HELP, right? Just poison spiders."

Nalini nodded. "There is no HELP, yes. Only spiders."

"So how come some people die in two days and others go as soon as they're bitten?"

The Spider Diva mustered up a tentative smile that made her dark eyes sparkle alluringly. She stretched her legs, revealing no hidden arachnids.

"It is very simple," she said, averting her eyes. "My pets are no different from other creatures. Some are male. Some are female. The bite of the male brings weakness and a slow death. Those whom my sisters bite succumb at once."

Remo grunted. "Okay, why?"

"It is my duty." She lay back, stretching her arms, arching her back like a supple brown cat. "If you are Sinanju, I do not have to explain duty to you."

"Who's your boss—Clancy?"

She closed her eyes. "Yes, my boss is Clancy."

Remo listened to her beating heart. It had been slowing down, and was now beating normally. She was telling the truth, he decided.

"What's his game?"

"To be President of the United States."

"Blotto? Who'd vote for him?"

"Grateful Americans, once he delivers them from the terrible Human Environmental Liability Paradox."

"Smart. All you gotta do is pull your spiders back and anything he does will look like a cure. But it won't work."

Nalini found his eyes with hers. Her voice grew pleading.

"It could work, Remo. If you were to join us."

Remo shook his head. "No chance."

"I am sorry you say that," she said petulantly, lying back. Her head fell on the pillow. More of the fruity scent billowed up and Remo found himself breathing more rapidly. "I looked forward to more lovemaking with you."

"Sorry."

"You will not kill me."

"It's my job," said Remo.

"I too have a job. I am sorry that your job and my job have made us adversaries. But we need not be enemies."

"That's the biz, sweetheart," said Remo, trying to decide whether to shatter her face or deliver a simple heart-stopping blow over the left breast.

"I understand," Nalini murmured. "But I do not think you will kill me."

"Why not?"

"Because you cannot."

"Wrong," said Remo. Lifting his right hand, he made the stiffening fingers into a spear point.

Nalini spread her legs apart in the darkness, and her scent filled Remo's head. She lay open to him like a burst plum.

"Kill me then—if you can."

And Remo found he could not strike. Instead, he desired her. It was against all his training, but his mind kept flashing back to their wild lovemaking of the night before. And his body yearned to join with hers.

"Mount me," Nalini whispered. "Take me. I will be your slave if I am allowed to live."

Remo started to laugh, but his manhood was stirring. He willed the engorging blood back, but his desire was stronger than his will.

Eyes dark with want, he got onto the bed and straddled her.

Nalini smiled wantonly. "I knew your blood would hear the call of my blood," she whispered.

Remo grasped her under the arms, squeezing the bushy hair hard as he could. The crunching of tiny insect bodies rewarded him.

Nalini's smile melted, her eyes widening with shock.

"You thought I didn't figure they'd be there," said Remo, reaching down to remove his pants.

Nalini closed her eyes in surrender. "You are wise for a man of the West. I want you, therefore I will not resist you."

Remo took her. She threw her head back and gave a tiny grunt that mixed pleasure and pain. Her features softened, and a slow cunning smile touched the dark corners of her lips.

And before he could begin the first return thrust, Remo felt tiny fangs puncture the tip of his swollen manhood.

28

The Master of Sinanju employed his long nails to
sever the cloth gag and bonds of Thrush Limburger.

"You are safe now," he intoned, stepping back, restoring his hands to his sleeves.

"Who the heck are you?" Limburger demanded,
shedding his bonds.

"I regret that I cannot speak my name to you, but
I am here to rescue you from a cruel fate."

Limburger blinked in the gloom. He looked around.
"Where am I anyway?"

"The house of Clancy."

"Not the Black Hole of Hyannisport?"

Chiun nodded. "The very same."

"Unbelievable. I guess Clancy must be behind
HELP, if they kidnapped me just to shut me up. I
knew those California Highway Patrol guys were fakes
the minute I laid eyes on them. But they had their
guns out and snapped off my mike before I could say
anything."

"Speak to me the truth. What did you discover?"

"There is no Human Environmental Liability Paradox. It's a scam. The bugs are harmless. What's killing
people are poison spiders."

"Yes. We have learned that much."

Limburger looked quizzical. "We?"

"How did you come upon the truth?" Chiun asked.

"I happened to drop in on the Ukiah coroner when

233

he was autopsying a local guy who died mysteriously. While we were talking, a red bug crawled out from under the dead guy's leg. We thought it was an ant, until its head split apart and two fangs popped out like switchblades. That was when I recognized the thing as a Ceylonese jumping spider, *Myrmarachne plataleoides*. I figured it got into the guy's clothes and bit him."

Chiun narrowed his eyes. "How do you know its name?"

Limburger grinned proudly. "I saw a picture of one once in a *National Geographic*. I just happen to have a photographic memory. That's how I knew those CHP guys were phonies. I recognized them as Clancy campaign aides. Just one of the varied talents of Thrush Limburger, Renaissance talk show genius."

"And how did you know this insect to be poison?"

"Simple. It up and bit the coroner. He keeled over, and his eyes turned blue." Limburger shook his head sadly. "Poor guy was dead in a New York minute."

"But you told no one?"

"Wasn't any time," Limburger protested. "I had to go on the air with it as soon as possible. The sooner I warned the world, the sooner people could avoid the damned spiders and lives would be saved. There was nothing I could do for Esterquest."

Chiun nodded. "This was wise, except that there are those who blamed you for the man's death."

"The media, right?"

"And certain others."

"That's what it is to be Thrush Limburger. If I cured cancer, they'd bitch that I overlooked the common cold. Well, let's get the heck out of this pest hole of permissiveness."

And from somewhere above, a voice emitted a startled cry of pain.

"What was that?" Limburger demanded.

"Remo!" cried Chiun. And because he could not have a human elephant stumbling after him, he felled

Thrush Limburger with a short, chopping blow to the side of his head.

The man fell like an up-ended rain barrel.

Nalini Toshi laughed with musical mockery as Remo pulled himself free of her, a jumping spider clinging to the tip of his male organ.

He whacked it off, crushed it under a stamping heel.

And Nalini cried, "It is a she-spider! Your death is upon you, Western fool!"

Remo felt his manhood wilt, and knew the toxin-filled blood was returning to his body. His crotch was already growing numb. And a coldness crept into his upper thighs and solar plexus. He fought to keep the blood in check, but the coldness was already spreading toward his heart.

"Die! Die!" shrieked Nalini. "But be sure to fall where the moonlight will show me your eyes. I want to see them turn blue. I want to look into your dying eyes, Sinanju fool."

Remo sank to his knees. His arms went as limp as liver. As if they were only balloons, all the air seemed to leak out of his muscles. Closing his eyes, he bowed his head.

For a moment, he was still. For a moment, his heart stopped. And for a moment, the air in his lungs began to escape with a steady tired hissing. Then, a long silence fell.

Nalini laughed. She climbed off the bed and took his dark hair in her grasping fingers.

"Show me your dying eyes," she sneered, jerking his head backward on its unresisting neck. "So I will know that my ancestors have been avenged."

Remo's eyes snapped open. The whites were bright blue. But deep in the black core of his pupils a red spark flickered angrily.

And out of his mouth, mixed with a hot black spray of expelled venom, came a hollow roar of a voice.

"I am created Shiva, the Destroyer; Death, the shatterer of worlds!"

With a startled shriek, Nalini Toshi recoiled.

"What is this! What is this!" she said, shrinking against a wall.

And as she watched, the figure on its knees began jerking as if reviving electricity were jumping through every lean muscle and sinew.

"What are you doing?" Nalini moaned. "You should not die like that!"

And the figure came to its feet, tall, unbowed, erect in every way. The eyes were red coals and the surrounding whites where white again.

The mouth dropped open. *"Who is this dog meat who stands before me?"*

Nalini pressed her back to the wall in fear. "I—I am the last living Spider Diva, Nalini."

"No," said the voice of Shiva the Destroyer. *"You are the dead Spider Diva, Nalini."*

Nalini Toshi watched the hand lift to her eyeline as if it were in slow motion. She realized the hand was not moving in slow motion. These were the last moments of her life and her senses were doing this— trying to hold on to every precious moment the turning wheel of destiny had allotted her.

She saw the hand, like a weaving cobra's head, form a wedge and aim blunt fingers toward her face. The cruel face behind the hand went out of focus as her eyes were mesmerized by the fingertips she knew had the power to obliterate her, just as other empty hands had obliterated those of her kind who came before.

"I consign you to a place of no returning," said the hollow voice.

And the hand struck.

There was nothing more after that. No thought. No fear. There was not enough time for her brain to call up in kaleidoscope all the images it had recorded in life.

Nalini Toshi collapsed, her face an inverted mask

of crushed bone and raw meat, onto the broken bodies of her children.

And in Remo's dark eyes, a red spark flared, then dwindled. He shook his head as if to clear it of cobwebs.

29

Remo was putting his pants on when the Master of Sinanju burst into the room. Chiun froze.

"What has happened here?" he demanded, his cold eyes switching between the calm figure of his pupil and the sprawled inert thing that was the last of the Spider Divas.

"Figure it out," said Remo, his voice stripped of all emotion.

"I see the Spider Diva, dead."

"That's all you need to know."

Chiun hovered over the dead woman, taking in her nakedness. "You could not resist her, could you?"

"That's between her and me," said Remo, avoiding his Master's searching eyes.

Chiun cocked his head to one side. "But you paid a price."

"How do you know?"

"I heard the mantra of Shiva."

"I don't know what you're talking about," said Remo, buckling his belt.

"We will speak of it later. I have found Thrush Limburger, a prisoner in the basement. He has told me all he knows."

"Clancy's behind this," said Remo.

"She told you that?"

"Yeah."

"And you believed her—a Hindu and a harlot?"

"Who else could it be?" said Remo, his voice returning to its normal timbre. "Come on, let's get out of here."

They stepped out into the corridor and a blue disk of a thing came wheeling toward them.

"What is that, Remo?" Chiun asked.

"A security robot. No big deal."

An orange light winked on and Remo stepped forward. His foot came up and down, and the robot broke like a china plate.

"See?" he said. "No big deal. They just came on the market. This is one of the cheaper models. All they do is beep out a warning."

"Ah."

"So where's Limburger?" Remo asked.

"I left him sleeping below."

"It might help if Smith sent in the cavalry and they found Limburger here."

"That is for Smith to decide."

Remo peered about, his thick wrists rotating absently. "So what is the best way out of here?"

"Have you forgotten something, Remo?"

Remo frowned. "What?"

"You left an old woman helpless."

"Oh, yeah. Pearl Clancy. That won't take a minute."

The Master of Sinanju followed his pupil to the great parlor in the center of the rambling house.

"The whole thing was a scheme to get Ned Clancy into the White House next time around," Remo was saying. "Nalini was the Eldress. She set up all the dominoes at the start, and once HELP was a big deal, started knocking them down so Clancy could rehabilitate himself politically."

"You walk unsteadily," Chiun pointed out.

"I caught a dose."

"It does not appear to trouble you very much."

They came to the door.

"Did I mention I saw the same thing that Sambari saw in the forest?" said Remo.

"And?"

Remo threw open the door. "Sambari was a fraidy cat."

Thinning his dry lips, the Master of Sinanju followed his insolent pupil into the room.

Pearl Clancy crouched in her wheelchair like a mummy refusing to die. Her head jerked around, and her eyes widened. She began bouncing in place.

"This poor woman has been through much," Chiun said.

"She could've done a better job of raising her kids," Remo said, kneeling down to reconnect the battery cables.

The wheelchair motor whined back into life and Pearl Clancy grabbed for the control stick. Since it wasn't there anymore, she made a fist and beat the armrest futilely.

Chiun regarded her with compassion.

"She is a pitiful sight. There is almost nothing left of her but her mind."

"If that," Remo grunted, restoring the silver pen to the universal socket on the wheelchair armrest. "Let's go, Little Father."

And as they started from the room, Pearl Clancy grasped the pen and pushed it forward. The wheelchair whined after them, and Pearl Clancy tried to run them down.

They walked faster.

Then Pearl Clancy bugged out her eyes, bringing her outstretched forefingers to her slack mouth. They began wriggling up and down, in and out.

"She is still following us," Chiun told Remo.

"Big deal."

And from the gray disorder of Pearl Clancy's hair emerged red matchstick heads that split to reveal curving black fangs.

Walking along, Remo felt something in his hair, and

brushed it off. He stomped the scuttling red thing into the floor.

"Musta missed one," he muttered.

"You smell of that harlot again," Chiun sniffed.

Then one landed on the bald top of his head.

The Master of Sinanju hissed, "What is this?" and shook his head once sharply.

A jumping spider landed in a corner and skittered out again. It lifted itself up on its rear set of legs and wriggled its fangs in their direction.

And behind them, Pearl Clancy wriggled her fore-fingers back.

As they watched, the jumping spider crouched and launched itself at her head. It crawled into her hair as two more heads poked out, separating.

"Chiun, do you see what I see?" Remo said.

"She is a Spider Diva too!" Chiun cried.

And Pearl Clancy leered at them, drool leaking from her slack mouth.

Two spiders jumped, one for Remo and one for Chiun.

They fended them off with quick blows, bringing their heels down on the dying things as soon as they hit the floor.

That seemed to be the end of the spiders.

"Remo, do not stand there. Dispatch that evil creature!"

"Hey, I don't snuff old ladies."

"I will not lower myself to kill an old woman."

"Well, I took care of Nalini."

"And you may take care of this one too," said Chiun.

"No way, Chiun. I'm not Dr. Doom."

Remo blinked. The Master of Sinanju looked up into his pupil's face.

"Maybe we'd better call Smith on this one," Remo muttered, keeping his distance from the agitated woman bouncing helplessly in her chair.

*   *   *

When Remo finished explaining himself, Harold Smith said, "Yes, I know."

"What do you mean, you know?" Remo said hotly.

"I deduced the truth—too late to communicate it to you. But it appears that you have neutralized the situation."

"Except for this old dingbat. I won't do her and neither will Chiun. Sorry."

"Have you secured the house?" Smith asked after a moment.

"There's a guard around somewhere, but that's all."

"Lock him up somewhere and keep Thrush Limburger out of sight," said Smith.

"And?"

"Wait."

"For who?"

Dr. Mordaunt Gregorian answered his beeper at a payphone outside San Francisco. Listening as his secretary informed him of the urgent need for his services in Massachusetts, his cracked dry lips quirked into a thin smile.

"Tell them I am on my way," he said, and drove his hearse to the airport. There was no business in California for him anyway.

He arrived at the walled compound as dawn was breaking. The electric gates opened automatically and he drove up the driveway past a guard in a box who seemed to be asleep, an empty liquor bottle in one hand.

The door opened before he could touch the pushbell.

"What kept you?" a man's voice said impatiently.

"Why is it so dark in here?" Dr. Gregorian wondered, looking around. There was a tall man standing in the gloomy vestibule. His face was indistinct. It was very dirty, as if smeared with coal dust.

"Power outage. It's straight ahead. Past the two doors. Here's a pillow."

"Pillow?"

"She specifically asked to be suffocated with her favorite pillow."

"But I have brought my medicide machine. Most people prefer to be eased across the River Styx chemically, I have found."

"Not this time. If you can't grant a dying woman's final wish, we'll get someone who can."

"That would be illegal. I offer physician-assisted suicide, not murder."

"I guess I had you wrong," the man said with a hint of flat amusement in his voice.

"I *could* do both, I suppose. . . ."

"Now you're talking."

"I will need to be alone with her," Dr. Gregorian said. "There must be no witnesses."

"Be gentle with her. She's as old as the hills."

"This should have been done long ago, you know. To allow a person to reach this state of debilitation, it's just criminal."

"Couldn't agree with you more," said the faceless man.

Dr. Gregorian stepped through the door and closed it behind him.

Thirty minutes later, he emerged, flushed of face, his eyes feverishly bright, his medicide machine tucked under one skinny arm.

"How'd it go?" asked the male voice.

"She struggled more than I expected."

"You look kinda funny. Hope you didn't catch anything."

"No, no," Dr. Gregorian said absently. "I always use a condom."

"What?"

"I mean, I always take precautions against infection."

"You dried-up old ghoul! No wonder you snuff only women!"

"You misunderstood me, I assure you." Dr. Gregorian suddenly passed a hand over his face. "I don't feel very well."

"Uh-oh."

"What is it?"

"The old bat had contracted HELP. Hope you didn't catch it."

Dr. Gregorian blinked. "HELP? But I have eaten no bugs."

"Not even one? Back at Nirvana West?"

"How did you know I have been to Nirvana West?"

"The same way I know you've killed your last little old lady. I was there and I saw a lot of HELP victims. You look just like one."

Dr. Gregorian took an involuntary step backward. "You—you mean I'm dying?"

"Your eyeballs are still white. That means you've got forty-eight hours."

"But I have so much work to do. So much suffering to end. My life's work will die with me." Dr. Gregorian looked back at the closed doors. "Should I— should I go back for seconds?"

"Not a good idea since the police are going to be here any minute now."

"What good will they do?"

"For you, not much. But when they find out you snuffed Senator Clancy's mother without family permission, they'll probably lock you up for Murder One."

"But I have your permission. You told me over the phone it was your mother."

"Not me. You must have talked to somebody else."

"I was asked to come here."

"You got that in writing?"

Dr. Gregorian's black eyes went dull. "No."

"Malpractice lawyers love guys like you."

Dr. Gregorian looked at his medicide machine.

"I think I need some of my own medicine. Could you help me?"

"Sorry, I have better things to do."

Woodenly, Dr. Mordaunt Gregorian sat himself down on the hard pine floor and hooked himself up. He was about to trip the switch that would pour the painless barbiturates into his own bloodstream when a tiny old Asian stepped from the shadows and said, "Next time, demand a fair price for correct services."

His last thoughts were a confused question. *What did that little man mean?*

When the police came, they recognized Mordaunt Gregorian from his TV appearances. No one could tell if he was dead or not, because he looked the same in life as he had in death. Which was to say, dead.

Just to be sure, they cuffed the corpse before they shoved it into the body bag.

30

"It is obvious," Harold Smith was saying two days later, "that Pearl Clancy was the true Eldress."

"No way she was traipsing around Nirvana West, whispering in people's ears," Remo said. He was in the kitchen of his home, steaming rice for the midday meal, the telephone receiver cradled under his chin. It buzzed with Smith's lemony tones.

"She was the Eldress, but Nalini Toshi served as her eyes, ears, and when necessary, personal assassin. It was her voice that spoke to Karl Sagacious and Theodore Magarac, precipitating the events that led to the discovery of the so-called thunderbug, the founding of PAPA and all the events that followed."

"The whole thing was loony, trying to get Blotto Clancy back on the presidential fast track."

"It had been a Clancy dream—some might say obsession—to get one of their sons elected President," Smith said.

"At the rate new Clancys are entering politics these days," Remo sighed, "it's bound to happen one of these days."

"Perhaps in your lifetime, Remo. But not in mine. In any case, we need not fear for Senator Clancy running for high office again."

"Why not?"

"It was announced today that Senator Clancy is vacating his Senate seat."

Remo checked the rice. It was almost done. "Grief over his mother's death?" he asked.

"Not from the sound of his plans. He has also filed for divorce and run off to Tahiti with his secretary."

"Guess the only thing keeping him in politics was family pressure," said Remo. "Do we go after him?"

"Not necessary. Acting on statements Thrush Limburger made to the FBI, three of Clancy's aides have been arrested for the Limburger kidnapping. They have confessed and have implicated the senator. Extradition may be difficult, but Clancy appears to be not much more than a drink-sodden pawn to his mother's ambitions. Needless to say, the HELP bill has been quietly killed in committee."

"One thing I don't understand. What was all that finger wriggling about?"

"I have looked into that, Remo. It is believed that arachnids, specifically certain species of jumping spider, communicate through semaphorelike signals using their palpi."

"Their what?"

"Palpi. They are in the nature of—um—sexual organs and situated on either side of a spider's head. From the behavior both the Toshi woman and Pearl Clancy exhibited, it appears they were bugging their eyes to give them the semblance of a spider's unwinking orbs, their fingers mimicking the palp signals. Obviously, this was a method of directing the deadly spiders to specific actions. The perfume scent you describe was some sort of olfactory signal to bite the wearer. As well as a natural pheromone of some sort, no doubt passed down along with the secret of communicating with spiders from Spider Diva to Spider Diva."

"That would explain why I couldn't keep my hands off her, even when I knew better," Remo said. "So why didn't the spiders just bite Nalini?"

"Perhaps they did. Perhaps she had built up an immunity to the spider venom. More likely, the spiders considered her one of their own species. No doubt the Toshi woman passed her secrets on to Pearl Clancy. The finger signals were clearly their method of communicating with one another."

"I'll try explaining that to Chiun, but I'm not sure he's gonna believe it. I'm not sure I do."

"Where is Master Chiun?"

"Upstairs, listening to Thrush Limburger."

"I have been monitoring his broadcast as well. He seems to have single-handedly quelled the HELP scare. Bug-eating has tailed off now that people understand the bug is neither a disease carrier nor nutritionally fulfilling."

"Tail off?" What's wrong with stopping altogether?"

"Certain people with eating disorders have been unable to cease eating them. Anorexics, mostly."

"Anything that can be done about that?"

"The FDA is looking into banning the bug, but we may have underground bug-eating in this country for years to come."

"Different strokes for different folks," said Remo. "How did the President take the news?"

Smith cleared his throat nervously. "The President is, as you know, a longtime admirer of the Clancy clan and their contribution to American politics. And Senator Clancy was one of his most important political allies in the Senate."

"He blew his top, huh?"

"He was relieved to know he would not have to fight Senator Clancy for his party's nomination in the next presidential election," said Smith.

"I guess he owes us one."

"He was not entirely pleased, since we were responsible for restoring Thrush Limburger to the airwaves again."

"Maybe there's something to that windbag after all," said Remo, laughing.

*   *   *

Later, rice in hand, Remo went upstairs, where the Master of Sinanju was seated on a tatami mat before a clock radio that was booming in sympathy with the voice of Thrush Limburger.

Limburger was saying, "Put away your sunblock, my friends. There is no ozone hole over northern California. But if you are a regular listener to this show, you knew that. Because here at the TTT Network, we always—but always—tell the truth."

"I guess he turned out to be useful after all," said Remo.

"Hush," admonished Chiun.

Limburger went on. "And there is no HELP. Oh, we have a lot of dead people out in California. But they're not dead because they've taken a bite from *Ingraticus Avalonicus*, an insect so retarded it commits suicide at the first opportunity. They're dead—and you might want to write this down—they're dead because they were the bitee, not the biter. Doing the biting—listen to these verb endings carefully now—is a rather venomous tropical spider salted into the California wilderness. Mercifully, they're all dead now, thanks to me and Mother Nature."

"Mother Nature!" said Remo. "Where does he get that?"

"You've heard me tell you," boomed Thrush Limburger, "that the California drought is no end-of-the-world catastrophe, but a mere inevitable cycle of nature, serving some useful but as yet unfathomable purpose in the great scheme of things. Well, I'm here to tell you, that purpose revealed itself. Yes, it did. Because if we hadn't had that drought, and if those northern California grasses hadn't been so crackly dry, and a careless match had not been dropped, we'd still have a jumping spider infestation out there on the coast and we'd still be here talking about Human Environmental Liability Paradox, the virus that does not, and never did exist. Investigated, unmasked, and eradicated by Yours Truly. Thrush Limburger."

A musical chime began ringing, signaling the close of another broadcast.

And without warning, the Master of Sinanju brought his hand crashing down on the radio.

"What'd he say to tick you off?" Remo demanded.

"It is not what he said, it is what he did not say."

"Which is?"

"He did not give proper credit where proper credit is due."

"He can't give us any credit. He doesn't even know who we are."

"He could have dropped a hint. I would have settled for a hint. Even a niggling one."

"You wouldn't have settled for anything less than a guest spot on his show and you know it."

"He does not have guests," Chiun spat. "He is an air hog. It is bad enough that he is a credit hog, but he is an air hog too."

"Forget him. I cooked you some of your favorite rice."

"I am not hungry. Instead, fetch me my scrolls. If that loud, fat white will not give Sinanju proper credit, at least I will record the truth for future generations. Taking care to correctly spell Flush Hamburger's name, of course."

And Remo laughed. After Nirvana West, it was good to be home again—such as it was.

ON THE FRONT LINES OF DRAMA

☐ **FIELDS OF HONOR #1: THE MEDAL OF HONOR by Donald E. Zlotnik.**
Here is the first novel in a magnificent saga of Americans who gave
their best in Vietnam. (167880 $4.99)

☐ **FIELDS OF HONOR #2: THE DISTINGUISHED SERVICE CROSS by Donald
E. Zlotnik.** A stirring novel about the live-saving bravery of an American
medic in Vietnam—and the very different bravery he would need twenty
years later to triumph over unthinkable memories. (168739—$4.50)

☐ **FIELDS OF HONOR #3: THE SILVER STAR by Donald E. Zlotnik.** In
a lethal labyrinth below the jungle floor, a showdown awaits two
brothers in arms and an NVA commander as brilliant and determined as
they. (169565—$4.99)

☐ **FIELDS OF HONOR #4: THE SOLDIER'S MEDAL by Donald E. Zlotnik.** A
fierce novel of an officer who rose from the ranks in the Vietnam
cauldron. (170164—$4.99)

☐ **FIELDS OF HONOR #5: THE BRONZE STAR by Donald E. Zlotnik.** An
American fighting man gets involved in a Vietnam mission impossible.
(171225—$4.99)

Prices slightly higher in Canada

There's an epidemic with 27 million victims. And no visible symptoms.

It's an epidemic of people who can't read.

Believe it or not, 27 million Americans are functionally illiterate, about one adult in five.

The solution to this problem is you... when you join the fight against illiteracy. So call the Coalition for Literacy at toll-free **1-800-228-8813** and volunteer.

Volunteer Against Illiteracy. The only degree you need is a degree of caring.